Philip K. Dick was born in Chicago in 1928 and lived most of his life in California. He attended college for a year at Berkeley. Apart from writing, his main interest was music. He won the Hugo Award for his classic novel of alternative history, *The Man in the High Castle* (1962). He was married five times and had three children. He died in March 1982.

'One of the most original practitioners writing any kind of fiction, Philip K. Dick made most of the European avant-garde seem navel-gazers in a cul-de-sac'   *The Sunday Times*

'No other writer of his generation had such a powerful intellectual presence. He has stamped himself not only on our memories but in our imaginations'
BRIAN ALDISS

'The most consistently brilliant SF writer in the world'   JOHN BRUNNER

'Dick quietly produced serious fiction in a popular form and there can be no greater praise'
MICHAEL MOORCOCK

Voyager

PHILIP K. DICK

We Can Build You

HarperCollins*Publishers*

Voyager
An Imprint of HarperCollins*Publishers*
77–85 Fulham Palace Road,
Hammersmith, London W6 8JB

The *Voyager* World Wide Web site address is
http://www.harpercollins.co.uk/voyager

This paperback edition 1997
1 3 5 7 9 8 6 4 2

Previously published in paperback by
Panther Books 1986

Copyright © Philip K Dick 1972

ISBN 0 00 648279 1

Set in Times

Printed and bound in Great Britain by
Caledonian International Book Manufacturing Ltd, Glasgow

To Robert and Ginny Heinlein,
whose kindness to us meant more
than ordinary words can answer.

1

Our sales technique was perfected in the early 1970s. First we put an ad in a local newspaper, in the classified.

Spinet piano, also electronic organ, repossessed, in perfect condition, SACRIFICE. Cash or good credit risk wanted in this area, to take over payments rather than transport back to Oregon. Contact Frauenzimmer Piano Company, Mr Rock Credit Manager, Ontario, Ore.

For years we've run this ad in newspapers in one town after another, all up and down the western states and as far inland as Colorado. The whole approach developed on a scientific, systematic basis; we use maps, and sweep along so that no town goes untouched. We own four turbine-powered trucks, out on the road constantly, one man to a truck.

Anyhow, we place the ad, say the San Rafael Independent-Journal, and soon letters start arriving at our office in Ontario, Oregon, where my partner Maury Rock takes care of all that. He sorts the letters and compiles lists, and then when he has enough contacts in a particular area, say around San Rafael, he night-wires the truck. Suppose it's Fred down there in Marin County. When Fred gets the wire he brings out his own map and lists the calls in proper sequence. And then he finds a pay phone and telephones the first prospect.

Meanwhile, Maury has airmailed an answer to each person who's written in response to the ad.

Dear Mr So-and-so:
    We were gratified to receive your response to our notice in the San Rafael Independent-Journal. The man who is handling

7

this matter has been away from the office for a few days now, so we've decided to forward to him your name and address with the request that he contact you and provide you with all the details.

The letter drones on, but for several years now it has done a good job for the company. However, of late, sales of the electronic organs have fallen off. For instance, in the Vallejo area we sold forty spinets not long ago, and not one single organ.

Now, this enormous balance in favor of the spinet over the electronic organ, in terms of sales, led to an exchange between I and my partner, Maury Rock; it was heated, too.

I got to Ontario, Oregon late, having been down south around Santa Monica discussing matters with certain do-gooders there who had invited law-enforcement officials in to scan our enterprise and method of operating . . . a gratuitous action which led to nothing, of course, since we're operating strictly legally.

Ontario isn't my hometown, or anybody else's. I hail from Wichita Falls, Kansas, and when I was high school age I moved to Denver and then to Boise, Idaho. In some respects Ontario is a suburb of Boise; it's near the Idaho border – you go across a long metal bridge – and it's a flat land, there, where they farm. The forests of eastern Oregon don't begin that far inland. The biggest industry is the Ore-Ida potato patty factory, especially its electronics division, and then there're a whole lot of Japanese farmers who were shuffled back that way during World War Two and who grow onions or something. The air is dry, real estate is cheap, people do their big shopping in Boise; the latter is a big town which I don't like because you can't get decent Chinese food there. It's near the old Oregon Trail, and the railroad goes through it on its way to Cheyenne.

Our office is located in a brick building in downtown

Ontario across from a hardware store. We've got root iris growing around our building. The colors of the iris look good when you come driving up the desert route from California and Nevada.

So anyhow I parked my dusty Chevrolet Magic Fire turbine convertible and crossed the sidewalk to our building and our sign:

MASA ASSOCIATES

MASA stands for MULTIPLEX ACOUSTICAL SYSTEM OF AMERICA, a made-up electronics type name which we developed due to our electronic organ factory, which, due to my family ties, I'm deeply involved with. It was Maury who came up with Frauenzimmer Piano Company, since as a name it fitted our trucking operation better. Frauenzimmer is Maury's original old-country name, Rock being made-up, too. My real name is as I give it: Louis Rosen, which is German for roses. One day I asked Maury what Frauenzimmer meant, and he said it means womankind. I asked where he specifically got the name Rock.

'I closed my eyes and touched a volume of the encyclopedia, and it said ROCK TO SUBUD.'

'You made a mistake,' I told him. 'You should have called yourself Maury Subud.'

The downstairs door of our building dates back to 1965 and ought to be replaced, but we just don't have the funds. I pushed the door open, it's massive and heavy but swings nicely, and walked to the elevator, one of those old automatic affairs. A minute later I was upstairs stepping out in our offices. The fellows were talking and drinking loudly.

'Time has passed us by,' Maury said at once to me. 'Our electronic organ is obsolete.'

'You're wrong,' I said. 'The trend is actually *toward* the electronic organ because that's the way America is going in its space exploration: electronic. In ten years we

9

won't sell one spinet a day; the spinet will be a relic of the past.'

'Louis,' Maury said, 'please look what our competitors have done. Electronics may be marching forward, but without us. Look at the Hammerstein Mood Organ. Look at the Waldteufel Euphoria. And tell me why anyone would be content like you merely to bang out music.'

Maury is a tall fellow, with the emotional excitability of the hyperthyroid. His hands tend to shake and he digests his food too fast; they're giving him pills, and if those don't work he has to take radioactive iodine someday. If he stood up straight he'd be six three. He's got, or did have once, black hair, very long but thinning, and large eyes, and he always had a sort of disconcerted look, as if things are going all wrong on every side.

'No good musical instrument becomes obsolete,' I said. But Maury had a point. What had undone us was the extensive brain-mapping of the mid 1960s and the depth-electrode techniques of Penfield and Jacobson and Olds, especially their discoveries about the mid-brain. The hypothalamus is where the emotions lie, and in developing and marketing our electronic organ we had not taken the hypothalamus into account. The Rosen factory never got in on the transmission of selective-frequency short range shock, which stimulate very specific cells of the mid-brain, and we certainly failed from the start to see how easy – and important – it would be to turn the circuit switches into a keyboard of eighty-eight black and whites.

Like most people, I've dabbled at the keys of a Hammerstein Mood Organ, and I enjoy it. But there's nothing creative about it. True, you can hit on new configurations of brain stimulation, and hence produce entirely new emotions in your head which would never otherwise show up there. You might – theoretically – even hit on the combination that will put you in the state of nirvana. Both the Hammerstein and Waldteufel corporations have a big prize for that. But that's not music. That's escape. Who wants it?

'I want it,' Maury had said back as early as December of 1978. And he had gone out and hired a cashiered electronics engineer of the Federal Space Agency, hoping he could rig up for us a new version of the hypothalamus-stimulation organ.

But Bob Bundy, for all his electronics genius, had no experience with organs. He had designed simulacra circuits for the Government. Simulacra are the synthetic humans which I always thought of as robots; they're used for Lunar exploration, sent up from time to time from the Cape.

Bundy's reasons for leaving the Cape are obscure. He drinks, but that doesn't dim his powers. He wenches. But so do we all. Probably he was dropped because he's a bad security risk; not a Communist – Bundy could never have doped out even the existence of political ideas – but a bad risk in that he appears to have a touch of hebephrenia. In other words, he tends to wander off without notice. His clothes are dirty, his hair uncombed, his chin unshaved, and he won't look you in the eye. He grins inanely. He's what the Federal Bureau of Mental Health psychiatrists call *dilapidated*. If someone asks him a question he can't figure out how to answer it; he has speech blockage. But with his hands – he's damn fine. He can do his job, and well. So the McHeston Act doesn't apply to him.

However, in the many months Bundy had worked for us, I had seen nothing invented. Maury in particular kept busy with him, since I'm out on the road.

'The only reason you stick up for that electric keyboard Hawaiian guitar,' Maury said to me, 'is because your dad and brother make the things. That's why you can't face the truth.'

I answered, 'You're using an ad hominum agreement.'

'Talmud scholarism,' Maury retorted. Obviously, he –

11

all of them, in fact – were well-loaded; they had been sopping up the Ancient Age bourbon while I was out on the road driving the long hard haul.

'You want to break up the partnership?' I said. And I was willing to, at that moment, because of Maury's drunken slur at my father and brother and the entire Rosen Electronic Organ Factory at Boise with its seventeen full-time employees.

'I say the news from Vallejo and environs spells the death of our principal product,' Maury said. 'Even with its six-hundred-thousand possible tone combinations, some never heard by human ears. You're a bug like the rest of your family for those outer-space voodoo noises your electronic dungheap makes. And you have the nerve to call it a musical instrument. None of you Rosens have an ear. I wouldn't have a Rosen electronic sixteen-hundred-dollar organ in my home if you gave it to me at cost; I'd rather have a set of vibes.'

'All right,' I yelled, 'you're a purist. And it isn't six-hundred-thousand; it's seven-hundred-thousand.'

'Those souped-up circuits bloop out one noise and one only,' Maury said, 'however much it's modified – it's just basically a whistle.'

'One can compose on it,' I pointed out.

'Compose? It's more like creating remedies for diseases that don't exist, using that thing. I say either burn down the part of your family's factory that makes those things or damn it, Louis, convert. Convert to something new and useful that mankind can lean on during its painful ascent upward. Do you hear?' He swayed back and forth, jabbing his long finger at me. 'We're in the sky, now. To the stars. Man's no longer hidebound. Do you hear?'

'I hear,' I said. 'But I recall that you and Bob Bundy were supposed to be the ones who were hatching up the new and useful solution to our problems. And that was months ago and nothing's come of it.'

'We've got something,' Maury said. 'And when you

12

see it you'll agree it's oriented toward the future in no uncertain terms.'

'Show it to me.'

'Okay, we'll take a drive over to the factory. Your dad and your brother Chester should be in on it; it's only fair, since it'll be them who produce it.'

Standing with his drink, Bundy grinned at me in his sneaky, indirect fashion. All this inter-personal communication probably made him nervous.

'You guys are going to bring ruin down on us,' I told him. 'I've got a feeling.'

'We face ruin anyhow,' Maury said, 'if we stick with your Rosen WOLFGANG MONTEVERDI electronic organ, or whatever the decal is this month your brother Chester's pasting on it.'

I had no answer. Gloomily, I fixed myself a drink.

2

The Mark VII Saloon Model Jaguar is an ancient huge white car, a collector's item, with fog lights, a grill like the Rolls, and naturally hand-rubbed walnut, leather seats, and many interior lights. Maury kept his priceless old 1954 Mark VII in mint condition and tuned perfectly, but we were able to go no faster than ninety miles an hour on the freeway which connects Ontario with Boise.

The languid pace made me restless. 'Listen Maury,' I said, 'I wish you would begin explaining. Bring the future to me right now, like you can in words.'

Behind the wheel, Maury smoked away at his Corina Sport cigar, leaned back and said, 'What's on the mind of America, these days?'

'Sexuality,' I said.

'No.'

'Dominating the inner planets of the solar system before Russia can, then.'

'No.'

'Okay, you tell me.'

'The Civil War of 1861.'

'Aw chrissakes,' I said.

'It's the truth, buddy. This nation is obsessed with the War Between the States. I'll tell you why. It was the only and first national epic in which we Americans participated; that's why.' He blew Corina Sport cigar smoke at me. 'It matured we Americans.'

'It's not on my mind,' I said.

'I could stop at a busy intersection of any big downtown city in the US and collar ten citizens, and six of those ten, if asked what was on their mind, would say, "The US Civil War of 1861." And I've been working on the implications – the practical side – ever since I figured that out, around six months ago. It has grave meaning for MASA ASSOCIATES, if we want it to, I mean; if we're alert. You know they had that Centennial a decade or so back; recall?'

'Yes,' I said. 'In 1961.'

'And it was a flop. A few souls got out and refought a few battles, but it was nothing. Look in the back seat.'

I switched on the interior lights of the car and twisting around I saw on the back seat a long newspaper-wrapped carton, shaped like a display window dummy, one of those manikins. From the lack of bulge up around the chest, I concluded it wasn't a female one.

'So?' I said.

'That's what I've been working on.'

'While I've been setting up areas for the trucks!'

'Right,' Maury said. 'And this, in time, will be so far long remembered over any sales of spinets or electronic organs that it'll make your head swim.'

He nodded emphatically. 'Now when we get to Boise – listen. I don't want your dad and Chester to give us a hard time. That's why it's necessary to inform you right now. That back there is worth a billion bucks to us or anyone else who happens to find it. I've got a notion to pull off the road and demonstrate it to you, maybe at some lunch counter. Or a gas station, even; any place that's light.' Maury seemed very tense and his hands were shaking more than usual.

'Are you sure,' I said, 'that isn't a Louis Rosen dummy, and you're going to knock me off and have it take my place?'

Maury glanced at me oddly. 'Why do you say that? No, that's not it, but by chance you're close, buddy. I can see that our brains still fuse, like they did in the old days, in the early 'seventies when we were new and green and without backing except maybe your dad and that warning-to-all-of-us younger brother of yours. I wonder, why

15

didn't Chester become a large-animal vet like he started out to be? It would have been safer for the rest of us; we would have been spared. But instead a spinet factory in Boise, Idaho. Madness!' He shook his head.

'Your family never even did that,' I said. 'Never built anything or created anything. Just middlemen, schlock hustlers in the garment industry. I mean, what did they do to set us up in business, like Chester and my dad did? What is that dummy in the back seat? I want to know, and I'm not stopping at any gas station or lunch counter; I've got the distinct intuition that you really do intend to do me in or some such thing. So let's keep driving.'

'I can't describe it in words.'

'Sure you can. You're an A-one snow-job artist.'

'Okay. I'll tell you why that Civil War Centennial failed. Because all the original participants who were willing to fight and lay down their lives and die for the Union, or for the Confederacy, are dead. Nobody lives to be a hundred, or if they do they're good for nothing – they can't fight, they can't handle a rifle. Right?'

I said. 'You mean you have a mummy back there, or one of what in the horror movies they call the "undead"?'

'I'll tell you exactly what I have. Wrapped up in those newspapers in the back seat I have Edwin M. Stanton.'

'Who's that?'

'He was Lincoln's Secretary of War.'

'Aw!'

'No, it's the truth.'

'When did he die?'

'A long time ago.'

'That's what I thought.'

'Listen,' Maury said, 'I have an electronic simulacrum back in the back seat, there. I built it, or rather we had Bundy build it. It cost me six thousand dollars but it was worth it. Let's stop at that roadside cafe and gas station up along the road, there, and I'll unwrap it and demonstrate it to you; that's the only way.'

16

I felt my flesh crawl. 'You will indeed.'

'Do you think this is just some bagatelle, buddy?'

'No. I think you're absolutely serious.'

'I am,' Maury said. He began to slow the car and flash the directional signal. 'I'm stopping where it says Tommy's Italian Fine Dinners and Lucky Lager Beer.'

'And then what? What's a demonstration?'

'We'll unwrap it and have it walk in with us and order a chicken and ham pizza; that's what I mean by a demonstration.'

Maury parked the Jaguar and came around to crawl into the back. He began tearing the newspaper from the human-shaped bundle, and sure enough, there presently emerged an elderly-looking gentleman with eyes shut and white beard, wearing archaically-styled clothing, his hands folded over his chest.

'You'll see how convincing this simulacrum is,' Maury said, 'when it orders its own pizza.' He began to tinker with switches which were available at the back of the thing.

All at once the face assumed a grumpy, taciturn expression and it said in a growl, 'My friend, remove your fingers from my body, if you will.' It pried Maury's hands loose from it, and Maury grinned at me.

'See?' Maury said. The thing had sat up slowly and was in the process of methodically brushing itself off; it had a stern, vengeful look, now, as if it believed we had done it some harm, possibly sapped it and knocked it out, and it was just recovering. I could see that the counter man in Tommy's Italian Fine Dinners would be fooled, all right; I could see that Maury had made his point already. If I hadn't seen it spring to life I would believe myself it was just a sour elderly gentleman in old-style clothes and a split white beard, brushing itself off with an attitude of outrage.

'I see,' I said.

Maury held open the back door of the Jaguar, and the

Edwin M. Stanton electronic simulacrum slid over and rose to a standing position in a dignified fashion.

'Does it have any money?' I asked.

'Sure,' Maury said. 'Don't ask trifling questions; this is the most serious matter you've ever had facing you.' As the three of us started across the gravel to the restaurant, Maury went on, 'Our entire economic future and that of America's involved in this. Ten years from now you and I could be wealthy, due to this thing, here.'

The three of us had a pizza at the restaurant, and the crust was burned at the edges. The Edwin M. Stanton made a noisy scene, shaking its fist at the proprietor, and then after finally paying our bill, we left.

By now we were an hour behind schedule, and I was beginning to wonder if we were going to get to the Rosen factory after all. So I asked Maury to step on it, as we got back into the Jaguar.

'This car'll crack two hundred,' Maury said, starting up, 'with that new dry rocket fuel they have out.'

'Don't take unnecessary chances,' the Edwin M. Stanton told him in a sullen voice as the car roared out onto the road. 'Unless the possible gains heavily outweigh the odds.'

'Same to you,' Maury told it.

The Rosen Spinet Piano & Electronic Organ Factory at Boise, Idaho doesn't attract much notice, since the structure itself, technically called the plant, is a flat, one-story building that looks like a single-layer cake, with a parking lot behind it, a sign over the office made of letters cut from heavy plastic, very modern, with recessed red lights behind. The only windows are in the office.

At this late hour the factory was dark and shut, with no one there. We drove on up into the residential section, then.

'What do you think of this neighborhood?' Maury asked the Edwin M. Stanton.

Seated upright in the back of the Jaguar the thing grunted, 'Rather unsavory and unworthy.'

'Listen,' I said, 'my family lives down here near the industrial part of Boise so as to be in easy walking distance from the factory.' It made me angry to hear a mere fake criticizing genuine humans, especially a fine person like my dad. And as to my brother – few radiation-mutants ever made the grade in the spinet and electronic organ industry outside of Chester Rosen. *Special birth* persons, as they are called. There is so much discrimination and prejudice in so many fields . . . most professions of high social status are closed to them.

It was always disappointing to the Rosen family that Chester's eyes are set beneath his nose, and his mouth is up where his eyes ought to be. But blame H-bomb testing in the 'fifties and 'sixties for him – and all the others similar to him in the world today. I can remember, as a kid, reading the many medical books on birth defects – the topic has naturally interested many people for a couple of decades, now – and there are some that make Chester nothing at all. One that always threw me into a week-long depression is where the embryo disintegrates in the womb and is born in pieces, a jaw, an arm, handful of teeth, separate fingers. Like one of those plastic kits out of which boys build a model airplane. Only, the pieces of the embryo don't add up to anything; there's no glue in this world to stick it together.

And there're embryos with hair growing all over them, like a slipper made from yak fur. And one that dries up so that the skin cracks; it looks like it's been maturing outdoors on the back step in the sun. So lay off Chester.

The Jaguar had halted at the curb before the family house, and there we were. I could see lights on inside the house, in the living room; my mother, father and brother were watching TV.

'Let's send the Edwin M. Stanton up the stairs alone,'

19

Maury said. 'Have it knock on the door, and we'll sit here in the car and watch.'

'My dad'll recognize it as a phony,' I said, 'a mile away. In fact he'll probably kick it back down the steps, and you'll be out the six hundred it cost you.' Or whatever it was Maury had paid for it, and no doubt charged against MASA's assets.

'I'll take the chance,' Maury said, holding the back door of the car open so that the contraption could get out. To it he said, 'Go up there to where it says 1429 and ring the bell. And when the man comes to the door, you say, "Now he belongs to the ages." And then just stand.'

'What does that mean?' I said. 'What kind of opening remark is that supposed to be?'

'It's Stanton's famous remark that got him into history,' Maury said. 'When Lincoln died.'

'"Now he belongs to the ages,"' the Stanton practiced as it crossed the sidewalk and started up the steps.

'I'll explain to you in due course how the Edwin M. Stanton was constructed,' Maury said to me. 'How we collected the entire body of data extant pertaining to Stanton and had it transcribed down at UCLA into instruction punch-tape to be fed to the ruling monad that serves the simulacrum as a brain.'

'You know what you're doing?' I said, disgusted. 'You're wrecking MASA, all this kidding around, this harebrained stuff – I never should have gotten mixed up with you.'

'Quiet,' Maury said, as the Stanton rang the doorbell.

The front door opened and there stood my father in his trousers, slippers, and the new bathrobe I had given him at Christmas. He was quite an imposing figure, and the Edwin M. Stanton, which had started on its little speech, halted and shifted gears.

'Sir,' it finally said, 'I have the privilege of knowing your boy Louis.'

20

'Oh yes,' my father said. 'He's down in Santa Monica right now.'

The Edwin M. Stanton did not seem to know what Santa Monica was, and it stood there at a loss. Beside me in the Jaguar, Maury swore with exasperation, but it struck me funny, the simulacrum standing there like some new, no-good salesman, unable to think up anything at all to say and so standing mute.

But it was impressive, the two old gentlemen standing there facing each other, the Stanton with its split white beard, its old-style garments, my father looking not much newer. The meeting of the patriarchs, I thought. Like in the synagogue.

My father at last said to it, 'Won't you step inside?' He held the door open, and the thing passed on inside and out of sight; the door shut, leaving the porch lit up and empty.

'How about that,' I said to Maury.

We followed after it. The door being unlocked, we went on inside.

There in the living room sat the Stanton, in the middle of the sofa, its hands on its knees, discoursing with my dad, while Chester and my mother went on watching the TV.

'Dad,' I said, 'you're wasting your time talking to that thing. You know what it is? A machine Maury threw together in his basement for six bucks.'

Both my father and the Edwin M. Stanton paused and glanced at me.

'This nice old man?' my father said, and he got an angry, righteous expression; his brows knitted and he said loudly, 'Remember, Louis, that man is a frail reed, the most feeble thing in nature, but goddamn it, mein Sohn, a thinking reed. The entire universe doesn't have to arm itself against him; a drop of water can kill him.' Pointing his finger at me excitedly, my dad roared on, 'But if the entire universe were to crush him, you know

21

what? You know what I say? Man would still be more noble!' He pounded on the arm of his chair for emphasis. 'You know why, mein Kind? Because he knows that he dies and I'll tell you something else; he's got the advantage over the goddamn universe because it doesn't know a thing of what's going on. And,' my dad concluded, calming down a little, 'all our dignity consists in just that. I mean, man's little and can't fill time and space, but he sure can make use of the brain God gave him. Like what you call this "thing," here. This is no thing. This is ein *Mensch*, a man. Say, I have to tell you a joke.' He launched, then, into a joke half in yiddish, half in English.

When it was over we all smiled, although it seemed to me that the Edwin M. Stanton's was somewhat formal, even forced.

Trying to think back to what I had read about Stanton, I recalled that he was considered a pretty harsh guy, both during the Civil War and the Reconstruction afterward, especially when he tangled with Andrew Johnson and tried to get him impeached. He probably did not appreciate my dad's humanitarian-type joke because he got the same stuff from Lincoln all day long during his job. But there was no way to stop my dad anyhow; his own father had been a Spinoza scholar, well known, and although my dad never went beyond the seventh grade himself he had read all sorts of books and documents and corresponded with literary persons throughout the world.

'I'm sorry, Jerome,' Maury said to my dad, when there was a pause, 'but I'm telling you the truth.' Crossing to the Edwin M. Stanton, he reached down and fiddled with it behind the ear.

'Glop,' the Stanton said, and then became rigid, as lifeless as a window-store dummy; the light in its eyes expired, its arms paused and stiffened. It was graphic, and I glanced to see how my dad was taking it. Even Chester and my mom looked up from the TV a moment. It really made one pause and consider. If there hadn't been philosophy in the air already that night, this would have started it; we all became solemn. My dad even got up and walked over to inspect the thing firsthand.

'Oy gewalt.' He shook his head.

'I could turn it back on,' Maury offered.

'Nein, das geht mir nicht.' My dad returned to his easy chair, made himself comfortable, and then asked in a resigned, sober voice, 'Well, how did the sales at Vallejo go, boys?' As we got ready to answer he brought out an Anthony & Cleopatra cigar, unwrapped it and lit up. It's a fine-quality Havana-filler cigar, with a green outer wrapper, and the odor filled the living room immediately. 'Sell lots of organs and AMADEUS GLUCK spinets?' He chuckled.

'Jerome,' Maury said, 'the spinets sold like lemmings, but not one organ moved.'

My father frowned.

'We've been involved in a high-level confab on this topic,' Maury said, 'with certain facts emerging. The Rosen electronic organ – '

'Wait,' my dad said. 'Not so fast, Maurice. On this side of the Iron Curtain the Rosen organ has no peer.' He produced from the coffee table one of those masonite boards on which we have mounted resistors, solar batteries, transistors, wiring and the like, for display. 'This demonstrates the workings of the Rosen true electronic organ,' he began. 'This is the rapid delay circuit, and – '

'Jerome, I know how the organ works. Allow me to make my point.'

'Go ahead.' My dad put aside the masonite board, but before Maury could speak, he went on, 'But if you expect us to abandon the mainstay of our livelihood simply because salesmanship – and I say this knowingly, not without direct experience of my own – when and because salesmanship has deteriorated, and there isn't the will to sell – '

23

Maury broke in, 'Jerome, listen. I'm suggesting expansion.'

My dad cocked an eyebrow.

'Now, you Rosens can go on making all the electronic organs you want,' Maury said, 'but I know they're going to diminish in sales volume all the time, unique and terrific as they are. What we need is something which is really new; because after all, Hammerstein makes those mood organs and they've gone over good, they've got that market sewed up airtight, so there's no use our trying that. So here it is, my idea.'

Reaching up, my father turned on his hearing aid.

'Thank you, Jerome,' Maury said. 'This Edwin M. Stanton electronic simulacrum. It's as good as if Stanton had been alive here tonight discussing topics with us. What a sales idea that is, for educational purposes, like in the schools. But that's nothing; I had that in mind at first, but here's the authentic deal. Listen. We propose to President Mendoza in our nation's Capitol that we abolish war and substitute for it a ten-year-spaced-apart centennial of the US Civil War, and what we do is, the Rosen factory supplies all the participants, simulacra – that's the plural, it's a Latin type word – of *everybody*. Lincoln, Stanton, Jeff Davis, Robert E. Lee, Longstreet, and around three million simple ones as soldiers we keep in stock all the time. And we have the battles fought with the participants really killed, these made-to-order simulacra blown to bits, instead of just a grade-B movie type business like a bunch of college kids doing Shakespeare. Do you get my point? You see the scope of this?'

We were all silent. Yes, I thought, there is scope to it.

'We could be as big as General Dynamics in five years,' Maury added.

My father eyed him, smoking his A & C. 'I don't know, Maurice. I don't know.' He shook his head.

'Why not? Tell me, Jerome, what's wrong with it?'

'The times have carried you away, perhaps,' my father

24

said in a slow voice tinged with weariness. He sighed. 'Or am I getting old?'

'Yeah, you're getting old!' Maury said, very upset and flushed.

'Maybe so, Maurice.' My father was silent for a little while and then he drew himself up and said, 'No, your idea is too – ambitious, Maurice. We are not that great. We must take care not to reach too high for maybe we will topple, nicht wahr?'

'Don't give me that German foreign language,' Maury grumbled. 'If you won't approve this . . . I'm too far into it already, I'm sorry but I'm going ahead. I've had a lot of good ideas in the past which we've used and this is the best so far. It is the times, Jerome. We have to *move*.'

Sadly, to himself, my father resumed smoking his cigar.

25

3

Still hoping my father would be won over, Maury left the Stanton – on consignment, so to speak – and we drove back to Ontario. By then it was nearly midnight, and since we both were depressed by my father's weariness and lack of enthusiasm Maury invited me to stay overnight at his house. I was glad to accept; I felt the need of company.

When we arrived we found his daughter Pris, who I had assumed was still back at Kasanin Clinic at Kansas City in the custody of the Federal Bureau of Mental Health. Pris, as I knew from what Maury had told me, had been a ward of the Federal Government since her third year in high school; tests administered routinely in the public schools had picked up her 'dynamism of difficulty,' as the psychiatrists are calling it now – in the popular vernacular, her schizophrenic condition.

'She'll cheer you up,' Maury said, when I hung back. 'That's what you and I both need. She's grown a lot since you saw her last; she's no child anymore. Come on.' He dragged me into the house by one arm.

She was seated on the floor in the living room wearing pink pedal pushers. Her hair was cut short and in the years since I had seen her she had lost weight. Spread around her lay colored tile; she was in the process of cracking the tile into irregular pits with a huge pair of long-handled cutting pliers.

'Come look at the bathroom,' she said, hopping up. I followed warily after her.

On the bathroom walls she had sketched all sorts of sea monsters and fish, even a mermaid; she had already partially tiled them with every color imaginable. The mermaid had red tiles for tits, one bright tile in the center of each breast.

The panorama both repelled and interested me.

'Why not have little light bulbs for nipples?' I said. 'When someone comes in to use the can and turns on the light the nipples light up and guide him on his way.'

No doubt she had gotten into this tiling orgy due to years of occupational therapy at Kansas City; the mental health people were keen on anything creative. The Government has literally tens of thousands of patients in their several clinics throughout the country, all busy weaving or painting or dancing or making jewelry or binding books or sewing costumes for plays. And all the patients are there involuntarily, committed by law. Like Pris, many of them had been picked up during puberty, which is the time psychosis tends to strike.

Undoubtedly Pris was much better now, or they would not have released her into the outer world. But she still did not look normal or natural to me. As we walked back to the living room together I took a close look at her; I saw a little hard, heart-shaped face, with a widow's crown, black hair, and due to her odd make-up, eyes outlined in black, a Harlequin effect, and almost purple lipstick; the whole color scheme made her appear unreal and doll-like, lost somewhere back behind the mask which she had created out of her face. And the skinniness of her body put the capper on the effect: she looked to me like a dance of death creation animated in some weird way, probably not through the usual assimilation of solid and liquid foods . . . perhaps she chewed only walnut shells. But anyhow, from one standpoint she looked good, although unusual to say the least. For my money, however, she looked less normal than the Stanton.

'Sweet Apple,' Maury said to her, 'we left the Edwin M. Stanton over at Louis' dad's house.'

Glancing up, she said, 'Is it off?' Her eyes burned with

a wild, intense flame, which both startled and impressed me.

'Pris,' I said, 'the mental health people broke the mold when they produced you. What an eerie yet fine-looking chick you turned out to be, now that you've grown up and gotten out of there.'

'Thanks,' she said, with no feeling at all; her tone had, in former times, been totally flat, no matter what the situation, including big crises. And that was the way with her still.

'Get the bed ready,' I said to Maury, 'so I can turn in.'

Together, he and I unfolded the guest bed in the spare room; we tossed sheets and blankets on it, and a pillow. His daughter made no move to help; she remained in the living room snipping tile.

'How long's she been working on that bathroom mural?' I asked.

'Since she got back from K.C. Which has been quite a while, now. For the first couple of weeks she had to report back to the mental health people in this area. She's not actually out; she's on probation and receiving outpatient therapy. In fact you could say she's on loan to the outside world.'

'Is she better or worse?'

'A lot better. I never told you how bad she got, there in high school before they picked it up on their test. We didn't know what was wrong. Frankly, I thank God for the McHeston Act; if they hadn't picked it up, if she had gone on getting sicker, she'd be either a total schizophrenic paranoid or a dilapidated hebephrenic, by now. Permanently institutionalized for sure.'

I said, 'She looks so strange.'

'What do you think of the tiling?'

'It won't increase the value of the house.'

Maury bristled. 'Sure it will.'

Appearing at the door of the spare room, Pris said, 'I

28

asked, *is it off?*' She glowered at us as if she had guessed we were discussing her.

'Yes,' Maury said, 'unless Jerome turned it back on to discourse about Spinoza with it.'

'What's it know?' I asked. 'Has it got a lot of spare random useless type facts in it? Because if not my dad won't be interested long.'

Pris said, 'It has the same facts that the original Edwin M. Stanton had. We researched his life to the nth degree.'

I got the two of them out of my bedroom, then took off my clothes and went to bed. Presently I heard Maury say goodnight to his daughter and go off to his own bedroom. And then I heard nothing – except, as I had expected, the snap-snap of tile being cut.

For an hour I lay in bed trying to sleep, falling off and then being brought back by the noise. At last I got up, turned on my light, put my clothes back on, smoothed my hair in place, rubbed my eyes, and came out of the spare room. She sat exactly as I had seen her first that evening, yogi-style, now with an enormous heap of broken tile around her.

'I can't sleep with that racket,' I told her.

'Too bad.' She did not even glance up.

'I'm a guest.'

'Go elsewhere.'

'I know what using that pliers symbolizes,' I told her. 'Emasculating thousands upon thousands of males, one after another. Is that why you left Kasanin Clinic? To sit here all night doing this?'

'No. I'm getting a job.'

'Doing what? The labor market's glutted.'

'I have no fears. There's no one like me in the world. I've already received an offer from a company that handles emigration processing. There's an enormous amount of statistical work involved.'

'So it's someone like you,' I said, 'who'll decide which of us can leave Earth.'

'I turned it down. I don't intend to be just another bureaucrat. Have you ever heard of Sam K. Barrows?'

'Naw,' I said. But the name did sound familiar.

'There was an article on him in *Look*. When he was twenty he always rose at five A.M., had a bowl of stewed prunes, ran two miles around the streets of Seattle, then returned to his room to shave and take a cold shower. And then he went off and studied his law books.'

'Then he's a lawyer.'

'Not anymore,' Pris said. 'Look over in the bookcase. The copy of *Look* is there.'

'Why should I care?' I said, but I went to get the magazine.

Sure enough, there on the cover in color was a man labeled:

SAM K. BARROWS, AMERICA'S MOST ENTER-PRISING NEW YOUNG MULTI-MILLIONAIRE.

It was dated June 18, 1981, so it was fairly recent. And sure enough, there came Sam, jogging up one of the waterfront streets of downtown Seattle, in khaki shorts and gray sweatshirt, at what appeared to be sunup, puffing happily, a man with head shining due to being smooth-shaven, his eyes like the dots stuck in a snow-man's face: expressionless, tiny. No emotion there; only the lower half of the face seemed to be grinning.

'If you saw him on TV – ' Pris said.

'Yeah,' I said, 'I saw him on TV.' I remembered now, because at the time – a year ago – the man had struck me unfavorably. His monotonous way of speaking . . . he had leaned close to the reporter and mumbled at him very rapidly. 'Why do you want to work for him?' I asked.

'Sam Barrows,' Pris said, 'is the greatest living land speculator in existence. Think about that.'

'That's probably because we're running out of land,' I said. 'All the realtors are going broke because there's

30

nothing to sell. Just people and no places to put them.'
And then I remembered.

Barrows had solved the real estate speculation problem.
In a series of far-reaching legal actions, he had managed
to get the United States Government to permit private
speculation in land on the other planets. Sam Barrows
had single-handedly opened the way for sub-dividers on
Luna, Mars and Venus. His name would go down in
history forever.

'So that's the man you want to work for,' I said. 'The
man who polluted the untouched other worlds.' His
salesmen sold from offices all over the United States his
glowingly-described Lunar lots.

'"Polluted untouched other worlds,"' Pris mimicked.
'A slogan of those conservationists.'

'But true,' I said. 'Listen, how are you going to make
use of your land, once you've bought it? How do you live
on it? No water, no air, no heat, no – '

'That will be provided,' Pris said.

'How?'

'That's what makes Barrows the great man he is,' Pris
said. 'His vision. Barrows Enterprises is working day and
night – '

'A racket,' I broke in.

There was silence, then. A strained silence.

'Have you ever actually spoken to Barrows?' I asked.
'It's one thing to have a hero; you're a young girl and it's
natural for you to worship a guy who's on the cover of
magazines and on TV and he's rich and single-handedly
he opened up the Moon to loan sharks and land speculators. But you were talking about getting a job.'

Pris said, 'I applied for a job at one of his companies.
And I told them I wanted to see him personally.'

'They laughed.'

'No, they sent me into his office. He sat there and
listened to me for a whole minute. Then, of course, he

31

had to take care of other business; they sent me on to the personnel manager's office.'

'What did you say to him in your minute?'

'I looked at him. He looked at me. You've never seen him in real life. He's incredibly handsome.'

'On television,' I said, 'he's a lizard.'

'I told him that I can screen dead beats. No time-wasters could get past me if I was his secretary. I know how to be tough and yet also I never turn away anyone who matters. You see, I can turn it on and off. Do you comprehend?'

'But can you open letters?' I said.

'They have machines who do that.'

'Your father does that. That's Maury's job with us.'

'And that's why I'd never work for you,' Pris said. 'Because you're so pathetically small. You hardly exist. No, I can't open letters. I can't do any routine jobs. I'll tell you what I can do. It was my idea to build the Edwin M. Stanton simulacrum.'

I felt a deep unease.

'Maury wouldn't have thought of it,' Pris said. 'Bundy – he's a genius. He's inspired. But it's idiot savantry that he has; the rest of his brain is totally deteriorated by the hebephrenic process. I designed the Stanton and he built it, and it's a success; you saw it. I don't even want or need the credit; it was fun. Like this.' She had resumed her tile-snipping. 'Creative work,' she said.

'What did Maury do? Tie its shoelaces?'

'Maury was the organizer. He saw to it that we had our supplies.'

I had the dreadful feeling that this calm account was god's truth. Naturally, I could check with Maury. And yet – it did not seem to me that this girl even knew how to lie; she was almost the opposite from her father. Perhaps she took after her mother, whom I had never met. They had been divorced, a broken family, long before I met Maury and became his partner.

'How's your out-patient psychoanalysis coming?' I asked her.

'Fine. How's yours?'

'I don't need it,' I said.

'That's where you're wrong. You're very sick, just like me.' She smiled up at me. 'Face facts.'

'Would you stop that snap-snapping? So I can go to sleep?'

'No,' she answered. 'I want to finish the octopus tonight.'

'If I don't get sleep,' I said. 'I'll drop dead.'

'So what?'

'Please,' I said.

'Another two hours,' Pris said.

'Are they all like you?' I asked her. 'The people who emerge from the Federal clinics? The new young people who get steered back onto course? No wonder we're having trouble selling organs.'

'What sort of organs?' Pris said. 'Personally I've got all the organs I want.'

'Ours are electronic.'

'Mine aren't. Mine are flesh and blood.'

'So what,' I said. 'Better they were electronic and you went to bed and let your houseguest sleep.'

'You're no guest of mine. Just my father's. And don't talk to me about going to bed or I'll wreck your life. I'll tell my father you propositioned me, and that'll end MASA ASSOCIATES and your career, and then you'll wish you never saw an organ of any kind, electronic or not. So toddle on to bed, buddy, and be glad you don't have worse troubles than not being able to sleep.' And she resumed her snap-snapping.

I stood for a moment, wondering what to do. Finally I turned and went back into the spare room, without having found any rejoinder.

My god, I thought. Beside her, the Stanton contraption is all warmth and friendliness.

And yet, she had no hostility toward me. She had no sense that she had said anything cruel or hard – she simply went on with her work. Nothing had happened, from her standpoint. I didn't matter to her.

If she had really disliked me – but could she do that? Did such a word mean anything in connection with her? Maybe it would be better, I thought as I locked my bedroom door. It would mean something more human, more comprehensible, to be disliked by her. But to be brushed off purposelessly, just so she would not be interfered with, so she could go on and finish her work – as if I were a variety of restraint, of possible interference and nothing more.

She must see only the most meager outer part of people, I decided. Must be aware of them in terms only of their coercive or non-coercive effects on her . . . thinking that, I lay with one ear pressed against the pillow, my arm over the other, dulling the snap-snapping noise, the endless procession of cuttings-off that passed one by one into infinity.

I could see why she felt attracted to Sam K. Barrows. Birds of a feather, or rather lizards of a scale. On the TV show, and again now, looking at the magazine cover . . . it was as if the brain part of Barrows, the shaved dome of his skull, had been lopped off and then skillfully replaced with some servo-system or some feedback circuit of selenoids and relays, all of which was operated from a distance off. Or operated by Something which sat upstairs there at the controls, pawing at the switches with tiny tricky convulsive motions.

And so odd that this girl had helped create the almost likable electronic simulacrum, as if on some subconscious level she was aware of the massive deficiency in herself, the emptiness dead center, and was busy compensating for it . . .

The next morning Maury and I had breakfast down the

street from the MASA building at a little cafe. As we faced each other across the booth I said,

'Listen, how sick is your daughter right now? If she's still a ward of the mental health people she must still be —'

'A condition like hers can't be cured,' Maury said, sipping his orange juice. 'It's a life-long process that either moves into less or into more difficult stages.'

'Would she still be classified under the McHeston Act as a 'phrenic if they were to administer the Benjamin Proverb Test at this moment to her?'

Maury said, 'It wouldn't be the Benjamin Proverb Test; they'd use the Soviet test, that Vigotsky-Luria colored blocks test, on her at this point. You just don't realize how early she branched off from the norm, if you could be said to be part of the "norm".'

'In school I passed the Benjamin Proverb Test.' That was the sine quo non for establishing the norm, ever since 1975, and in some states before that.

'I would say,' Maury said 'from what they told me at Kasanin, when I went to pick her up, that right now she wouldn't be classified as a schizophrenic. She was that for only three years, more or less. They've rolled her condition back to before that point, to her level of integration of about her twelfth year. And that's a non-psychotic state and hence it doesn't come in under the McHeston Act . . . so she's free to roam around.'

'Then she's a neurotic.'

'No, it's what they call *atypical* development or latent or borderline psychosis. It can develop either into a neurosis, the obsessional type, or it can flower into full schizophrenia, which it did in Pris' case in her third year in high school.'

While he ate his breakfast Maury told me about her development. Originally she had been a withdrawn child, what they call encapsulated or introverted. She kept to herself, had all sorts of secrets, such as a diary and private spots in the garden. Then, when she was about nine years old she started having fears at night, fears so great that by ten she was up a good deal of the night roaming about the house. When she was eleven she had gotten interested in science; she owned a chemistry set and did nothing after school but fiddle with that – she had few or no friends, and didn't seem to want any.

It was in high school that real trouble had begun. She had become afraid to enter large buildings, such as classrooms, and even feared the bus. When the doors of the bus closed she thought she was being suffocated. And she couldn't eat in public. Even if one single person was watching her, that was enough, and she had to drag her food off by herself, like a wild animal. And at the same time she had become compulsively neat. Everything had to be in its exact spot. She'd wander about the house all day, restlessly, making certain everything was clean – she'd wash her hands ten to fifteen times in a row.

'And remember,' Maury added, 'she was getting very fat. She was hefty when you first met her. Then she started dieting. She starved herself to lose weight. And she's still losing it. She's always avoiding one food after another; she does that even now.'

'And it took the Proverb Test to tell you that she was mentally ill?' I said. 'With a history like that?'

He shrugged. 'We deluded ourselves. We told ourselves she was merely neurotic. Phobias and rituals and the like . . .'

What bothered Maury the most was that his daughter, somewhere along the line, had lost her sense of humor. Instead of being giggly and silly and sloppy as she had once been she had now become as precise as a calculator. And not only that. Once she had cared about animals. And then, during her stay at Kansas City, she had suddenly gotten so she couldn't stand a dog or a cat. She had gone on with her interest in chemistry, however. And that – a profession – seemed to him a good thing.

36

'Has the out-patient therapy here helped her?'

'It keeps her at a stable level; she doesn't slide back. She still has a strong hypochondriacal trend and she still washes her hands a lot. She'll never stop that. And she's still overprecise and withdrawn; I can tell you what they call it. Schizoid personality. I saw the results of the inkblot test Doctor Horstowski made.' He was silent for a time. 'That's her out-patient doctor, here in this area, Region Five – counting the way the mental health Bureau counts. Horstowski is supposed to be good, but he's in private practice, so it costs us a hell of a lot.'

'Plenty of people are paying for that,' I said. 'You're not alone, according to the TV ads. What is it, one person out of every four has served time in a Federal Mental Health Clinic?'

'I don't mind the clinic part because that's free; what I object to is this expensive out-patient follow up. It was her idea to come home from Kasanin Clinic, not mine. I keep thinking she's going to go back there, but she threw herself into designing the simulacrum, and when she wasn't doing that she was mosaicing the bathroom walls. She never stops being active. I don't know where she gets the energy.'

I said, 'When I consider all the people I know who've been victims of mental illness it's amazing. My aunt Gretchen, who's at the Harry Stack Sullivan Clinic at San Diego. My cousin Leo Roggis. My English teacher in high school, Mr Haskins. The old Italian down the street who was on a pension, George Oliveri. I remember a buddy of mine in the Service, Art Boles; he had 'phrenia and went to the Fromm-Reichmann Clinic at Rochester, New York. There was Alys Johnson, a girl I went with in college; she's at Samuel Anderson Clinic in Area Three, which would be in Baton Rouge, La. And a man I worked for, Ed Yeats; he had 'phrenia that became paranoia. And Waldo Dangerfield, another buddy of mine. Gloria Milstein, a girl I knew who had really enormous breasts like pears; she's god knows where, but she was picked up by a personnel psych test when she was applying for a typing job; the Federal people swooped down and grabbed her – off she went. She was cute. And John Franklin Mann, a used car salesman I knew; he tested out as a dilapidated 'phrenic and was carted off, probably to Kasanin, because he's got relatives in Missouri. And Marge Morrison, another girl I knew; she had the hebe' version, which always bothers me. She's out again, though; I got a card from her. And Bob Ackers, a roommate I had. And Eddy Weiss – '

Maury had risen to his feet. 'We better get going.'

Together we left the cafe. 'You know this Sam Barrows?' I asked.

'Sure. I mean, not personally; I know him by reputation. He's the darndest fellow. He'll bet on anything. If one of his mistresses – and that's a story in itself – if one of his mistresses dived out of a hotel window he'd bet on which end hit the pavement first, her head or her tail. He's like one of the old-time speculators reborn, one of those captains of finance. Life's a gamble to a guy like that. I admire him.'

'So does Pris.'

'Admire, hell – adores. She met him. They stared each other down – it was a draw. He galvanized or magnetized her or some darn thing. For weeks afterwards she could hardly talk.'

'Was that when she was job-hunting?'

Maury nodded. 'She didn't get the job, but she did get into the sanctum sanctorum. Louis, that guy can scent out possibilities on all sides, opportunities no one else could see in a million years. You ought to dip into *Fortune*, sometime; they did a big write-up on him around ten months ago.'

'From what she told me Pris made quite a pitch to him that day.'

'She told him she had incredible worth that no one

recognized. He was supposed to recognize it, evidently. Anyhow, she said that in his organization, working for him, she'd rise to the top and be known all over the universe. But otherwise, she'd just go on as she was. She told him she was a gambler, too; she wanted to stake everything on going to work for him. Can you beat that?'

'No,' I said. She hadn't told me that part.

After a pause Maury said, 'The Edwin M. Stanton was her idea.'

Then it was true. That made me feel really bad, to hear that. 'And it was her idea that it would be of Stanton?'

'No, it was my idea. She wanted it to look like Sam Barrows. But there wasn't enough data to feed to its ruling monad guidance system, so we got reference books on historical characters. And I was always interested in the Civil War; it was a hobby of mine years ago. So that settled that.'

'I see,' I said.

'She still has Barrows on her mind all the time. It's what her analyst calls an obsessive idea.'

We walked on toward the office of MASA ASSOCIATES.

4

When we entered our office we found my brother Chester on the phone from Boise, reminding us that we had left the Edwin M. Stanton in the family living room, and asking us to pick it up, please.

'Well, we'll try to get out sometime today,' I promised him.

Chester said, 'It's sitting where you left it. Father turned it on for a few minutes this morning to see if it got the news.'

'What news?'

'The morning news. The summary, like David Brinkley.'

He meant *gave* the news. So my family had in the meantime decided that I was right; it was a machine after all and not a person.

'Did it?' I asked.

'No,' Chester said. 'It talked about the unnatural impudence of commanders in the field.'

When I had hung up the phone Maury said, 'Maybe Pris would get it.'

'Does she have a car?' I asked.

'She can take the Jag. Maybe you better go along with her, though, in case there's still a chance your dad's interested.'

Later in the day Pris showed up at the office, and soon we were on our way back to Boise.

For the first part of the trip we drove in silence, Pris behind the wheel. All at once she said, 'Do you have connections with someone who's interested in the Edwin M. Stanton?' She eyed me.

'No. What a strange question.'

'What's your real motive for coming along on this trip? You do have a concealed motive . . . it radiates from every pore of your body. If it were up to me I wouldn't let you within a hundred yards of the Stanton.'

As she continued to eye me, I knew I was in for more dissection.

'Why aren't you married?' she asked.

'I don't know.'

'Are you a homosexual?'

'No!'

'Did some girl you fell in love with find you too ugly?'

I groaned.

'How old are you?'

That seemed reasonable enough, and yet, in view of the general attitude she held, I was wary of even that. 'Ummm,' I murmured.

'Forty?'

'No. Thirty-three.'

'But your hair is gray on the sides and you have funny-looking snaggly teeth.'

I wished I was dead.

'What was your first reaction to the Stanton?' Pris asked.

I said, 'I thought, "What a kindly-looking old gentleman that is there."'

'You're lying, aren't you?'

'Yes!'

'What did you actually think?'

'I thought, "What a kindly-looking old gentleman that is there, wrapped up in newspapers."'

Pris said thoughtfully, 'You probably are queer for old men. So your opinion isn't worth anything.'

'Listen, Pris, somebody is going to brain you with a tire iron, someday. You understand?'

'You can barely handle your hostility, can you? Is that because you're a failure in your own eyes? Maybe you're

41

being too hard on yourself. Tell me your childhood dreams and goals and I'll tell you if – '

'Not for a billion dollars.'

'Are they shameful?' She continued to study me intently. 'Did you do shameful sexual things with yourself, like it tells about in the psych books?'

I felt as if I were about to pass out.

'Obviously I hit on a sensitive topic with you,' Pris said. 'But don't be ashamed. You don't do it anymore, do you? I suppose you still might . . . you're not married, and normal sexual outlets are denied you.' She pondered that. 'I wonder what Sam does, along the sex line.'

'Sam Vogel? Our driver, now in the Reno, Nevada area?'

'No. Sam K. Barrows.'

'You're obsessed,' I said. 'Your thoughts, your speech, your tiling the bathroom – your involvement in the Stanton.'

'The simulacrum is brilliantly original.'

'What would your analyst say about it?'

'Milt Horstowski? I told him. He already said.'

'Tell me,' I said. 'Didn't he say this is a deranged manic compulsion of some kind?'

'No, he agreed that I should be doing something creative. When I told him about the Stanton he complimented me on it and hoped it would work out.'

'Probably you gave him one hell of a biased account.'

'No. I told him the truth.'

'About *refighting the Civil War with robots*?'

'Yes. He said it had flair.'

'Jesus Christ,' I said. 'They're all crazy.'

'All,' Pris said, reaching out and ruffling my hair, 'but you, buddy boy. Right?'

I could say nothing.

'You take things too seriously,' Pris drawled. 'Relax and enjoy life. You're an anal type. Duty bound. You ought to let those old sphincter muscles let go for once

. . . see how it feels. You want to be bad; that's the secret desire of the anal type. They feel they must do their duty, though; that's why they're so pedantic and given to having doubts all the time. Like this; you have doubts about this.'

'I don't have doubts. I just have a yawning sense of absolute dread.'

Pris laughed, rumpled my hair.

'It's funny,' I said. 'My overwhelming fear.'

'It's not an overwhelming fear you feel,' Pris said matter-of-factly. 'It's simply a little bit of natural carnal earthly lust. Some for me. Some for loot. Some for power. Some for fame.' She indicated, with her thumb and first finger, a small amount. 'About that much in total. That's the size of your great big overwhelming emotions.' Lazily, she glanced at me, enjoying herself.

We drove on.

In Boise, at my family's home, we picked up the simulacrum, re-wrapped it in newspapers, and lugged it to the car. We returned to Ontario and Pris let me off at the office. There was little conversation between us on the return trip; Pris was withdrawn and I smoldered with anxiety and resentment toward her. My attitude seemed to amuse her. I was wise enough, however, to keep my mouth closed.

When I entered the office I found a short, plump, dark-haired woman waiting for me. She wore a heavy coat and carried a briefcase. 'Mr Rosen?'

'Yeah,' I said, wondering if she was a process server.

'I'm Colleen Nild. From Mr Barrows' office. Mr Barrows asked me to drop by here and speak to you, if you have a moment.' She had a low, rather uncertain voice, and looked, I thought, like someone's niece.

'What does Mr Barrows want?' I asked guardedly, showing her to a chair. I seated myself facing her.

'Mr Barrows had me make a carbon of a letter he has

prepared for Miss Pris Frauenzimmer, a carbon for you.' She held out three thin sheets, onion-skin, in fact; I saw somewhat blurred, dimmed, but obviously very correctly-typed business correspondence. 'You're the Rosen family from Boise, aren't you? The people who propose to manufacture the simulacra?'

Scanning the letter, I saw the word Stanton pop up again and again; Barrows was answering a letter from Pris having to do with it. But I could not get the hang of Barrows' thoughts; it was all too diffuse.

Then all at once I got the drift.

Barrows had obviously misunderstood Pris. He thought the idea of refighting the Civil War with electronic simulacra, manufactured at our factory in Boise, was a civic enterprise, a do-gooding patriotic effort along the lines of improving the schools and reclaiming the deserts, not a business proposition at all. That's what she gets, I said to myself. Yes, I was right; Barrows was thanking her for her idea, for thinking of him in connection with it . . . but, he said, he received requests of this sort daily, and already had his hands full with worthy efforts. For instance a good deal of his time was spent in fighting condemnation of a war-time housing tract somewhere in Oregon . . . the letter became so vague, at that point, that I lost the thread completely.

'Can I keep this?' I asked Miss Nild.

'Please do. And if you'd like to comment, I'm sure Mr Barrows would be interested in anything you have to say.'

I said, 'How long have you worked for Mr Barrows?'

'Eight years, Mr Rosen.' She sounded happy about it.

'Is he a billionaire, like the papers say?'

'I suppose so, Mr Rosen.' Her brown eyes twinkled, enlarged by her glasses.

'Does he treat his employees good?'

She smiled without answering.

44

'What's this housing project, this Green Peach Hat, that Barrows is talking about in the letter?'

'That's a term for Gracious Prospect Heights, one of the greatest multiple-unit housing developments in the Pacific Northwest. Mr Barrows always calls it that, although originally it was a term of derision. The people who want to tear it down invented the term and Mr Barrows took it over – the term, I mean – to protect the people who live there, so they won't feel spat upon. They appreciate that. They got up a petition thanking him for his help in blocking condemnation proceedings; there were almost two thousand signatures.'

'Then the people who live there don't want it torn down?'

'Oh no. They're fiercely loyal to it. A group of do-gooders have taken it upon themselves to meddle, house-wives and some society people who want to increase their own property values. They want to see the land used for a country club or something on that order. Their group is called the Northwest Citizens' Committee for Better Housing. A Mrs Devorac heads it.'

I recalled having read about her in the Oregon papers; she was quite up in the fashionable circles, always involved in causes. Her picture appeared on the first page of section two regularly.

'Why does Mr Barrows want to save this housing tract?' I asked.

'He is incensed at the idea of American citizens deprived of their rights. Most of them are poorer people. They'd have no place to go. Mr Barrows understands how they feel because he lived in rooming houses for years . . . you know that his family had no more money than anyone else? That he made his money on his own, through his own hard work and efforts?'

'Yes,' I said. She seemed to be waiting for me to go on, so I said, 'It's nice he still is able to identify with the working class, even though he's now a billionaire.'

'Since most of Mr Barrows' money was made in real estate, he has an acute awareness of the problems people face in their struggle to obtain decent housing. To society ladies such as Silvia Devorac, Green Peach Hat is merely an unsightly conglomeration of old buildings; none of them have gone inside – it would never occur to them to do so.'

'You know,' I said, 'hearing this about Mr Barrows goes a long way to make me feel that our civilization isn't declining.'

She smiled her informal, warm smile at me.

'What do you know about this Stanton electronic simulacrum?' I asked her.

'I know that one has been built. Miss Frauenzimmer mentioned that in her communications both by mail and over the phone to Mr Barrows. I believe Mr Barrows also told me that Miss Frauenzimmer wanted to put the Stanton electronic simulacrum onto a Greyhound bus and have it ride unaccompanied to Seattle, where Mr Barrows is currently. That would be her way of demonstrating graphically its ability to merge with humans and be unnoticed.'

'Except for its funny split beard and old-fashioned vest.'

'I was unaware of those factors.'

'Possibly the simulacrum could argue with a cab driver as to the shortest route from the bus terminal to Mr Barrows' office,' I said. 'That would be an additional proof of its humanness.'

Colleen Nild said, 'I'll mention that to Mr Barrows.'

'Do you know the Rosen electronic organ, or possibly our spinet pianos?'

'I'm not sure.'

'The Rosen factory at Boise produces the finest electronic chord organ in existence. Far superior to the Hammerstein Mood Organ, which emits a noise nothing more adequate than a modified flute-sound.'

'I was unaware of that, too,' Miss or Mrs Nild said. 'I'll mention that to Mr Barrows. He has always been a music lover.'

I was still involved in reading Barrows' letter when my partner returned from his mid-day coffee break. I showed it to him.

'Barrows writing to Pris,' he said, seating himself to pore over it. 'Maybe we're in, Louis. Could it be? I guess it isn't a figment of Pris' mind after all. Gosh, the man's hard to follow; is he saying he is or he isn't interested in the Stanton?'

'Barrows seems to say he's completely tied up right now with a pet project of his own, that housing tract called Green Peach Hat.'

'I lived there,' Maury said. 'In the late 'fifties.'

'What's it like?'

'Louis, it's hell. The dump ought to be burned to the ground; only a match – nothing else – would help that place.'

'Some do-gooders agree with you.'

Maury said in a low, tense voice, 'If they want someone to burn it down I'll do it personally for them. You can quote me, too. Sam Barrows owns that place.'

'Ah,' I said.

'He's making a fortune in rentals off it. Slum rentals is one of the biggest rackets in the world today; you get back like five to six hundred per cent return on your investment. Well, I suppose we can't let personal opinion enter into business. Barrows is still a shrewd businessman and the best person to back the simulacra, even if he is a rich fink. But you say this letter is a rejection of the idea?'

'You could phone him and find out. Pris seems to have phoned him.'

Picking up the phone, Maury dialed.

'Wait,' I said.

47

He glared at me.

'I've got an intuition,' I said, 'of doom.'

Into the phone, Maury said, 'Mr Barrows.'

I grabbed the phone from him and hung it up.

'You – ' He quivered with anger. 'What a coward.' Lifting the receiver he once more dialed. 'Operator, I was cut off.' He looked around for the letter; it had Barrows' number on it. I picked up the letter and crumpled it into a ball and tossed it across the room.

Cursing at me he slammed down the receiver.

We faced each other, breathing heavily.

'What's wrong with you?' Maury said.

'I don't think we should get tangled up with a man like that.'

'*Like what?*'

I said, 'Whom the gods would destroy they first make mad!'

That shook him. 'What do you mean?' he mumbled, tipping his head and regarding me bird-like. 'You think I'm batty to call, do you? Ought to be at the funny clinic. Maybe so. But anyhow I intend to.' Going past me he fished up the crumpled ball of paper, smoothed it, memorized the number, and returned to the phone. Again he placed the call.

'It's the end of us,' I said.

An interval passed. 'Hello,' Maury said suddenly. 'Let me talk to Mr Barrows, please. This is Maury Rock in Ontario, Oregon.'

Another interval.

'Mr Barrows! This is Maury Rock.' He got a set grin on his face; he bent over, resting his elbow on his thigh. 'I have your letter here, sir, to my daughter, Pris Frauenzimmer . . . regarding our world-shaking invention, the electronic simulacrum, as personified by the charming, old-time characterization of Lincoln's Secretary of War, Edwin McMasters Stanton.' A pause in which he gaped at me vacantly. 'Are you interested, sir?' Another pause, much longer this time.

You're not going to make the sale, Maury, I said to myself.

'Mr Barrows,' Maury said. 'Yes, I see what you mean. That's true, sir. But let me point this out to you, in case you overlooked it.'

The conversation rambled on for what seemed an endless time. At last Maury thanked Barrows, said goodbye, and hung up.

'No dice,' I said.

He glowered at me wearily. 'Wow.'

'What did he say?'

'The same as in the letter. He still doesn't see it as a commercial venture. He thinks we're a patriotic organization.' He blinked, shook his head wonderingly, 'No dice, like you said.'

'Too bad.'

'Maybe it's for the better,' Maury said. But he sounded merely resigned; he did not sound as if he believed it. Someday he would try again. He still hoped.

We were as far apart as ever.

5

During the next two weeks Maury Rock's predictions as to the decline of the Rosen electronic organ seemed to be borne out. All trucks reported few if any sales of organs. And we noticed that the Hammerstein people had begun to advertise one of their mood organs for less than a thousand dollars. Of course their price did not include shipping charges or the bench. But still – it was bad news for us.

Meanwhile, the Stanton was in and out of our office. Maury had the idea of building a showroom for sidewalk traffic and having the Stanton demonstrate spinets. He got my permission to call in a contractor to remodel the ground floor of the building; the work began, while the Stanton puttered about upstairs, helping Maury with the mail and hearing what it was going to have to do when the showroom had been completed. Maury advanced the suggestion that it shave off its beard, but after an argument between him and the Stanton he withdrew his idea and the Stanton went about as before, with its long white side whiskers.

'Later on,' Maury explained to me when the Stanton was not present, 'I'm going to have it demonstrate itself. I'm in the process of finalizing on a sales pitch to that effect.' He intended, he explained, to feed the pitch into the Stanton's ruling monad brain in the form of punched instruction tape. That way there would be no arguments, as there had been over the whiskers.

All this time Maury was busy concocting a second simulacrum. It was in MASA's truck-repair shop, on one of the workbenches, in the process of being assembled.

On Thursday the powers that decreed our new direction permitted me to view it for the first time.

'Who's it going to be?' I asked, studying it with a feeling of gloom. It consisted of no more than a large complex of selenoids, wiring, circuit breakers, and the like, all mounted on aluminum panels. Bundy was busy testing a central monad turret; he had his volt-meter in the midst of the wiring, studying the reading on the dial.

Maury said, 'This is Abraham Lincoln.'

'You've lost control of your reason.'

'Not at all. I want something really big to take to Barrows when I visit him next month.'

'Oh I see,' I said. 'You hadn't told me about that.'

'You think I'm going to give up?'

'No,' I admitted. 'I knew you wouldn't give up; I know you.'

'I've got the instinct,' Maury said.

The next afternoon, after some gloomy pondering, I looked up Doctor Horstowski in the phonebook. The office of Pris' out-patient psychiatrist was in the better residential section of Boise. I telephoned him and asked for an appointment as soon as possible.

'May I ask who recommended you?' his nurse said.

With distaste I said, 'Miss Priscilla Frauenzimmer.'

'All right, Mr Rosen; Doctor Horstowski can see you tomorrow at one-thirty.'

Technically, I was supposed to be out on the road, again, setting up communities to receive our trucks. I was supposed to be making maps and inserting ads in newspapers. But ever since Maury's phonecall to Sam Barrows something had been the matter with me.

Perhaps it had to do with my father. Since the day he had set eyes on the Stanton – and found out it was a machine built to resemble a man – he had become progressively more feeble. Instead of going down to the factory every morning he often remained at home, generally hunched in a chair before the TV; the times I had seen him he had a troubled expression and his faculties seemed clouded.

I mentioned it to Maury.

'Poor old guy,' Maury said. 'Louis, I hate to say this to you, but Jerome is getting frail.'

'I realize that.'

'He can't compete much longer.'

'What do you suggest I do?'

'Keep him out of the bustle and strife of the market place. Consult with your mother and brother; find out what Jerome has always wanted to do hobby-wise. Maybe carve flying model World War One airplanes, such as the Fokker Triplane or the Spad. You should look into that, Louis, for the old man's sake. Am I right, buddy?'

I nodded.

'It's partly your fault,' Maury said. 'You haven't cared for him properly. When a man gets his age he needs support. I don't mean financial; I mean – hell, I mean *spiritual*.'

The next day I drove to Boise and, at one-twenty parked before the modern, architect-designed office building of Doctor Horstowski.

When Doctor Horstowski appeared in the hallway to usher me into his office, I found myself facing a man built along the lines of an egg. His body was rounded; his head was rounded; he wore tiny round glasses; there were no straight or broken lines about him, and when he walked he progressed in a flowing smooth motion as if he was rolling. His voice, too, was soft and smooth. And yet, when I entered his office and seated myself and got a closer look, I saw that there was one feature of him which I had not noticed: he had a tough, harsh-looking nose, as flat and sharp as a parrot's beak. And now that I noticed that, I could hear in his voice a suppressed tearing edge of great harshness.

He seated himself with a pad of lined paper and a pen,

crossed his legs, and began to ask me dull, routine questions.

'What did you wish to see me about?' he asked at last, in a voice barely at the fringe of audibility but at the same time clearly distinct.

'Well, I'm having this problem. I'm a partner in this firm, MASA ASSOCIATES. And I feel that my partner and his daughter are against me and plotting behind my back. Especially I feel they're out to degrade and destroy my family, in particular my elderly father, Jerome, who isn't well enough or strong enough anymore to take that sort of thing.'

'What "sort of thing"?'

'This deliberate and ruthless destruction of the Rosen spinet and electronic organ factory and our entire retail system. In favor of a mad, grandiose scheme for saving mankind or defeating the Russians or something like that; I can't make out what it is, to be honest.'

'Why can't you "make it out"?' His pen scratch-scratched.

'Because it changes from day to day.' I paused. The pen paused, too. 'It seems to be designed to reduce me to helplessness. And as a result Maury will take over the business and maybe the factory as well. And they're mixed up with an incredibly wealthy and powerful sinister figure, Sam K. Barrows of Seattle, whose picture you possibly saw on the cover of *Look* magazine.'

I was silent.

'Go. On.' He enunciated as if he were a speech instructor.

'Well, in addition I feel that my partner's daughter, who is the prime mover in all this, is a dangerous ex-psychotic who can only be said to be as hard as iron and utterly without scruples.' I looked at the doctor expectantly, but he said nothing, and showed no visible reaction. 'Pris Frauenzimmer,' I said.

He nodded.

'What's your opinion?' I asked.

'Pris,' Doctor Horstowski said, sticking his tongue out and down and staring at his notes, 'is a dynamic personality.'

I waited, but that was all.

'You think it's in my mind?' I demanded.

'What do you think is their *motive* for doing all this?' he asked.

That took me by surprise. 'I don't know. Is it my business to figure that out? Hell, they want to peddle the simulacra to Barrows and make a mint; what else? And get a lot of prestige and power, I guess. They have maniacal dreams.'

'And you stand in their way?'

'Right,' I said.

'You have no such dreams.'

'I'm a realist. Or at least I try to be. As far as I'm concerned that Stanton – have you seen it?'

'Pris came in here once with it. It sat in the waiting room while she had her hour.'

'What did it do?'

'It read *Life* magazine.'

'Didn't it make your blood crawl?' I asked.

'I don't think so.'

'You weren't frightened to think that those two, Maury and Pris, could dream up something unnatural and dangerous like that?'

Doctor Horstowski shrugged.

'Christ,' I said bitterly, 'you're insulated. You're in here safe in this office. What do you care what goes on in the world?'

Doctor Horstowski gave what seemed to me to be a fleeting but smug smile. That made me furious.

'Doctor,' I said, 'I'll let you in on it. Pris is playing a cruel prank on you. She sent me in here. I'm a simulacrum, like the Stanton. I wasn't supposed to give the show away, but I can't go on with it any longer. I'm just

54

a machine, made out of circuits and relay switches. You see how sinister all this is? She'd do it even to you. What do you say to that?'

Halting in his writing, Doctor Horstowski said, 'Did you tell me you're married? If so, what is your wife's name, age, and does she have an occupation? And where born?'

'I'm not married. I used to have a girl friend, an Italian girl who sang in a night club. She was tall and had dark hair. Her name was Lucrezia but she asked us to call her Mimi. Later on she died of t.b. That was after we split up. We used to fight.'

The doctor carefully wrote those facts down.

'Aren't you going to answer my question?' I asked.

It was hopeless. The doctor, if he had a reaction to the simulacrum sitting in his office reading *Life*, was not going to reveal it. Or maybe he didn't have one; maybe he didn't care who he found sitting across from him or among his magazines – maybe he had taught himself long ago to accept anyone and anything he found there.

But at least I could get an answer out of him regarding Pris, who I regarded as a worse evil than the simulacra.

'I've got my .45 Service revolver and shells,' I said. 'That's all I need; the opportunity will take care of itself. It's just a question of time before she tries the same cruelty on someone else as she did on me. I consider it my sacred task to rub her out – that's god's truth.'

Scrutinizing me, Horstowski said, 'Your real problem, as you've phrased it – and I believe accurately – is the hostility you feel, a very mute and baffled hostility, seeking an outlet, toward your partner and this eighteen-year-old girl, who has difficulties of her own and who is actively seeking solutions in her own way as best she can.'

Put like that, it did not sound so good. It was my own feelings which harried me, not the enemy. *There was no enemy*. There was only my own emotional life, suppressed and denied.

'Well, what can you do for me?' I asked.

'I can't make your reality-situation palatable to you. But I can help you comprehend it.' He opened a drawer of his desk; I saw boxes and bottles and envelopes of pills, a rat's nest of physician's samples, scattered and heaped. After rooting, Horstowski came up with a small bottle, which he opened. 'I can give you these. Take two a day, one when you get up and one on retiring. Hubrizine.' He passed me the bottle.

'What's it do?' I put the bottle away in my inside pocket.

'I can explain it to you because you are professionally familiar with the Mood Organ. Hubrizine stimulates the anterior portion of the spetal region of the brain. Stimulation in that area, Mr Rosen, will bring about greater alertness, plus cheerfulness and a belief that events will work out all right on their own. It compares to this setting on the Hammerstein Mood Organ.' He passed me a small glossy folded printed piece of paper; I saw Hammerstein stop-setting indications on it. 'But the effect of the drug is much more intense; as you know, the amplitude of affect-shock produced by the Mood Organ is severely limited by law.'

I read the setting critically. By god, when translated into notes it was close to the opening of the Beethoven Sixteenth Quartet. What a vindication for enthusiasta of the Beethoven Third Period, I said to myself. Just looked at, the stop-setting numbers made me feel better.

'I can almost hum this drug,' I said. 'Want me to try?'

'No thank you. Now, you understand that if drug therapy does not avail in your case we can always attempt brain-slicing in the region of the temporal lobes – based, of course, on extensive brain-mapping which would have to be conducted at U.C. Hospital in San Francisco or Mount Zion; we have no facilities here. I prefer to avoid that myself if possible, since it often develops that the section of the temporal lobes involved can't be spared. The Government has abandoned that at its clinics, you know.'

'I'd rather not be sliced,' I agreed. 'I've had friends who've had that done . . . but personally it gives me the shivers. Let me ask you this. Do you by any chance have a drug whose setting in terms of the Mood Organ corresponds to portions of the Choral Movement of the Beethoven Ninth?'

'I've never looked into it,' Horstowski said.

'On a Mood Organ I'm particularly affected when I play the part where the choir sings, "*Mus' ein Lieber Vater wohnen*," and then very high up, like angels, the violins and the soprano part of the choir sing as an answer, "*Ubrem Sternenzelt*."'

'I'm not familiar with it to that extent,' Horstowski admitted.

'They're asking whether a Heavenly Father exists, and then very high up they answer, yes, above the realm of stars. That part – if you could find the correspondence in terms of pharmacology, I might benefit enormously.'

Doctor Horstowski got out a massive loose-leaf binder and began to thumb through it. 'I'm afraid I can't locate a pill corresponding to that. You might consult with the Hammerstein engineers, however.'

'Good idea,' I said.

'Now, as to your dealings with Pris. I think you're a little strong in your view of her as a menace. After all, you are free not to associate with her *at all*, aren't you?' He eyed me slyly.

'I guess so.'

'Pris has challenged you. She's a provocative personality . . . most people who know her, I'd imagine, get to feeling as you do. That's Pris' way of stirring them up, making them react. It is probably allied to her scientific

57

bent . . . it's a form of curiosity; she wants to see what makes people tick.' He smiled.

'In this case,' I said, 'she almost killed the specimen while trying to investigate it.'

'Pardon?' He cupped his ear. 'Yes, a specimen. She perceives other people sometimes in that aspect. But I wouldn't let that throw me. We live in a society where detachment is almost essential.'

While he was saying this, Doctor Horstowski was writing in his appointment book.

'What do you think of,' he murmured, 'when you think of Pris.'

'Milk,' I said.

'Milk!' His eyes opened wide. 'Interesting. Milk . . .'

'I'm not coming back here,' I told him. 'It's no use giving me that card.' However, I accepted the appointment card. 'Our time is up for today, is it?'

'Regrettably,' Doctor Horstowski said, 'it is.'

'I was not kidding when I told you I'm one of Pris' simulacra. There used to be a Louis Rosen, but no more. Now there's only me. And if anything happens to me, Pris and Maury have the instructional tapes to create another. Pris makes the body out of bathroom tile. It's pretty good, isn't it? It fooled you and my brother Chester and almost my father. That's the actual reason he's so unhappy; he guessed the truth.' Having said that I nodded goodbye and walked from the office, along the hall and through the waiting room, to the street.

But you, I said to myself. You'll never guess, Doctor Horstowski, not in a million years. I'm good enough to fool you and all the rest of them like you.

Getting into my Chevrolet Magic Fire, I drove slowly back to the office.

6

After having told Doctor Horstowski that I was a simulacrum I could not get the idea out of my mind. Once there had been a real Louis Rosen but now he was gone and I stood in this spot, fooling almost everyone, including myself.

This idea persisted for the next week, growing a little dimmer each day but not quite fading out.

And yet on another level I knew it was a preposterous idea, just a lot of drivel I had come up with because of my resentment toward Doctor Horstowski.

The immediate effect of the idea was to cause me to look up the Edwin M. Stanton simulacrum; when I got back to the office from my visit to the doctor I asked Maury where the thing could be found.

'Bundy's feeding a new tape to it,' Maury said. 'Pris came across a biography of Stanton that had some new material.' He returned to his letter-reading.

I found Bundy in the shop with the Stanton; having finished, he was putting it back together. Now he was asking it questions.

'Andrew Johnson betrayed the Union by his inability to conceive the rebellious states as – ' Seeing me, Bundy broke off. 'Hi, Rosen.'

'I want to talk to the thing. Okay?'

Bundy departed, leaving me alone with the Stanton. It was seated in a brown, cloth-covered armchair, with a book open on its lap; it regarded me sternly.

'Sir,' I said, 'do you recall me?'

'Yes sir, I do. You are Mr Louis Rosen of Boise, Idaho. I recall a pleasant overnight stay with your father. Is he well?'

'Not as well as I wish he was.'

'A pity.'

'Sir, I'd like to ask you a question. Doesn't it seem odd to you that although you were born around 1800 you are still alive in 1982? And doesn't it seem odd to you to be shut off every now and then? And what about your being made out of transistors and relays? You didn't used to be, because in 1800 they didn't have transistors and relays.' I paused, waiting.

'Yes,' the Stanton agreed, 'those are oddities. I have here a volume – ' He held up his book. 'Which deals with the new science of cybernetics and this science has shed light on my perplexity.'

That excited me. 'Your perplexity!'

'Yes sir. During my stay with your father I discussed puzzling matters of this nature with him. When I consider the brief span of my life, swallowed up in the eternity before and behind it, the small space that I fill, or even see, engulfed in the infinite immensity of spaces which I know not, and which know not me, I am afraid.'

'I should think so,' I said.

'I am afraid, sir, and wonder to see myself here rather than there. For there is no reason why I should be here rather than there, now rather than then.'

'Did you come to any conclusion?'

The Stanton cleared its throat, then got out a folded linen handkerchief and carefully blew its nose. 'It seems to me that time must move in strange jumps, passing over intervening epochs. But why it would do that, or even how, I do not know. At a certain point the mind cannot fathom anything further.'

'You want to hear my theory?'

'Yes sir.'

'I claim there is no Edwin M. Stanton or Louis Rosen anymore. There was once, but they're dead. We're machines.'

The Stanton regarded me, its round, wrinkled face

twisted up. 'There may be some truth in that,' it said finally.

'And,' I said, 'Maury Rock and Pris Frauenzimmer designed us and Bob Bundy built us. And right now they're working on an Abe Lincoln simulacrum.'

The round, wrinkled face darkened. 'Mr Lincoln is dead.'

'I know.'

'You mean they are going to bring him back?'

'Yes,' I said.

'*Why*?'

'To impress Mr Barrows.'

'Who is Mr Barrows?' The old man's voice grated.

'A multi-millionaire who lives in Seattle, Washington. It was his influence that got sub-dividers started on the Moon.'

'Sir, have you ever heard of Artemus Ward?'

'No,' I admitted.

'If Mr Lincoln is revived you will be subjected to endless humorous selections from the writings of Mr Ward.' Scowling, the Stanton picked up its book and once more read. Its face was red and its hands shook.

Obviously I had said the wrong thing.

There was really not much that I knew about Edwin M. Stanton. Since everybody today looks up to Abraham Lincoln it hadn't occurred to me that the Stanton would feel otherwise. But you live and learn. After all, the simulacrum's attitude was formed well over a century ago, and there's not much you can do to change an attitude that old.

I excused myself – the Stanton barely glanced up and nodded – and set off down the street to the library. Fifteen minutes later I had the Britannica out and laid flat on a table; I looked up both Lincoln and Stanton and then the Civil War itself.

The article on Stanton was short but interesting. Stanton had started out hating Lincoln; the old man had been a Democrat, and he both hated and distrusted the new Republican Party. It described Stanton as being harsh, which I had already noticed, and it told of many squabbles with generals, especially Sherman. But, the article said, the old man was good in his job under Lincoln; he booted out fraudulent contractors and kept the troops well-equipped. And at the end of hostilities he was able to demobilize 800,000 men, no mean feat after a bloody Civil War.

The trouble hadn't started until Lincoln's death. It had really been hot-going there for a while, between Stanton and President Johnson; in fact it looked as if the Congress were going to take over and be the sole governing body. As I read the article I began to get a pretty good idea of the old man. He was a real tiger. He had a violent temper and a sharp tongue. He almost got Johnson out and himself in as a military dictator.

But the Britannica added, too, that Stanton was thoroughly honest and a genuine patriot.

The article on Johnson stated bluntly that Stanton was disloyal to his chief and in league with his enemies. It called Stanton obnoxious. It was a miracle that Johnson got the old man out.

When I put the volumes of the Britannica back on the shelf I breathed a sigh of relief; just in those little articles you could catch the atmosphere of pure poison which reigned in those days, the intrigues and hates, like something out of Medieval Russia. In fact all the plotting at the end of Stalin's lifetime – it was much like that.

As I walked slowly back to the office I thought, Kindly old gentleman hell. The Rock-Frauenzimmer combine, in their greed, had reawakened more than a man; they had reawakened what had been an awesome and awful force in this country's history. Better they should have made a Zachary Taylor simulacrum. No doubt it was Pris and her perverse, nihilistic mind that had conceived this great joker in the deck, this choice out of all the possible thousands, even millions. Why not Socrates? Or Gandhi?

And so now they expected calmly and happily to bring to life a second simulacrum: someone whom Edwin M. Stanton had a good deal of animosity toward. Idiots!

I entered our shop once more and found the Stanton reading as before. It had almost finished its cybernetics book.

There, not more than ten feet away, on the largest of MASA's workbenches, lay the mass of half-completed circuits which would one day be the Abraham Lincoln. Had the Stanton made it out? Had it connected this electronic confusion with what I had said? I stole a glance at the new simulacrum. It did not look as if anyone – or anything – had meddled inappropriately. Bundy's careful work could be seen, nothing else. Surely if the Stanton had gone at it in my absence, there would be a few broken or burned segments . . . I saw nothing like that.

Pris, I decided, was probably at home these days, putting the final life-like colors into the sunken cheeks of the Abe Lincoln shell which would house all these parts. That in itself was a full-time job. The beard, the big hands, skinny legs, the sad eyes. A field for her creativity, her artistic soul, to run and howl rampant. She would not show up until she had done a top-notch job.

Going back upstairs I confronted Maury. 'Listen, friend. That Stanton thing is going to up and bang Honest Abe over the head. Or haven't you bothered to read the history books?' And then I saw it. 'You *had* to read the books in order to make the instruction tapes. So you know better than I what the Stanton feels toward Lincoln! You know he's apt to roast the Lincoln into charred rust any minute!'

'Don't get mixed up in last year's politics.' Maury put down his letters for a moment, sighing. 'The other day it was my daughter; now it's the Stanton. There's always

63

some dark horror lurking. You have the mind of an old maid, you know that? Lay off and let me work.'

I went back downstairs to the shop again.

There, as before, sat the Stanton, but now it had finished its book; it sat pondering.

'Young man,' it called to me, 'give me more information about this Barrows. Did you say he lives at our nation's Capitol?'

'No sir, the state of Washington.' I explained where it was.

'And is it true, as Mr Rock tells me, that this Barrows arranged for the World's Fair to be held in that city through his great influence?'

'I've heard that. Of course, when a man is that rich and eccentric all sorts of legends crop up about him.'

'Is the fair still in progress?'

'No, that was years ago.'

'A pity,' the Stanton murmured. 'I wanted to go.'

That touched me to the heart. Again I reexperienced my first impression of it: that in many ways it was more human – god help us! – than we were, than Pris or Maury or even me, Louis Rosen. Only my father stood above it in dignity. Doctor Horstowski – another only partly-human creature, dwarfed by this electronic simulacrum. And, I thought, what about Barrows? How will he look when compared, face to face, with the Stanton?

And then I thought, How about the Lincoln? I wonder how that will make us feel and make us look.

'I'd like your opinion about Miss Frauenzimmer, sir,' I said to the simulacrum. 'If you have the time to spare.'

'I have the time, Mr Rosen.'

I seated myself on a truck tire opposite its brown easy-chair.

'I have known Miss Frauenzimmer for some time. I am not certain precisely how long, but no matter; we are well-acquainted. She has recently left the Kasanin Medical Clinic at Kansas City, Missouri and returned here to her family. As a matter of fact I live at the Frauenzimmer home. She has light gray eyes and stands five feet six inches. Her weight is one-hundred-twenty-pounds at this time. She has been losing weight, I am told. I cannot recall her as anything but beauteous. Now I shall dilate on deeper matters. Her stock is of the highest, although immigrant; for it has imbibed of the American vision, which is: that a person is only limited by his abilities and may rise to whatever station in life is best-suited to those abilities. It does not follow from that however, that all men will rise equally; far from it. But Miss Frauenzimmer is quite right in refusing to accept any arrangement which denies her expression of those abilities and she senses any infringement with a flash of fire in her gray eyes.'

I said, 'It sounds as if you've worked out your view thoroughly.'

'Sir, it is a topic deserving of some consideration; you yourself have erected it for our mutual inspection, have you not?' Its hard but wise eyes sparkled momentarily. 'Miss Frauenzimmer is basically good, at heart. She will come through. There is in her just a bit of impatience, and she does have a temper. But sir, temper is the anvil of justice, on which the hard facts of reality must be smitten. Men without temper are like animals without life; it is the spark that turns a lump of fur, flesh, bones and fat into a breathing expression of the Creator.'

I had to admit that I was impressed by the Stanton's harangue.

'What I am concerned with in Priscilla,' the Stanton continued, 'is not her fire and spirit; far from that. When she trusts her heart she trusts correctly. But Priscilla does not always listen to the dictates of her heart. Sorry to say, sir, she often pays heed to the dictates of her head. And there the difficulty arises.'

'Ah,' I said.

'For the logic of a woman is not the logic of the philosopher. It is in fact a vitiated and pale shadow of the knowledge of the heart, and, as a shade rather than an entity, it is not a proper guide. Women, when they heed their mind and not their heart, fall readily into error, and this may all too easily be seen in Priscilla Frauenzimmer's case. For when she hearkens there, a coldness falls over her.'

'Ah!' I interjected excitedly.

'Exactly.' The Stanton nodded and waggled his finger at me. 'You, too, Mr Rosen, have marked that shadow, that special coldness which emanates from Miss Frauenzimmer. And I see that it has troubled your soul, as well as mine. How she will deal with this in the future I do not know, but deal with it she must. For her Creator meant for her to come to terms with herself, and at present it is not in her to view with tolerance this part, this cold, impatient, abundantly-reasonable – but alas – *calculating* side of her character. For she has what many of us find in our own selves: a tendency to permit the insidious entrance of a meager and purblind philosophy into our everyday transactions, those we have with our fellows, our daily neighbors . . . and nothing is more dangerous than this puerile, ancient, venerated compendium of opinion, belief, prejudice, and the now-discarded sciences of the past – all of these cast off rationalisms forming a sterile and truncated source for her deeds; whereas were she merely to bend, to listen, she would hear the individual and wholesome expression of her own heart, her own being.'

The Stanton ceased speaking. It had finished its little speech on the topic of Pris. Where had it gotten it? Made it up? Or had Maury stuck the speech there in the form of an instruction tape, ready to be used on an occasion of this kind? It certainly did not sound like Maury. Was Pris herself responsible? Was this some bitter, weird irony of hers, inserting in the mouth of this mechanical contraption this penetrating analysis of herself? *I had the feeling it was. It demonstrated the great schizophrenic process still active in her, this strange split.*

I couldn't help comparing this to the sly, easy answers which Doctor Horstowski had given me.

'Thanks,' I said to the Stanton. 'I have to admit I'm very impressed by your off-the-cuff remarks.'

'"Off the cuff",' it echoed.

'Without preparation.'

'But this, sir, came from much preparation. For I have been gravely worried about Miss Frauenzimmer.'

'Me, too,' I said.

'And now, sir. I would be obliged if you would tell me about Mr Barrows. I understand he has expressed an interest in me.'

'Maybe I can get you the *Look* article. Actually I've never met him; I talked to his secretary recently, and I have a letter from him – '

'May I see the letter?'

'I'll bring it around tomorrow.'

'Was it your impression, too, that Mr Barrows is interested in me?' The Stanton eyed me intently.

'I – guess so.'

'You seem hesitant.'

'You ought to talk to him yourself.'

'Perhaps I will.' The Stanton reflected, scratching the side of its nose with its finger. 'I will ask either Mr Rock or Miss Frauenzimmer to convey me there and assist me in meeting tete-a-tete Mr Barrows.' It nodded to itself, evidently having made its decision.

7

Now that the Stanton had decided to visit Sam K. Barrows it was obvious that only the question of time remained. Even I could see the inevitability of it.

And at the same time, the Abraham Lincoln simulacrum neared completion. Maury set the next weekend for the date of the first test of the totality of the components. All the hardware would be in the case, mounted and ready to function.

The Lincoln container, when Pris and Maury brought it into the office, flabbergasted me. Even in its inert stage, lacking its working parts, it was so lifelike as to seem ready at any moment to rise into its day's activity. Pris and Maury, with Bob Bundy's help, carried the long thing downstairs to the shop; I trailed along and watched while they laid it out on the workbench.

To Pris I said, 'I have to hand it to you.'

Standing with her hands in her coat pockets, she somberly supervised. Her eyes seemed dark, deeper set; her skin was quite noticeably pale – she had on no make-up, and I guessed that she had been up all hours every night, finishing her task. It seemed to me, too, that she had lost weight; now she appeared actually thin. She wore a striped cotton t-shirt and blue jeans under her coat, and apparently she did not even need to wear a bra. She had on her low-heeled leather slippers and her hair had been tied back and held with a ribbon.

'Hi,' she murmured, rocking back and forth on her heels and biting her lip as she watched Bundy and Maury lower the Lincoln onto the bench.

'You did a swell job,' I said.

'Louis,' Pris said, 'take me out of here; take me

somewhere and buy me a cup of coffee, or let's just walk.' She started toward the door and after a moment of hesitation I followed.

Together, we strolled along the sidewalk, Pris staring down and kicking a pebble ahead of her.

'The first one was nothing,' she said, 'compared to this. Stanton is just another person and yet even so it was almost too much for us. I have a book at home with every picture taken of Lincoln. I've studied them until I know his face better than my own.' She kicked her pebble into the gutter. 'It's amazing how good those old photographs were. They used glass plates and the subject had to sit without moving. They had special chairs they built, to prop the subject's head so it wouldn't wobble. Louis.' At the curb she halted. 'Can he really come to life?'

'I dunno, Pris.'

'It's all self-deception. We can't really restore life to something that's dead.'

'Is that what you're doing? Is that how you think of it? If you put it like that I agree. Sounds like you're too deep in it emotionally. You better back away and get perspective.'

'You mean we're just making an imitation that walks and talks like the real thing. The spirit isn't there, just the appearance.'

'Yes,' I said.

'Did you ever go to a Catholic mass, Louis?'

'Naw.'

'They believe the bread and wine actually are the body and blood. That's a miracle. Maybe if we get the tapes perfect here, and the voice and the physical appearance and – '

'Pris,' I said, 'I never thought I'd see you frightened.'

'I'm not frightened. It's just too much for me. When I was a kid in junior high Lincoln was my hero; I gave a report on him in the eighth grade. You know how it is when you're a kid, everything you read in books is real. Lincoln was real to me. But of course I really spun it out of my own mind. So what I mean is, my own fantasies were real to me. It took me years to shake them, fantasies about the Union cavalry and battles and Ulysses S. Grant . . . you know.'

'Yeah.'

'Do you think someday somebody will make a simulacrum of you and me? And we'll have to come back to life?'

'What a morbid thought.'

'There we'll be, dead and oblivious to everything . . . and then we'll feel something stirring. Maybe see a snatch of light. And then it'll all come flooding in on us, reality once more. We'll be helpless to stop the process, we'll have to come back. Resurrected!' She shuddered.

'It's not that, what you're doing; get that idea out of your mind. You have to separate the actual Lincoln from this – '

'The real Lincoln exists in my mind,' Pris said.

I was astonished. 'You don't believe that. What do you mean by saying that? You mean you have the *idea* in your mind.'

She cocked her head on one side and eyed me. 'No, Louis. I really have Lincoln in my mind. And I've been working night after night to transfer him out of my mind, back into the outside world.'

I laughed.

'It's a dreadful world to bring him into,' Pris said. 'Listen Louis. I'll tell you something. I know a way to get rid of those awful yellowjackets that sting everybody. You don't take any risk . . . and it doesn't cost anything; all you need is a bucket of sand.'

'Okay.'

'You wait until night. So the yellowjackets are all down below in their nest asleep. Then you show up at their hole and you pour the bucket of sand over it, so the sand

70

forms a mound. Now listen. You think the sand suffocates them. But it's not quite like that. Here's what happens. The next morning the yellowjackets wake up and find their entrance blocked with this sand, so they start burrowing up into the sand to clear it away. They have no place to carry it except to other parts of their nest. So they start a bucket brigade; they carry the sand grain by grain to the back of their nest, but as they take sand from the entrance more falls in its place.'

'I see.'

'Isn't it awful?'

'Yes,' I agreed.

'What they do is they gradually fill their own nest with sand. They do it themselves. The harder they work to clear their entrance the faster it happens, and they suffocate. It's like an Oriental torture, isn't it? When I heard about this, Louis, I said to myself, I wish I was dead. I don't want to live in a world where such things can be.'

'When did you learn about this sand technique?'

'Years ago; I was seven. Louis, I used to imagine what it was like down there in the nest. I'd be asleep.' Walking along beside me, she suddenly took hold of my arm and shut her eyes tight. 'Absolutely dark. All around me, others like me. Then – thump. That's the noise from above. Somebody dumping the sand. But it means nothing . . . we all sleep on.' She let me guide her along the sidewalk, pressing tightly against me. 'Then we doze; we doze for the rest of the night, because it's cold . . . but then daylight comes and the ground gets warm. But it's still dark. We wake up. Why is there no light? We head for the entrance. All those particles, they block it. We're frightened. What's going on? We all pitch in; we try not to get panicked. We don't use up all the oxygen; we're organized into teams. We work silently. Efficiently.'

I led her across the street; she still had her eyes shut. It was like leading a very tiny girl.

'We never see daylight, Louis. No matter how many

grains of sand we haul away. We work and we wait, but it never comes. Never.' In a despairing, strangled voice she said, 'We die, Louis, down there.'

I wound my fingers through hers. 'What about the cup of coffee now?'

'No,' she said. 'I just want to walk.' We went on for a distance.

'Louis,' Pris said, 'those insects like wasps and ants . . . they do so much down in their nests; it's very complicated.'

'Yes. Also spiders.'

'Spiders in particular. Like the trap-door spider. I wonder how a spider feels when someone breaks its web to pieces.'

'It probably says "drat",' I said.

'No,' Pris said solemnly. 'It gets furious and then it abandons hope. First it's sore – it would sting you to death if it could get hold of you. And then this slow, awful blind despair creeps over it. It knows that even if it rebuilds, the same thing is going to happen again.'

'But spiders get right out there and rebuild.'

'They have to. It's inherited in them. That's why their lives are worse than ours; they can't give up and die – they have to go on.'

'You ought to look on the bright side once in a while. You do fine creative work, like those tiles, like your work on the simulacra; think about that. Doesn't that cheer you? Don't you feel inspired by the sight of your own creativity?'

'No,' Pris said. 'Because what I do doesn't matter. It isn't enough.'

'What would be enough?'

Pris considered. She had opened her eyes, now, and all at once she disengaged her fingers from mine. It seemed automatic; she showed no awareness of doing it. A reflex, I thought. Such as spiders have.

'I don't know,' she said. 'But I know that no matter

72

how hard I work or how long or what I achieve – *it won't be enough.*'

'Who judges?'

'I do.'

'You don't think that when you see the Lincoln come to life you'll feel pride?'

'I know what I'll feel. Greater despair than ever.'

I glanced at her. Why that? I wondered. Despair at success . . . it makes no sense. What would failure bring for you, then? Elation?

'I'll tell you one, out of the world of nature,' I said. 'See what you make of it.'

'Okay.' She listened intently.

'One day I was starting into a post office in some town down in California and there were birds' nests up in the eaves of the building. And a young bird had flown or dropped out and was sitting on the pavement. And its parents were flying around anxiously. I walked up to it with the idea of picking it up and putting it back up in the nest, if I could reach the nest.' I paused. 'Do you know what it did as I came near?'

'What?'

I said, 'It opened its mouth. Expecting that I would feed it.'

Wrinkling her brow, Pris pondered.

'See,' I explained, 'that shows that it had known only life forms which fed and protected it and when it saw me even though I didn't look like any living thing it had ever known it assumed I would feed it.'

'What does that mean to you?'

'It shows that there's benevolence and kindness and mutual love and selfless assistance in nature as well as cold awful things.'

Pris said, 'No, Louis; it was ignorance on the bird's part. You weren't going to feed it.'

'But I was going to help it. It was right to trust me.'

73

'I wish I could see that side of life, Louis, like you do. But to me – it's just ignorance.'

'Innocence,' I corrected.

'That's the same; innocence of reality. It would be great if you could keep that, I wish I had kept it. But you lose that by living, because living means to experience, and that means – '

'You're cynical,' I told her.

'No, Louis. Just realistic.'

'I can see it's hopeless,' I said. 'Nobody can break through and reach you. And you know why? Because you want to be the way you are; you prefer it. It's easier, it's the easiest way of all. You're lazy, on a ghastly scale, and you'll keep on until you're forced to be otherwise. You'll never change by yourself. In fact you'll just get worse.'

Pris laughed, sharply and coldly.

So we walked back without saying anything more to each other.

When we returned to the repair shop we found the Stanton watching Bob Bundy as he labored on the Lincoln.

To the Stanton, Pris said, 'This is going to be that man who used to write you all those letters about getting soldiers pardoned.'

The Stanton said nothing; it gazed fixedly at the prone figure, its face lined and stiff with a sort of haughty aloofness. 'So I see,' it replied at last. It cleared its throat noisily, coughed, struck a pose in which it put its arms behind its back and clasped its fingers together; it rocked back and forth, still with the same expression. This is my business, it seemed to be saying. Everything of public importance is my business.

It had, I decided, taken up much the same stance that it had assumed during its authentic earlier lifetime. It was returning to its customary posture. Whether this was good or not I could not say. Certainly, as we watched the Lincoln we were all acutely aware of the Stanton behind us; we could not ignore it or forget it. Maybe that's how Stanton had been during his lifetime, always there – no one could ignore him or forget him, no matter how they felt about him otherwise, whether they hated him or feared him or worshiped him.

Pris said, 'Maury, I think this one's already working out better than the Stanton one. Look, it's stirring.'

Yes, the prone Lincoln simulacrum had stirred.

'Sam Barrows ought to be here,' Pris said excitedly, clasping her hands together. 'What's wrong with us? If he could see it he'd be overwhelmed – I know he'd be. Even he, Maury, even Sam K. Barrows!'

It was impressive. No doubt of it.

'I remember when the factory turned out our first electronic organ,' Maury said to me. 'And we all played it, all day long, until one in the morning; you remember?'

'Yes.'

'You and me and Jerome and that brother of yours with the upside down face, we made the darn thing sound like a harpsichord and a Hawaiian guitar and a steam calliope. We played all sorts of stuff on it, Bach and Gershwin, and then remember we made those frozen rum drinks with the blender – and after that, what did we do. We made up our own compositions and we found all types of tone settings, thousands of them; we made up new musical instruments that didn't exist. We composed! And we got that tape recorded and turned it on while we composed. Boy. That was something.'

'That was the day.'

'And I lay down on the floor and worked the foot pedals that get those low notes – I passed out on the low G, as I recall. And it kept playing; when I came to the next morning that goddam low G was still sounding like a fog horn. Wow. That organ – where do you suppose it is now, Louis?'

'In someone's living room. They never wear out because they don't generate any heat. And they never need to be tuned. Someone's playing tunes on it right now.'

'I'll bet you're right.'

Pris said, 'Help it sit up.'

The Lincoln simulacrum had begun struggling, flailing with its big hands in an effort to sit up. It blinked its eyes, grimaced; its heavy features stirred. Both Maury and I jumped over and helped support it; god, it weighed a lot, like solid lead. But we managed to get it up to a sitting position at last; we propped it against the wall so it wouldn't slide back down again.

It groaned.

Something about the noise made me shiver. Turning to Bob Bundy I said, 'What do you think? Is it okay? It's not suffering, is it?'

'I don't know.' Bundy drew his fingers nervously again and again through his hair; I noticed that his hands were shaking. 'I can check it over. The pain-circuits.'

'Pain-circuits!'

'Yeah. It has to have them or it'll run into a wall or some goddam object and massacre itself.' Bundy jerked a thumb towards the silent, watching Stanton. 'That's got 'em, too. What else, for crissakes?'

We were, beyond doubt, watching a living creature being born. It now had begun to take note of us; its eyes, jet black, moved up and down, from side to side, taking us all in, the vision of us. In the eyes no emotion showed only pure perception of us. Wariness beyond the capacity of man to imagine. The cunning of a life form from beyond the lip of our universe, from another land entirely. A creature plopped into our time and our space, conscious of us and itself, its existence, here; the black, opaque eyes rolled, focusing and yet not focusing, seeing everything and in a sense not picking out any one thing. As if it were primarily in suspension, yet; waiting with such infinite reserve that I could glimpse thereby the dreadful fear it felt, fear so great that it could not be called an emotion. It was fear as absolute existence: the basis of its life. It had become separate, yanked away from some fusion that we could not experience – at least, not now. Maybe once we all had lain quietly in that fusion. For us, the rupturing was long past; for the Lincoln it had just now occurred – was now taking place.

Its moving eyes still did not alight anywhere, on anything; it refused to perceive any given, individual thing.

'Gosh,' Maury muttered. 'It sure looks at us funny.'

Some deep skill was imbedded in this thing. Imparted to it by Pris? I doubted it. By Maury? Out of the question. Neither of them did this, nor had Bob Bundy whose idea of a good time was to drive like hell down to Reno to gamble and whore around. They had dropped life into this thing's ear, but it was just a transfer, not an invention; they had passed life on, but it did not originate in any or all of them. It was a contagion; they had caught it once and now these materials had contracted it – for a time. And what a transformation. Life is a form which matter takes . . . I made that up as I watched the Lincoln thing perceive us and itself. It is something which matter does. The most astonishing – the one truly astonishing – form in the universe; the one which, if it did not exist, could never have been predicted or even imagined.

And, as I watched the Lincoln come by degrees to a relationship with what it saw, I understood something: the basis of life is not a greed to exist, not a desire of any kind. It's fear, the fear which I saw here. And not even fear; much worse. Absolute *dread*. Paralyzing dread so great as to produce apathy. Yet the Lincoln stirred, rose out of this. Why? Because it had to. Movement, action, were implied by the extensiveness of the dread. That state, by its own nature, could not be endured.

All the activity of life was an effort to relieve this one

state. Attempts to mitigate the condition which we saw before us now.

Birth, I decided, is not pleasant. It is worse than death; you can philosophize about death – and you probably will: everyone else has. But birth! There is no philosophizing, no easing of the condition. And the prognosis is terrible: all your actions and deeds and thoughts will only embroil you in living the more deeply.

Again the Lincoln groaned. And then in a hoarse growl it mumbled words.

'What?' Maury said. 'What'd it say?'

Bundy giggled. 'Hell, it's a voice-tape but it's running through the transport backwards.'

The first words uttered by the Lincoln thing: uttered backward, due to an error in wiring.

8

It took several days to rewire the Lincoln simulacrum. During those days I drove from Ontario west through the Oregon Sierras, through the little logging town of John Day which had always been my favorite town in the western United States. I did not stop there, however; I was too restless. I kept on west until I joined the north-south highway. That straight road, the old route 99, goes through hundreds of miles of conifers. At the California end you find yourself going by volcanic mountains, black, dull and ashy, left over from the age of giants.

Two tiny yellow finches, playing and fighting in the air, swept up against the hood of my car; I heard and felt nothing but I knew by their disappearance and the sudden silence that they had gone into the radiator grill. Cooked and dead in an instant, I said to myself, slowing the car. And sure enough, at the next service station the attendant found them. Bright yellow, caught in the grill. Wrapping them in Kleenex I carried them to the edge of the highway and dropped them into the litter of plastic beer cans and moldering paper cartons there.

Ahead lay Mount Shasta and the border station of California. I did not feel like going on. That night I slept in a motel at Klamath Falls and the next day I started back up the coast the way I had come.

It was only seven-thirty in the morning and there was little traffic on the road. Overhead I saw something which caused me to pull off onto the shoulder and watch. I had seen such sights before and they always made me feel deeply humble and at the same time buoyed up. An enormous ship, on its way back from Luna or one of the planets, was passing slowly by, to its landing somewhere in the Nevada desert. A number of Air Force jets were accompanying it. Near it they looked no larger than black dots.

What few other cars there were on the highway had also stopped to watch. People had gotten out and one man was taking a snapshot. A woman and a small child waved. The great rocketship passed on, shaking the ground with its stupendous retro-blasts. Its hull, I could see, was pitted, scarred and burned from its re-entry into the atmosphere.

There goes our hope, I said to myself, shielding my eyes against the sun to follow its course. What's it got aboard? Soil samples? The first non-terrestrial life to be found? Broken pots discovered in the ash of an extinct volcano – evidence of some ancient civilized race?

More likely just a flock of bureaucrats. Federal officials, Congressmen, technicians, military observers, rocket scientists coming back, possibly some *Life* and *Look* reporters and photographers and maybe crews from NBC and CBS television. But even so it was impressive. I waved, like the woman with the small boy.

As I got back into my car I thought, Someday there'll be little neat houses in rows up there on the Lunar surface. TV antennae, maybe Rosen spinet pianos in living rooms . . .

Maybe I'll be putting repossession ads in newspapers on other worlds, in another decade or so.

Isn't that heroic? Doesn't that tie our business to the stars?

But we had a much more direct tie. Yes, I could catch a glimpse of the passion dominating Pris, this obsession about Barrows. He was the link, moral, physical and spiritual, between us mere mortals and the sidereal universe. He spanned both realms, one foot on Luna, the other in real estate in Seattle Washington and Oakland, California. Without Barrows it was all a mere dream; he made it tangible. I had to admire him as a man, too. He wasn't awed by the idea of settling people on the Moon; to him, it was one more – one more very vast – business opportunity. A chance for high returns on an investment, higher even than on slum rentals.

So back to Ontario, I said to myself. And face the simulacra, our new and enticing product, designed to lure out Mr Barrows, to make us perceptible to him. To make us a part of the new world. To make us *alive*.

When I got back to Ontario I went directly to MASA ASSOCIATES. As I drove up the street, searching for a place to park, I saw a crowd gathered at our office building. They were looking into the new showroom which Maury had built. Ah so, I said to myself with a deep fatalism.

As soon as I had parked I hurried on foot to join the crowd.

There, inside the showroom, sat the tall, bearded, hunched, twilight figure of Abraham Lincoln. He sat at an old-fashioned rolltop walnut desk; a familiar desk; it belonged to my father. They had removed it from the factory in Boise to here for the Lincoln simulacrum to make use of.

It angered me. Yet I had to admit it was apropos. The simulacrum, wearing much the same sort of clothing as the Stanton, was busy writing a letter with a quill pen. I was amazed at the realistic appearance which the simulacrum gave; if I had not known better I would have assumed that it was Lincoln reincarnated in some unnatural fashion. And, after all, wasn't that precisely what it was? Wasn't Pris right after all?

Presently, I noticed a sign in the window; professionally lettered, it explained to the crowd what was going on.

THIS IS AN AUTHENTIC RECONSTRUCT OF ABRAHAM LINCOLN, SIXTEENTH PRESIDENT OF THE UNITED STATES. IT WAS MANUFACTURED BY MASA

ASSOCIATES IN CONJUNCTION WITH THE ROSEN ELECTRONIC ORGAN FACTORY OF BOISE, IDAHO. IT IS THE FIRST OF ITS KIND. THE ENTIRE MEMORY AND NEURAL SYSTEM OF OUR GREAT CIVIL WAR PRESIDENT HAS BEEN FAITHFULLY REPRODUCED IN THE RULING MONAD STRUCTURE OF THIS MACHINE, AND IT IS CAPABLE OF RENDERING ALL ACTIONS, SPEECH AND DECISIONS OF THE SIXTEENTH PRESIDENT TO A STATISTICALLY PERFECT DEGREE.

INQUIRIES INVITED.

The corny phrasing gave it away as Maury's work. Infuriated, I pushed through the crowd and rattled the showroom door; it was locked, but having a key I unlocked it and passed on inside.

There in the corner on a newly-purchased couch sat Maury, Bob Bundy and my father. They were quietly watching the Lincoln.

'Hi, buddy boy!' Maury said to me.

'Made your cost back yet?' I asked him.

'No. We're not charging anybody for anything. We're just demonstrating.'

'You dreamed up that sixth-grader type sign, didn't you? I know you did. What sort of sidewalk traffic did you expect to make an inquiry? Why don't you have the thing sell cans of auto wax or dishwasher soap? Why just have it sit and write? Or is it entering some breakfastfood contest?'

Maury said, 'It's going over its regular correspondence.' He and my dad and Bundy all seemed sobered.

'Where's your daughter?'

'She'll be back.'

To my dad I said, 'You mind it using your desk?'

'No, mein Kind,' he answered. 'Go speak with it; it maintains a calmness when interrupted that astonishes me. This I could well learn.'

I had never seen my father so chastened.

'Okay,' I said, and walked over to the rolltop desk and the writing figure. Outside the showroom window the crowd gawked.

'Mr President,' I murmured. My throat felt dry. 'Sir, I hate to bother you.' I felt nervous, and yet at the same time I knew perfectly well that this was a machine I was facing. My going up to it and speaking to it this way put me into the fiction, the drama, as an actor like the machine itself; nobody had fed me an instruction tape – they didn't have to. I was acting out my part of the foolishness voluntarily. And yet I couldn't help myself. Why not say to it, 'Mr Simulacrum?' After all that was the truth.

The truth! What did that mean? Like a kid going up to the department store Santa; to know the truth was to drop dead. Did I want to do that? In a situation like this, to face the truth would mean the end of everything, of me before all. The simulacrum wouldn't have suffered. Maury, Bob Bundy and my dad wouldn't even have noticed. So I went on, because it was myself I was protecting; and I knew it, better than anyone else in the room, including the crowd outside gawking in.

Glancing up, the Lincoln put aside its quill pen and said in a rather high-pitched, pleasant voice, 'Good afternoon. I take it you are Mr Louis Rosen.'

'Yes sir,' I said.

And then the room blew up in my face. The rolltop desk flew into a million pieces; they burst up at me, flying slowly, and I shut my eyes and fell forward, flat on the floor; I did not even put out my hands. I felt it hit me; I smashed into bits against it, and darkness covered me up.

I had fainted. It was too much for me. I had passed out cold.

Next I knew I was upstairs in the office, propped up in a corner. Maury Rock sat beside me, smoking one of his

Corina Larks, glaring at me and holding a bottle of household ammonia under my nose.

'Christ,' he said, when he realized I had come to. 'You got a bump on your forehead and a split lip.'

I put up my hand and felt the bump; it seemed to be as big as a lemon. And I could taste the shreds of my lip. 'I passed out,' I said.

'Yeah, didn't you.'

Now I saw my dad hovering nearby. And – disagreeably – Pris Frauenzimmer in her long gray cloth coat, pacing back and forth, glancing at me with exasperation and the faint hint of contemptuous amusement.

'One word from it,' she said to me, 'and you're out. Good grief.'

'So what,' I managed to say feebly.

To his daughter, Maury said, grinning, 'It proves what I said; it's effective.'

'What – did the Lincoln do?' I asked. 'When I passed out?'

Maury said, 'It got up, picked you up and carried you up here.'

'Jesus,' I murmured.

'Why did you faint?' Pris said, bending down to peer at me intently. 'What a bump. You idiot. Anyhow, it got the crowd; you should have heard them. I was outside with them, trying to get through. You'd think we had produced God or something; they were actually praying and a couple of old ladies were crossing themselves. And some of them, if you can believe it – '

'Okay,' I broke in.

'Let me finish.'

'No,' I said. 'Shut up. Okay?'

We glared at each other and then Pris rose to her feet. 'Did you know your lip is badly gashed? You better get a couple of stitches put in it.'

Touching my lip with my fingers I discovered that it was still dribbling blood. Perhaps she was right.

'I'll drive you to a doctor,' Pris said. She walked to the door and stood waiting. 'Come on, Louis.'

'I don't need any stitches,' I said, but I rose and shakily followed after her.

As we waited in the hall for the elevator Pris said, 'You're not very brave, are you?'

I did not answer.

'You reacted worse than I did, worse than any of us. I'm surprised. There must be a far less stable streak in you than any of us knows about. And I bet someday, under stress, it shows up. Someday you're going to reveal grave psychological problems.'

The elevator door opened; we entered and the doors shut.

'Is it so bad to react?' I said.

'At Kansas City I learned how not to react unless it was in my interest to. That was what saved me and got me out of there and out of my illness. That was what they did for me. It's always a bad sign when there's effect, as in your case; it's always a sign of failure in adjustment. They call it parataxis, at Kansas City; it's emotionality that enters inter-personal relations and makes them complicated. It doesn't matter if it's hate or envy or, as in your case, fear – they're all parataxis. And when they get strong enough you have mental illness. And, when they take control, you have 'phrenia, like I had. That's the worst.'

I held a handkerchief to my lip, dabbing and fussing with the cut. There was no way I could explain my reaction to Pris; I did not try.

'Shall I kiss it?' Pris said. 'And make it well?'

I glared at her, but then I saw that on her face there was vibrant concern.

'Hell!' I said, flustered. 'It'll be okay.' I was embarrassed and I couldn't look at her. I felt like a little boy again. 'Adults don't talk to each other like that,' I

85

mumbled. 'Kissing and making well – what sort of dumb diction is that?'

'I want to help you.' Her mouth quivered. 'Oh, Louis – it's all over.'

'What's all over?'

'It's alive. I can never touch it again. Now what'll I do? I have no further purpose in life.'

'Christ,' I said.

'My life is empty – I might as well be dead. All I've done and thought has been the Lincoln.' The elevator door opened and Pris started out into the lobby of the building. I followed. 'Do you care what doctor you go to? I'll just take you down the street, I guess.'

'Fine.'

As we got into the white Jaguar, Pris said, 'Tell me what to do, Louis. I have to do something right away.'

At a loss I said, 'You'll get over this depression.'

'I never felt like this before.'

'I'm thinking. Maybe you could run for Pope.' It was the first thing that popped into my mind; it was inane.

'I wish I were a man. Women are cut off from so much. You could be anything, Louis. What can a woman be? A housewife or a clerk or a typist or a teacher.'

'Be a doctor,' I said. 'Stitch up wounded lips.'

'I can't stand sick or damaged or defective creatures. You know that, Louis. That's why I'm taking you to the doctor; I have to avert my gaze – maimed as you are.'

'I'm not maimed! I've just got a cut lip!'

Pris started up the car and we drove out into traffic. 'I'm going to forget the Lincoln. I'll never think of it again as living; it's just an object to me from this minute on. Something to market.'

I nodded.

'I'm going to see to it that Sam Barrows buys it. I have no other task in life but that. From now on all I will think or do will have Sam Barrows at the core of it.'

If I felt like laughing at what she was saying I had only

to look at her face; her expression was so bleak, so devoid of happiness or joy or even humor, that I could only nod. While driving me to the doctor to have my lip stitched up, Pris had dedicated her entire life, her future and everything in it. It was a kind of maniacal whim, and I could see that it had swum up to the surface out of desperation. Pris could not bear to spend a single moment without something to occupy her; she had to have a goal. It was her way of forcing the universe to make sense.

'Pris,' I said, 'the difficulty with you is that you're rational.'

'I'm not; everybody says I do exactly what I feel like.'

'You're driven by iron-clad logic. It's terrible. It has to be gotten rid of. Tell Horstowski that; tell him to free you from logic. You function as if a geometric proof were cranking the handle of your life. Relent, Pris. Be carefree and foolish and stupid. Do something that has no purpose. Okay? Don't even take me to the doctor; instead, dump me off in front of a shoeshine parlor and I'll get my shoes shined.'

'Your shoes are already shined.'

'See? See how you have to be logical all the time? Stop the car at the next intersection and we'll both get out and leave it, or go to a flower shop and buy flowers and throw them at other motorists.'

'Who'll pay for the flowers?'

'We'll steal them. We'll run out the door without paying.'

'Let me think it over,' Pris said.

'Don't think! Did you ever steal anything when you were a kid? Or bust something just for the hell of it, maybe some public property like a street lamp?'

'I once stole a candy bar from a drugstore.'

'We'll do that now.' I said. 'We'll find a drugstore and we'll be kids again; we'll steal a dime candy bar apiece, and we'll go find a shady place and sit like on a lawn for instance and eat it.'

'You can't, because of your lip.'

I said in a reasonable, urgent voice, 'Okay. I admit that. But you could. Isn't that so? Admit it. You could go into a drugstore right now and do that, even without me.'

'Would you come along anyhow?'

'If you want me to. Or I could park at the curb with the motor running and drive you the second you appeared. So you'd get away.'

'No,' Pris said, 'I want you to come into the store with me and be right there beside me. You could show me which candy bar to take; I need your help.'

'I'll do it.'

'What's the penalty for something like that?'

'Life everlasting,' I said.

'You're kidding me.'

'No,' I said. 'I mean it.' And I did; I was deeply serious.

'Are you making fun of me? I see you are. Why would you do that? Am I ridiculous, is that it?'

'God no.'

But she had made up her mind. 'You know I'll believe anything. They always kidded me in school about my gullibility. "Gullible's travels," they called me.'

I said, 'Come into the drugstore, Pris, and I'll show you; let me prove it to you. To save you.'

'Save me from what?'

'From the certitude of your own mind.'

She wavered; I saw her swallow, struggle with herself, try to see what she should do and if she had made a mistake – she turned and said to me earnestly, 'Louis, I believe you about the drugstore, I know you wouldn't make fun of me; you might hate me – you do hate me, on many levels – but you're not the kind of person who enjoys taunting the weak.'

'You're not weak.'

'I am. But you have no instinct to sense it. That's

good, Louis. I'm the other way around; I have that instinct and I'm not good.'

'Good, schmood,' I said loudly. 'Stop all this, Pris. You're depressed, because you've finished your creative work with the Lincoln, you're temporarily at loose ends and like a lot of creative people you suffer a letdown between one – '

'There's the doctor's place,' Pris said, slowing the car.

After the doctor had examined me – and sent me off without seeing the need of stitching me up – I was able to persuade Pris to stop at a bar. I felt I had to have a drink. I explained to her that it was a method of celebrating, that it was something which had to be done; it was expected of us. We had seen the Lincoln come to life and it was a great moment, perhaps the greatest moment, of our lives. And yet, as great as it was, there was in it something ominous and sad, something upsetting to all of us, that was just too much for us to handle.

'I'll have just one beer,' Pris said as we crossed the sidewalk.

At the bar I ordered a beer for her and an Irish coffee for myself.

'I can see you're at home, here,' Pris said, 'in a place like this. You spend a lot of time bumming around bars, don't you?'

I said, 'There's something I've been thinking about you that I have to ask you. Do you believe the cutting observations you make about other people? Or are they just offhand, for the purpose of making people feel bad? And if so – '

'What do you think?' Pris said in a level voice.

'I don't know.'

'Why do you care anyhow?'

'I'm insatiably curious about you, for every detail and tittle.'

'Why?'

'You've had a fascinating history. Schizoid by ten, compulsive-obsessive neurotic by thirteen, full-blown schizophrenic by seventeen and a ward of the Federal Government, now halfway cured and back among human beings again but still – ' I broke off. That was not the reason, her lurid history. 'I'll tell you the truth. I'm in love with you.'

'You're lying.'

Amending my statement I said, 'I *could* be in love with you.'

'If what?' She seemed terribly nervous; her voice shook.

'I don't know. Something holds me back.'

'Fear.'

'Maybe so,' I said. 'Maybe it's plain simple fear.'

'Are you kidding me, Louis? When you said that? Love, I mean?'

'No, I'm not kidding.'

She laughed tremulously. 'If you could conquer your fear you could win a woman; not me but some woman. I can't get over you saying that to me. Louis, you and I are opposites, did you know that? You show your feelings, I always keep mine in. I'm much deeper. If we had a child, what would it be like? I can't understand women who are always having children, they're like mother dogs . . . a litter every year. It must be nice to be biological and earthy like that.' She glanced at me out of the corner of her eye. 'That's a closed book to me. They fulfill themselves through their reproductive system, don't they? Golly, I've known women like that but I could never be that way. I'm never happy unless I'm doing things with my hands. Why is that, I wonder?'

'No knowing.'

'There has to be an explanation; everything has a cause. Louis, I can't remember for sure, but I don't think any boy ever said he was in love with me before.'

'Oh, they must have. Boys in school.'

'No, you're the first. I hardly know how to act . . . I'm not even sure if I like it. It feels strange.'

'Accept it,' I said.

'Love and creativity,' Pris said, half to herself. 'It's birth we're bringing about with the Stanton and the Lincoln; love and birth – the two are tied together, aren't they? You love what you give birth to, and since you love me, Louis, you must want to join me in bringing something new to life, don't you?'

'Guess so.'

'We're like gods,' Pris said, 'in what we've done, this task of ours, this great labor. Stanton and Lincoln, the new race . . . and yet by giving them life we empty ourselves. Don't you feel hollow, now?'

'Heck no.'

'Well, you're so different from me. You have no real sense of this task. Coming here to this bar . . . it was a momentary impulse that you yielded to. Maury and Bob and your dad and the Stanton are back at MASA with the Lincoln – you have no consciousness of that because you *want* to sit in a bar and have a drink.' She smiled at me genially, tolerantly.

'Suppose so,' I said.

'I'm boring you, aren't I? You really have no interest in me; you're only interested in yourself.'

'That's so. I realize you're right.'

'Why did you say you wanted to know everything about me? Why did you say you were almost in love with me except that fear held you back?'

'I dunno.'

'Don't you ever try to look yourself in the face and understand your own motives? I'm always analyzing myself.'

I said, 'Pris, be sensible for a moment. You're only one person among many, no better and no worse. Thousands of Americans go to – are right now in – mental health clinics, get schizophrenia and are committed under

91

the McHeston Act. You're attractive, I'll admit, but any number of movie starlets in Sweden and Italy are more so. Your intelligence is – '

'It's yourself you're trying to convince.'

'Pardon?' I said, taken aback.

'You're the one who idolizes me and is fighting against recognizing it,' Pris said calmly.

I pushed away my drink. 'Let's get back to MASA.' The alcohol made my cut lip burn searingly.

'Did I say the wrong thing?' For a moment she looked disconcerted; she was thinking back over what she had said, amending it, improving it. 'I mean, you're ambivalent about me . . .'

I took hold of her arm. 'Finish your beer and let's leave.'

As we left the bar she said wanly, 'You're sore at me again.'

'No.'

'I try to be nice to you but I always rub people the wrong way when I make a deliberate effort to be polite to them and say what I ought to say . . . it's wrong of me to be artificial. I told you I shouldn't adopt a set of behavior-patterns that are false to me. It never works out.' She spoke accusingly, as if it had been my idea.

'Listen,' I said as we got back into the car and set out into the traffic. 'We'll go back and resume our dedicated task of making Sam Barrows the core of all that we do – right?'

'No,' Pris said. 'Only I can do that. That's not within your power.'

I patted her on the shoulder. 'You know, I'm much more sympathetic to you, too, than I was. I think we're beginning to work out a very good, wholesome, stable relationship between us.'

'Maybe so,' Pris said, unaware of any overtone of sarcasm. She smiled at me. 'I hope so, Louis. People should understand one another.'

* * *

When we got back to MASA, Maury greeted us excitedly. 'What took you so long?' He produced a piece of paper. 'I sent a wire to Sam Barrows. Read it – here.' He pushed it into my hands.

Uneasily, I unfolded the paper and read Maury's writing.

ADVISE YOU FLY HERE AT ONCE. LINCOLN SIMU-
LACRUM INCREDIBLE SUCCESS. REQUEST YOUR
DECISION. SAVING ITEM FOR YOUR FIRST INSPEC-
TION AS PER PHONE CALL. EXCEEDS WILDEST
HOPES. EXPECT TO HEAR FROM YOU WITHIN DAY.
                            MAURY ROCK,
                            MASA ASSOCIATES

'Has he answered yet?' I asked.

'Not yet, but we just phoned in the wire.'

There was a commotion and Bob Bundy appeared. To me he said, 'Mr Lincoln asked me to express his regrets and find out how you are.' He looked pretty shaky, himself.

'Tell him I'm okay,' I added. 'And thank him.'

'Right,' Bundy departed; the office door shut after him.

To Maury I said, 'I have to admit it, Rock. You're onto something. I was wrong.'

'Thanks for coming around.'

Pris said, 'You're wasting your thanks on him.'

Puffing on his Corina agitatedly Maury said, 'We've got a lot of work ahead of us. I know we'll get Barrows' interest now. But what we have to be careful of – ' He lowered his voice. 'A man like that could sweep us aside like a lot of kindling. Am I right, buddy?'

'Right,' I answered. I had thought of that, too.

'He's probably done it a million times to small operators along the way. We got to close ranks, all four of us; five, if you include Bob Bundy. Right?' He looked around at Pris and me and my dad.

My dad said, 'Maury, maybe you should take this to the Federal Government.' He looked timidly at me. 'Hab' Ich nicht Recht, mein Sohn?'

'He's already contacted Barrows,' I said. 'For all we know, Barrows is on his way here.'

'We could tell him no,' Maury said, 'even if he shows up. If we feel this should go to Washington DC instead.'

'Ask the Lincoln,' I said.

'What?' Pris said sharply. 'Oh, for god's sake.'

'I mean it,' I said. 'Get its advice.'

'What would a hick politician from the last century know about Sam K. Barrows?' Pris shot at me sardonically.

In as calm a voice as possible, I said, 'Pris, watch it. Honest to god.'

Maury said quickly, 'Let's not get to quarreling. We all have a right to express our opinions. I think we should go ahead and show the Lincoln to Barrows and if for some crazy reason – ' He broke off. The office phone was ringing. Striding over he picked it up. 'MASA ASSOCIATES. Maury Rock speaking.'

Silence.

Turning towards us Maury mouthed silently: *Barrows*.

That's it, I said to myself. The die is cast.

'Yes, sir,' Maury was saying into the phone. 'We'll pick you up at the Boise airfield. Yes, we'll see you there.' His face glowed; he winked at me.

To my dad I said, 'Where's the Stanton?'

'What, mein Sohn?'

'The Stanton simulacrum – I don't see it around.' Recalling its expression of hostility towards the Lincoln I got up and went over to where Pris stood trying to hear the other end of Maury's phone conversation. 'Where's the Stanton?' I said loudly to her.

'I don't know. Bundy put it somewhere; it's probably down in the shop.'

'Wait a minute,' Maury lowered the phone. To me,

with a strange expression on his face, he said, 'The Stanton is in Seattle. With Barrows.'

'Oh no,' I heard Pris say.

Maury said, 'It took the Greyhound bus last night. Got there this morning and looked him right up. Barrows says he's been having a good long talk with it.' Maury covered the phone with his hand. 'He hasn't gotten our wire yet. It's the Stanton he's interested in. Shall I tell him about the Lincoln?'

'You might as well,' I said. 'He'll be getting the wire.'

'Mr Barrows,' Maury said into the phone, 'we just sent you a wire. Yes – we have the Lincoln electronic simulacrum operating and it's an incredible success, even more so than the Stanton.' Glancing at me with an uneasy grimace he said, 'Sir, you'll be accompanied on the plane flight by the Stanton, will you not? We're anxious to get it back.' Silence, and then Maury once more lowered the phone. 'Barrows says the Stanton told him it intends to stay in Seattle a day or so and look at the sights. It intends to get a haircut and visit the library and if it likes the town maybe even think about opening a law office and settling down there.'

'Christ's cross,' Pris said, clenching her fists. 'Tell Barrows to talk it into coming back here!'

Maury said into the phone, 'Can't you persuade it to come with you, Mr Barrows?' Again silence. 'It's gone,' Maury said to us, this time not covering the phone. 'It said goodbye to Barrows and took off.' He frowned, looking deeply distressed.

I said, 'Anyhow, finish up as to the flight.'

'Right.' Maury drew himself together and again addressed the phone. 'I'm sure the damn thing'll be all right; it had money, didn't it?' Silence. 'And you gave it twenty dollars, too; good. Anyhow, we'll see you. The Lincoln one is even better. Yes sir. Thanks. Goodbye.' He hung up and sat staring down at the floor, his lips twisting. 'I didn't even notice it was gone. You think it was sore about the Lincoln? Maybe so; it's got one hell of a temper.'

'No use crying over spilt milk,' I said.

'True,' Maury murmured, chewing his lip. 'And it's got a battery good for six months! We may not see it until next year. My god, we've got thousands of dollars tied up in it – and what if Barrows is stringing us? Maybe he's got the thing locked up in a vault somewhere.'

'If he had,' Pris said, 'he wouldn't be coming here. In fact, maybe this is all for the good; maybe Barrows wouldn't be coming here except for the Stanton, what it said and did – he got to see it and maybe the wire wouldn't have brought him. And if it hadn't run off and ditched him maybe he would have snared it and we'd be out in the cold; right?'

'Yeah,' Maury agreed morosely.

My dad said, 'Mr Barrows is reputable, isn't he? A man with so much social concern as he expresses, this letter my son showed me about that housing unit with those poor people he's protecting.'

Maury nodded again, still morosely.

Patting my dad on the arm Pris said, 'Yes, Jerome; he's a civic-minded fellow. You'll like him.'

My dad beamed at Pris and then at me. 'It looks as if everything is turning out good, nicht Wahr?'

We all nodded, with a mixture of gloom and fear.

The door opened and Bob Bundy appeared, holding a folded piece of paper. Coming up to me he said, 'Here's a note from Lincoln.'

I unfolded it. It was a short note of sympathy:

Mr Louis Rosen.
My Dear Sir:
   I wish to enquire of your condition, with hope that you have improved somewhat. Yours Truly,

A. Lincoln

'I'll go out and thank him,' I said to Maury.

'Do that,' Maury said.

9

As we waited in the cold wind at the concourse entrance for the flight from Seattle to land I said to myself, How'll he differ from the other people?

The Boeing 900 landed; it taxied along the runway. The ramps were run out, the doors opened, stewardesses helped people out, and at the bottom of each ramp airline employees made sure the passengers did not take pratfalls onto the asphalt ground. Meanwhile, luggage-carrying vehicles raced around like large bugs, and off to one side a Standard Stations truck had parked with its red lights on.

Every sort of passenger started appearing, issuing forth from the plane at both doors and swarming rapidly down the ramps. Around us friends and relatives pushed forward and out as far onto the field as was allowed. Beside me Maury stirred restlessly.

'Let's get out there and greet him.'

Both he and Pris started going, so I went along with them. We were halted by an airline official in a blue uniform who waved us back. However Maury and Pris ignored him; I did so, too, and we reached the bottom of the first class ramp. There we halted. The passengers, one by one, descended, some of them smiling, the businessmen with no expression on their faces. Some of them looked tired.

'There he is,' Maury said.

Down the first class ramp came a slender man in a gray suit, smiling slightly, his topcoat over his arm. As he got nearer to us it seemed to me that his suit fitted more naturally than the other men's. No doubt custom-tailored, probably in England or Hong Kong. And he looked more relaxed. He wore greenish dark glasses, rimless; his hair, as in the photos, was cut extra short, almost a GI sort of crewcut. Behind him came a jolly-looking woman I knew: Colleen Nild, with a clipboard and papers under her arm.

'Three in the party,' Pris observed. There was another man, very short, portly, in an ill-fitting brown suit with sleeves and trousers too long, a reddish-faced man with a Doctor Doolittle nose and long thinning lank black hair combed across his domed skull. He wore a stickpin in his tie, and the way he strode after Barrows with his short legs convinced me that here was an attorney; this was the way trial lawyers take off from their seat in court, like the manager of a baseball team striding out onto the field to protest a decision. The gesture of protest, I decided as I watched him, is the same in all professions; you get right out there, talking and waving your arms as you come.

The lawyer was beaming in an alert, active fashion, talking away at a great rate to Colleen Nild; he looked to me to be a likable sort of guy, someone with enormous bouncy energy, just the sort of attorney I would have expected Barrows to have on retainer. Colleen, as before, wore a heavy blueblack quilted cloth coat that hung like lead. This time she was dressed up: she had on gloves, a hat, new leather mailpouch type purse. She was listening to the attorney; as he talked away he gestured in all directions, like an interior decorator or the foreman of a construction crew. Something about him gave me a friendly warm feeling and I felt less tense, now. The lawyer looked, I decided, like a great kidder. I felt I understood him.

Now here came Barrows to the bottom of the ramp, his eyes invisible behind his dark glasses, his head down slightly so as to keep an eye on what his feet were doing. He was listening to the attorney. As he started out onto the field Maury stepped forward.

'Mr Barrows!'

Turning and halting, moving out of the way so those behind him could step from the ramp, Barrows in one movement of his body lithely swiveled and held out his hand. 'Mr Rock?'

'Yes sir,' Maury said, shaking hands. Colleen Nild and the attorney clustered around; so did I and Pris. 'This is Pris Frauenzimmer. And this is my partner, Louis Rosen.'

'Happy, Mr Rosen.' Barrows shook hands with me. 'This is Mrs Nild, my secretary. This gentleman is Mr Blunk, my council.' We all shook hands around. 'Cold out here on the field, isn't it?' Barrows started for the entrance of the building. He moved so swiftly that we all had to gallop after him like a flock of big awkward animals. Mr Blunk's short legs pumped away as in a speeded-up old movie; he did not seem to mind, however; he continued to radiate cheerfulness.

'Boise,' he declared, gazing around him. 'Boise, Idaho. What will they think of next?'

Colleen Nild falling in beside me, greeted me. 'Nice to see you again, Mr Rosen. We found the Stanton creature quite delightful.'

'A fabulous construct,' Blunk boomed back at us; we were lagging behind. 'We thought it was from the Bureau of Internal Revenue.' He gave me a hearty personal smile.

Up front walked Barrows and Maury; Pris had dropped back because the concourse door was so narrow. Barrows and Maury passed on inside and Pris followed next, then Mr Blunk, then Colleen Nild and I taking up the rear. By the time we had passed through the building and outside again onto the street entrance where the taxis waited, Barrows and Maury had already located the limousine; the uniformed driver was holding one of the rear doors open and Barrows and Maury were crawling inside.

'Luggage?' I said to Mrs Nild.

'No luggage. Too time-consuming to wait for it. We're only going to be here a few hours and then we're flying back. Probably late tonight. If we should stay over we'll buy what we need.'

'Um,' I said, impressed.

The rest of us also crawled into the limousine; the driver hopped around, and soon we were out in traffic, on our way into Boise proper.

'I don't see how the Stanton can set up a law office in Seattle,' Maury was saying to Barrows. 'It's not licensed to practice law in the State of Washington.'

'Yes, I think you'll be seeing it again one of these days.' Barrows offered Maury, then me, a cigarette from his case.

Summing it up I decided that Barrows differed from the rest of us in that he looked as if he had grown his gray English wool suit the way an animal grows its fur; it was simply part of him, like his nails and his teeth. He was utterly unconscious of it, as well as of his tie, his shoes, his cigarette case – he was unconscious of everything about his appearance.

So that's how it is to be a multi-millionaire, I decided.

A long jump from the bottom rung like myself, where the preoccupation is, I wonder if my fly is unzipped. That's the dregs. People like me, stealing swift covert glances down. Sam K. Barrows never stole a covert look at his fly in his life. If it was unzipped he'd simply zip it up. I wish I was rich, I said to myself.

I felt depressed. My condition was hopeless. I had not even gotten to the stage of worrying about the knot of my necktie, like other men. I probably never would.

And in addition Barrows was a really good-looking guy, sort of Robert Montgomery-shaped. Not handsome like Montgomery; for now Barrows had removed his dark glasses and I saw that he had puffy wrinkled skin beneath his eyes. But he's got that athletic build, probably from playing handball in a five thousand dollar private handball court. And he's got a top-notch doctor who doesn't let him swill cheap liquor or beer of any kind; he never eats in drive-ins . . . probably never eats any cut of pork, and only those eye lambchops, and only steak and roast type cuts of beef.

Naturally he hasn't got an ounce of extra flab on him, with a diet like that. It depressed me even more.

Now I could see how those bowls of stewed prunes at six o'clock in the morning and those four-mile jogs through the deserted early dawn streets at five A.M. fitted in. The eccentric young millionaire whose picture appeared in *Look* was not going to drop dead at forty from heart trouble; he intended to live and enjoy his wealth. No widow would inherit it, contrary to the national pattern.

Eccentric, hell.

Smart.

The time was a little after seven in the evening as our limousine entered Boise itself, and Mr Barrows and his two companions announced that they had not eaten dinner. Did we know of a good restaurant in Boise?

There is no good restaurant in Boise.

'Just a place where we can get fried prawns,' Barrows said. 'A light supper of that sort. We had a few drinks on the plane but none of us ate; we were too busy yakking.'

We found a passable restaurant. The head waiter led us to a leather horseshoe-shaped booth in the rear; we took off our coats and seated ourselves.

We ordered drinks.

'Did you really make your first pile playing poker in the Service?' I asked Barrows.

'No, craps it was. A six-month floating crapgame. Poker takes skill; I have luck.'

Pris said, 'It wasn't luck that got you into real estate.'

'No, it was because my mother used to rent out rooms in our old place in LA.' Barrows eyed her.

'Nor,' Pris said in the same tense voice, 'was it luck that has made you the Don Quixote who successfully tilted the Supreme Court of the United States into ruling against the Space Agency and its greedy monopolizing of entire moons and planets.'

Barrows nodded to her. 'You're generous in your description. I had in my possession what I believed to be valid title to parcels on Luna, and wanted to test the validity of those titles in such a way that they'd never be challenged again. Say, I've met you.'

'Yes,' Pris said, bright eyed.

'Can't place you, though.'

'It was only for a moment. In your office. I don't blame you for not remembering. I remember you, however.' She had not taken her eyes from the man.

'You're Rock's daughter?'

'Yes, Mr Barrows.'

She looked a lot better, tonight. Her hair had been done, and she wore enough make-up to hide her paleness, but not so much as to give her the garish mask-like appearance which I had noticed in the past. Now that she had taken off her coat I saw that she wore an attractive fluffy jersey sweater, short-sleeved, with one piece of gold jewelry – a pin shaped like a snake – over her right breast. By god, I decided, she had a bra on, too, the kind that created bulk where there was no bulk. For this extraordinary occasion Pris had obtained a bosom. And, when she rose to hang up her coat, I saw that in her high, very thin heels she appeared to have nice legs. So, when the occasion demanded, she could fix herself up more than correctly.

'Let me take that,' Blunk said, sweeping her coat away from her and bouncing over to the rack to hang it on a hanger. He returned, bowed, smiled merrily at her and reseated himself. 'Are you sure,' he boomed, 'that this dirty old man – ' He indicated Maury. 'Is actually your father? Or is it not the case that you're committing a sin, the sin of statutory rape, sir!' He pointed a finger in a

102

mock-epic manner at Maury. 'Shame sir!' He smiled at us all.

'You just want her for yourself,' Barrows said, biting off the fantail of a prawn and laying it aside. 'How do you know she's not another of those simulacrum things, like the Stanton one?'

'I'll take a dozen gross!' Blunk cried, his eyes shining.

Maury said, 'She really is my daughter. She's been away at school.' He looked uncomfortable.

'And come back – ' Blunk lowered his voice. In an exaggerated aside he whispered hoarsely to Maury, '*In the family way*, is that it?'

Maury grinned uneasily.

Changing the subject I said, 'It's nice to see you again, Mrs Nild.'

'Thank you.'

'That Stanton robot scared the slats out of us,' Barrows said to Maury and I, his elbows resting on the table, arms folded. He had finished his prawns and he looked well-fed and sleek. For a man who started out on stewed prunes he seemed to enjoy his food to the hilt. I had to approve of that, personally; it seemed to me to be an encouraging sign.

'You people are to be congratulated!' Blunk said. 'You produced a monster!' He laughed loudly, enjoying himself. 'I say kill the thing! Get a mob with torches! Onward!'

We all had to laugh at that.

'How did the Frankenstein monster finally die?' Colleen asked.

'Ice,' Maury said. 'The castle burned down and they sprayed hoses on it and the water became ice.'

'But the monster was found frozen in the ice in the next movie,' I said. 'And they revived him.'

'He disappeared into a pit of bubbling lava,' Blunk said. 'I was there. I kept a button from his coat.' From his coat pocket he produced a button which he displayed to each of us in turn. 'Off the world-famous Frankenstein monster.'

Colleen said, 'It's off your vest, David.'

'What!' Blunk glanced down scowling. 'So it is! It's my own button!' Again he laughed.

Barrows, investigating his teeth with the edge of his thumb nail, said to Maury and me, 'How much did it set you back to put together the Stanton robot?'

'Around five thousand,' Maury said.

'And how much can it be produced in quantity for? Say, if several hundred thousand are run off.'

'Hell,' Maury said quickly, 'I would say around six hundred dollars. That assumes they're identical, have the same ruling monads and are fed the same tapes.'

'What it is,' Barrows said to him, 'is a life-size version of the talking dolls that were so popular in the past; correct – '

'No,' Maury said, 'not exactly.'

'Well, it talks and walks around,' Barrows said. 'It took a bus to Seattle. Isn't that the automaton principle made a little more complex?' Before Maury could answer he continued, 'What I'm getting at is, there really isn't anything *new* here, is there?'

Silence.

'Sure,' Maury said. He did not look very merry, now. And I noticed that Pris, too, seemed abruptly humorless.

'Well, would you spell it out, please,' Barrows said, still with his pleasant tone, his informality. Picking up his glass of Green Hungarian he sipped. 'Go ahead, Rock.'

'It's not an automaton at all,' Maury said. 'You know the work of Grey Walter in England? The turtles? It's what's called a homeostatic system. It's cut off from its environment; it produces its own responses. It's like the fully automated factory which repairs itself. Do you know what "feedback" refers to? In electrical systems there – '

Dave Blunk put his hand on Maury's shoulder. 'What

104

Mr Barrows wants to know has to do with the patentability, if I may use such an unwieldly term, of your Stanton and Lincoln robots.'

Pris spoke up in a low, controlled voice. 'We're fully covered at the patent office. We have expert legal representatation.'

'That's good to hear,' Barrows said, smiling at her as he picked his teeth. 'Because otherwise there's nothing to buy.'

'Many new principles are involved,' Maury said. 'The Stanton electronic simulacrum represents work developed over a period of years by many research teams in and out of Government and if I may say so myself we're all abundantly pleased, even amazed, at the terrific results . . . as you saw yourself when the Stanton got off the Greyhound bus at Seattle and took a taxi to your office.'

'It walked,' Barrows said.

'Pardon?'

'I say, it walked to my office from the Greyhound bus station.'

'In any case,' Maury said, 'what we've achieved here has no precedent in the electronics trade.'

After dinner we drove to Ontario, arriving at the office of MASA ASSOCIATES at ten o'clock.

'Funny little town,' Dave Blunk said, surveying the empty streets. 'Everybody in bed.'

'Wait until you see the Lincoln,' Maury said as we got out from the car.

They had stopped at the showroom window and were reading the sign that had to do with the Lincoln.

'I'll be a son of a gun,' Barrows said. He put his face to the glass, peering in. 'No sign of it right now, though. What does it do, sleep at night? Or do you have it assassinated, every evening around five, when sidewalk traffic is heaviest?'

Maury said, 'The Lincoln is probably down in the shop.

We'll go down there.' He unlocked the door and stood aside to let us enter.

Presently we were standing at the entrance to the dark repairshop as Maury groped for the light switch. At last he found it.

There, seated in meditation, the Lincoln. It had been sitting quietly in the darkness.

Barrows said at once, 'Mr President.' I saw him nudge Colleen Nild. Blunk grinned, looking enthusiastic, with the greedy, good-humored warmth of a hungry but confident cat. Clearly, he was getting enormous enjoyment out of all this. Mrs Nild craned her neck, gasped faintly, obviously impressed. Barrows, of course, walked on into the repairshop without hesitation, knowing exactly what to do. He did not hold his hand out to the Lincoln; he halted a few paces from it, showing respect.

Turning his head the Lincoln regarded him with a melancholy expression. I had never seen such despair on a face before, and I shrank back; so did Maury. Pris did not react at all; she merely remained standing in the doorway. The Lincoln rose to its feet, hesitated, and then by degrees the expression of pain faded from its face; it said in a broken, reedy voice – completely at contrast to its tall frame, 'Yes sir.' It inspected Barrows from its height, with kindliness and interest, its eyes twinkling a little.

'My name is Sam Barrows,' Barrows said. 'It's a great honor to meet you, Mr President.'

'Thank you, Mr Barrows,' the Lincoln said. 'Won't you and your friends enter and accommodate yourselves?'

To me Dave Blunk gave a wide-eyed silent whistle of astonishment and awe. He clapped me on the back. 'Wheee,' he said softly.

'You remember me, Mr President,' I said to the simulacrum.

'Yes, Mr Rosen.'

'What about me?' Pris said drily.

The simulacrum made a faint, clumsy, formal bow. 'Miss Frauenzimmer. And you, Mr Rock . . . the person on which this edifice rests, does it not?' The simulacrum chuckled. 'The owner, or co-owner, if I am not mistook.'

'What have you been doing,' Maury asked it.

'I was thinking about a remark of Lyman Trumbull's. As you know, Judge Douglas met with Buchanan and they talked over the Lecompton Constitution and Kansas. Judge Douglas later came out and fought Buchanan, despite the threat, it being an Administration measure. I did not support Judge Douglas, as did a number of those dear to me among my own party, the Republicans and their cause. But in Bloomington, where I was towards the end of 1857, I saw no Republicans going over to Douglas, as one saw in the New York *Tribune*. I asked Lyman Trumbull to write me in Springfield to tell me whether – '

Barrows interrupted the Lincoln simulacrum, at that point. 'Sir, if you'll excuse me. We have business to conduct, and then I and this gentleman, Mr Blunk, and Mrs Nild, here, have to fly back to Seattle.'

The Lincoln bowed. 'Mrs Nild.' He held out his hand, and, with a snorting laugh, Colleen Nild went forward to shake hands with him. 'Mr Blunk.' He gravely shook hands with the short plump attorney. 'You're not related to Nathan Blunk of Cleveland, are you, sir?'

'No, I'm not,' Blunk answered, shaking hands vigorously. 'You were an attorney at one time, weren't you, Mr Lincoln?'

'Yes sir,' the Lincoln replied.

'My profession.'

'I see,' the Lincoln said, with a smile. 'You have the divine ability to wrangle over trifles.'

Blunk boomed out a hearty laugh.

Coming up beside Blunk, Barrows said to the simulacrum, 'We flew here from Seattle to discuss with Mr Rosen and Mr Rock a financial transaction involving backing of MASA ASSOCIATES by Barrows Enterprises. Before we finalize we wanted to meet you and have a talk. We met the Stanton recently; he came to visit us on a bus. We'd acquire you and Stanton both as assets of MASA ASSOCIATES, as well as basic patents. As an ex-attorney you're probably familiar with transactions of this sort. I'd be curious to ask you something. What's your sense of the modern world? Do you know what a *vitamin* is, for instance? Do you know what year this is?' He scrutinized the simulacrum keenly.

The Lincoln did not answer immediately, and while it was getting ready, Maury waved Barrows over to one side. I joined them.

'That's all beside the point,' Maury said. 'You know perfectly well it wasn't made to handle topics like that.'

'True,' Barrows agreed. 'But I'm curious.'

'Don't be. You'd feel funny if you burned out one of its primary circuits.'

'Is it that delicate?'

'No,' Maury said, 'but you're needling it.'

'No I'm not. It's so convincingly life-like that I want to know how conscious it is of its new existence.'

'Leave it alone,' Maury said.

Barrows gestured abruptly. 'Certainly.' He beckoned to Colleen Nild and their attorney. 'Let's conclude our business and start back to Seattle. David, are you satisfied by what you see?'

'No,' Blunk said, as he joined us. Colleen remained with Pris and the simulacrum; they were asking it something about the debates with Stephen Douglas. 'It doesn't seem to function nearly as well as the Stanton one, in my opinion.'

'How so?' Maury demanded.

'It's – halting.'

'It just came to,' I said.

'No, it's not that,' Maury said. 'It's a different personality. Stanton's more inflexible, dogmatic.' To me he said,

108

"I know a hell of a lot about those two people. Lincoln was this way. I made up the tapes. He had periods of brooding, he was brooding here just now when we came in. Other times he's more cheerful.' To Blunk he said, 'That's his character. If you stick around awhile you'll see him in other moods. Moody – that's what he is. Not like Stanton, not positive. I mean it's not an electrical failure; it's supposed to be that way.'

'I see,' Blunk said, but he did not sound convinced.

'I know what you refer to,' Barrows said. 'It seems to stick.'

'Right,' Blunk said. 'I'm not sure in my own mind that they've got this perfected. There may be a lot of bugs left to iron out.'

'And this cover-up line,' Barrows said, 'about not questioning it as to contemporary topics – you caught that?'

'I certainly did,' Blunk said.

'Sam,' I said to Barrows, plunging in, 'you don't get the point at all. Maybe that's due to you having just made that plane flight from Seattle and then that long drive by car from Boise. Frankly, I thought you grasped the principle underlying the simulacrum, but let's let the subject go, for the sake of amicability. Okay?' I smiled.

Barrows contemplated me without answering; so did Blunk. Off in the corner Maury perched on a workstool, with his cigar giving off clouds of lonely blue smoke.

'I understand your disappointment with the Lincoln,' I said. 'I sympathize. To be frank, the Stanton one was coached.'

'Ah,' Blunk said, his eyes twinkling.

'It wasn't my idea. My partner here was nervous and he wanted it all set up.' I wagged my head in Maury's direction. 'He was wrong to do it, but anyhow that's a dead issue; what we want to deal with is the Lincoln simulacrum because that's the basis of MASA ASSOCIATES' genuine discovery. Let's walk back and query it further.'

The three of us walked back to where Mrs Nild and Pris stood listening to the tall, bearded, stooped simulacrum.

'. . . quoted me to the effect that the Negro was included in that clause of the Declaration of Independence which says that all men were created equal. That was at Chicago Judge Douglas says I said that, and then he goes on to say that at Charleston I said the Negro belonged to an inferior race. And that I held it was not a moral issue, but a question of degree, and yet at Galesburg I went back and said it was a moral question once more.' The simulacrum smiled its gentle, painted smile at us. 'Thereupon some fellow in the audience called out, "He's right." I was glad somebody thought me right, because it seemed to myself that Judge Douglas had me by the coat tails.'

Pris and Mrs Nild laughed appreciatively. The rest of us stood silently.

'About the best applause Judge Douglas got was when he said that the whole Republican Party in the northern part of the state stands committed to the doctrine of no more slave states, and that this same doctrine is repudiated by the Republicans in the other part of the state . . . and the Judge wondered whether Mr Lincoln and his party do not present the case which Mr Lincoln cited from the Scriptures, of a house divided against itself which cannot stand.' The simulacrum's voice had assumed a droll quality. 'And the Judge wondered if my principles were the same as the Republican Party's. Of course, I don't get the chance to answer the Judge until October at Quincy. But I told him there, that he could argue that a horse-chestnut is the same as a chestnut horse. I certainly had no purpose to introduce political and social equality between the white and black races. There is a physical difference between the two, which, in my judgment, will probably forever forbid their living together on the footing of perfect equality. But I hold the Negro as much entitled to the right of life, liberty and the pursuit of

110

happiness as any white man. He is not my equal in many respects, certainly not in color – perhaps not in intellectual and moral endowments. But in the right to eat the bread which his own hand earns, without leave of anybody else, he is my equal and the equal of Judge Douglas, and the equal of every other man.' The simulacrum paused. 'I received a few good cheers myself at that moment.'

To me Sam Barrows said, 'You've got quite a tape reeling itself off inside the thing, don't you?'

'It's free to say what it wants,' I told him.

'Anything? *You mean it wants to speechify?*' Barrows obviously did not believe me. 'I don't see that it's anything but the familiar mechanical man gimmick, with this dressed-up historical guise. The same thing was demonstrated at the 1939 San Francisco World's Fair, Pedro the Vodor.'

This exchange between Barrows and I had not escaped the attention of the Lincoln simulacrum. In fact both it and Pris and Mrs Nild were now watching us and listening to us.

The Lincoln said to Mr Barrows, 'Did I not hear you, a short while ago, express the notion of "acquiring me", as an asset of some kind? Do I recall fairly? If so, I would wonder how you could acquire me or anyone else, when Miss Frauenzimmer tells me that there is a stronger impartiality between the races now than ever before. I am a bit mixed on some of this but I believe there is no more "acquiring" of any human in the world today, even in Russia where it is notorious.'

Barrows said, 'That doesn't include mechanical men.'

'You refer to myself?' the simulacrum said.

With a laugh Barrows said, 'All right, yes I do.'

Beside him the short lawyer David Blunk stood plucking at his chin thoughtfully, glancing from Barrows to the simulacrum and back.

'Would you tell me, sir,' the simulacrum said, 'what a man is?'

'Yes,' I would,' Barrows said. He caught Blunk's eye;

obviously, Barrows was enjoying this. 'A man is a forked radish.' He added, 'Is that definition familiar to you, Mr Lincoln?'

'Yes sir, it is,' the simulacrum said. 'Shakespeare has his Falstaff speak that, does he not?'

'Right,' Barrows said. 'And I'd add to that. A man can be defined as an animal that carries a pocket handkerchief. How about that? Mr Shakespeare didn't say that.'

'No sir,' the simulacrum agreed. 'He did not.' The simulacrum laughed heartily. 'I appreciate your humor, Mr Barrows. May I use that remark in a speech?'

Barrows nodded.

'Thank you,' the simulacrum said. 'Now, you've defined a man as an animal which carries a pocket handkerchief. But what is an animal?'

'I can tell you you're not,' Barrows said, his hands in his trouser pockets; he looked perfectly confident. 'An animal has a biological heritage and makeup which you lack. You've got valves and wires and switches. You're a machine. Like a – ' He considered. 'Spinning jenny. Like a steam engine.' He winked at Blunk. 'Can a steam engine consider itself entitled to protection under the clause of the Constitution which you quoted? Has it got a right to eat the bread it produces, like a white man?'

The simulacrum said, 'Can a machine talk?'

'Sure. Radios, phonographs, tape recorders, telephones – they all yak away like mad.'

The simulacrum considered. It did not know what those were, but it could make a shrewd guess; it had had enough time by itself to do a good deal of thinking. We could all appreciate that.

'Then what, sir, is a machine?' the simulacrum asked Barrows.

'You're one. These fellows made you. You belong to them.'

The long, lined, dark-bearded face twisted with weary amusement as the simulacrum gazed down at Barrows.

112

'Then you, sir, are a machine. For you have a Creator, too. And, like "these fellows," He made you in His image. I believe Spinoza, the great Hebrew scholar, held that opinion regarding animals; that they were clever machines. The critical thing, I think, is the soul. A machine can do anything a man can – you'll agree to that. But it doesn't have a soul.'

'There is no soul,' Barrows said. 'That's pap.'

'Then,' the simulacrum said, 'a machine is the same as an animal.' It went on slowly in its dry, patient way, 'And an animal is the same as a man. Is that not correct?'

'An animal is made out of flesh and blood, and a machine is made out of wiring and tubes, like you. What's the point of all this? You know darn well you're a machine; when we came in here you were sitting here alone in the dark thinking about it. So what? I know you're a machine; I don't care. All I care is whether you work or not. As far as I'm concerned you don't work well enough to interest me. Maybe later on when you have fewer bugs. All you can do is spout on about Judge Douglas and a lot of political, social twaddle that nobody gives a damn about.'

His attorney, Dave Blunk, turned to regard him thoughtfully, still plucking at his chin.

'I think we should start back to Seattle,' Barrows said to him. To me and Maury he said, 'Here's my decision. We'll come in, but we have to have a controlling interest so we can direct policy. For instance, this Civil War notion is pure absurdity. As it stands.'

Taken absolutely by surprise I stammered, 'W-what?'

'The Civil War scheme could be made to bring in a reasonable return in only one way. You'd never think of it in a million years. Refight the Civil War with robots; yes. But the return comes in when it's set up so you can bet on the outcome.'

'What outcome?' I said.

113

'Outcome as to which side prevails,' Barrows said. 'The blue or the gray.'

'Like the World Series,' Dave Blunk said, frowning thoughtfully.

'Exactly.' Barrows nodded.

'The South couldn't win,' Maury said. 'It had no industry.'

'Then set up a handicap system,' Barrows said.

Maury and I were at a loss for words.

'You're not serious,' I finally managed.

'I am serious.'

'A national epic made into a horse-race? A dog race? A lottery?'

Barrows shrugged. 'I've given you a million-dollar idea. You can throw it away; that's your privilege. I can tell you that there's no other way a Civil War use of your dolls can be made to pay. Myself, I would put them to a different use entirely. I know where your engineer, Robert Bundy, came from; I'm aware that he formerly was employed by the Federal Space Agency in designing circuits for their simulacra. After all, it's of the utmost importance to me to know as much about space-exploration hardware as can be known. I'm aware that your Stanton and Lincoln are minor modifications of Government systems.'

'Major,' Maury corrected hoarsely. 'The Government simulacra are simply mobile machines that creep about on an airless surface where no humans could exist.'

Barrows said, 'I'll tell you what I envision. Can you produce simulacra that are friendly-like?'

'What?' both I and Maury said together.

'I could use a number of them designed to look exactly like the family next door. A friendly, helpful family that would make a good neighbor. People you'd want to move in near, people like you remember from your childhood back in Omaha, Nebraska.'

After a pause Maury said, 'He means that he's going to sell lots to them. So they can build.'

'Not sell,' Barrows said. '*Give*. Colonization has to begin; it's been put off too long as it is. The Moon is barren and desolate. People are going to be lonely, there. It's difficult, we've found, to get anyone to go first. They'll buy the land but they won't settle on it. We want towns to spring up. To do that possibly we've got to prime the pump.'

'Would the actual human settlers know that their neighbors are merely simulacra?' I asked.

'Of course,' Barrows said smoothly.

'You wouldn't try to deceive them?'

'Hell no,' Dave Blunk said. 'That would be fraud.' I looked at Maury; he looked at me.

'You'd give them names,' I said to Barrows. 'Good old homey American names. The Edwards family, Bill and Mary Edwards and their son Tim who's seven. They're going to the Moon; they're not afraid of the cold and the lack of air and the empty, barren wastes.'

Barrows eyed me.

'And as more and more people got hooked,' I said, 'you could quietly begin to pull the simulacra back out. The Edwards family and the Jones family and the rest – they'd sell their houses and move on. Until finally your sub-divisions, your tract houses, would be populated by authentic people. And no one would ever know.'

'I wouldn't count on it working,' Maury said. 'Some authentic settler might try to sleep with Mrs Edwards and then he'd find out. You know how life is in housing tracts.'

Dave Blunk brayed out in a hee-haw of laughter. 'Very good!'

Placidly, Barrows said, 'I think it would work.'

'You have to,' Maury said. 'You've got all those parcels of land up there in the sky. So people are loath to emigrate . . . I thought there was a constant clamor, and all that was holding them back was the strict laws.'

'The laws are strict,' Barrows said, 'but – let's be realistic. It's an environment up there that once you've seen it . . . well, let's put it this way. About ten minutes is enough for most people. I've been there. I'm not going again.'

I said, 'Thanks for being so candid with us, Barrows.'

Barrows said, 'I know that the Government simulacra have functioned to good effect on the Lunar surface. I know what you have: a good modification of those simulacra. I know how you acquired the modification. I want the modification, once again modified, this time to my own concept. Any other arrangement is out of the question. Except for planetary exploration your simulacra have no genuine market value. It's a foolish pipe dream, this Civil War stunt. I won't do business with you on any understanding except as I've outlined. And I want it in writing.' He turned to Blunk, and Blunk nodded soberly.

I gaped at Barrows, not knowing whether to believe him; was this serious? Simulacra posing as human colonists, living on the Moon in order to create an illusion of prosperity? Man, woman and child simulacra in little living rooms, eating phony dinners, going to phony bathrooms . . . it was horrible. It was a way of bailing this man out of the troubles he had run into; did we want to hang our fortunes and lives onto that?

Maury sat puffing away miserably on his cigar; he was no doubt thinking along the lines I was.

And yet I could see Barrows' position. He had to persuade people in the mass that emigration to the Moon was desirable; his economic holdings hinged on it. And perhaps the end justified the means. The human race had to conquer its fear, its squeamishness, and enter an alien environment for the first time in its history. This might help entice it; there was comfort in solidarity. Heat and air domes protecting the great tracts would be built . . .

living would not be physically bad – it was only the psychological reality which was terrible, the aura of the Lunar environment. Nothing living, nothing growing . . . changeless forever. A brightly-lit house next door, with a family seated at their breakfast table, chatting and enjoying themselves: Barrows could provide them, as he would provide air, heat, houses and water.

I had to hand it to the man. From my standpoint it was fine except for one single joker. Obviously, every effort would be made to keep the secret. But if the efforts were a failure, if news got out, probably Barrows would be financially ruined, possibly even prosecuted and sent to jail. And we would go with him.

How much else in Barrows' empire had been concocted in this manner? Appearance built up over the fake . . .

I managed to switch the topic to the problems involved in a trip back to Seattle that night; I persuaded Barrows to phone a nearby motel for rooms. He and his party would stay until tomorrow and then return.

The interlude gave me a chance to do some phoning of my own. Off by myself where no one could overhear me I telephoned my dad at Boise.

'He's dragging us into something too deep for us,' I told my dad. 'We're out of our depth and none of us know what to do. We just can't handle this man.'

Naturally my dad had already gone to bed. He sounded befuddled. 'This Barrows, he is here now?'

'Yes. And he's got a brilliant mind. He even debated with the Lincoln and thinks he won. Maybe he did win; he quoted Spinoza, about animals being clever machines instead of alive. Not Barrows – Lincoln. Did Spinoza really say that?'

'Regretfully I must confess it.'

'When can you get down here?'

'Not tonight,' my father said.

'Tomorrow, then. They're staying over. We'll knock off

117

and resume tomorrow. We need your gentle humanism so be damn sure to show up.'

I hung up and returned to the group. The five of them – six, if you counted the simulacrum – were together in the main office, chatting.

'We're going down the street for a drink before we turn in,' Barrows said to me. 'You'll join us, of course.' He nodded toward the simulacrum. 'I'd like it to come along, too.'

I groaned to myself. But aloud I agreed.

Presently we were seated in a bar and the bartender was fixing our drinks.

The Lincoln had remained silent during the ordering, but Barrows had ordered a Tom Collins for it. Now Barrows handed it the glass.

'Cheers,' Dave Blunk said to the simulacrum, raising his whiskey sour.

'Although I am not a temperance man,' the simulacrum said in its cold, high-pitched voice, 'I seldom drink.' It examined its drink dubiously, then sipped it.

'You fellows would have been on firmer ground,' Barrows said, 'if you'd worked out the logic of your position a little further. But it's too late to accomplish that now. I say whatever this full-sized doll of yours is worth as a salable idea, the idea of utilizing it in space exploration is worth at least as much – maybe more. So the two cancel each other out. Wouldn't you agree?' He glanced inquiringly around.

'The idea of space exploration,' I said, 'was the Federal Government's.'

'My modification of that idea, then,' Barrows said. 'My point is that it's an even trade.'

'I don't see what you mean, Mr Barrows,' Pris said. 'What is?'

'Your idea, the simulacrum that looks so much like a human being that you can't tell it from one . . . and ours, of putting it on Luna in a modern two-bedroom California ranch-style house and calling it the Edwards family.'

'That was Louis' idea!' Maury exclaimed desperately. 'About the Edwards family!' He gazed wildly around at me. 'Wasn't it, Louis?'

'Yes,' I said. At least, I thought it was. We have to get out of here, I told myself. We're being backed farther and farther against the wall.

To itself the Lincoln sipped its Tom Collins.

'How do you like that drink?' Barrows asked it.

'Flavorful. But it blurs the senses.' It continued to sip, however.

That's all we need, I thought. Blurred senses!

119

10

At that point we managed to call a halt for the night.

'Nice meeting you, Mr Barrows,' I said, holding out my hand to him.

'Likewise.' He shook hands with me, then with Maury and Pris. The Lincoln stood a little apart, watching in its sad way . . . Barrows did not offer to shake hands with it, nor did he say goodbye to it.

Shortly, the four in our group were walking back up the dark sidewalks to MASA ASSOCIATES, taking in deep breaths of clear cold night air. The air smelled good and it cleansed our minds.

As soon as were back in our office, without the Barrows crew anywhere around, we got out the Old Crow using Dixie cups, we poured ourselves bourbon and water.

'We're in trouble,' Maury said.

The rest of us nodded.

'What do you say?' Maury asked the simulacrum. 'What's your opinion about him?'

The Lincoln said, 'He is like the crab, which makes progress forward by crawling sideways.'

'Meaning?' Pris said.

'I know what he means,' Maury said. 'The man has forced us down so far we don't know what we're doing. We're babes. Babes! And you and I – ' He gestured at me. 'We call ourselves salesmen. Why, we've been taken to the cleaners; if we hadn't adjourned he'd have the place, lock, stock and barrel right now.'

'My dad,' I began.

'Your dad!' Maury said bitterly. 'He's stupider than we are. I wish we never had gotten mixed up with this

Barrows. Now we'll never get rid of him – not until he gets what he wants.'

'We don't have to do business with him,' Pris said.

'We can tell him to go back to Seattle,' I said.

'Don't kid me! We can't tell him anything, he'll be knocking at the door bright and early tomorrow, like he said. Grinding us down, hounding us – ' Maury gaped at me.

'Don't let him bother you,' Pris said.

I said, 'I think Barrows is a desperate man. His vast economic venture is failing, this colonizing the Moon; don't you all feel that? This is not a powerful, successful man we're facing. It's a man who put everything behind buying real estate on the Moon and then subdividing it and building domes to hold in heat and air, and building converters to turn ice into water – and he can't get people to go there. I feel sorry for him.'

They all regarded me intently.

'Barrows has turned to this fraud as a last-ditch effort,' I said, 'this fakery of setting up villages of simulacra posing as human settlers. It's a scheme hatched out of despair. When I first heard it I thought possibly I was hearing another one of those bold visions that men like Barrows get, that the rest of us never have because we're mere mortals. But now I'm not sure at all. I think he's running scared, so scared that he's lost his senses. This idea isn't reasonable. He can't hope to fool anyone. The Federal Government would catch on right away.'

'How?' Maury asked.

'The Department of Health inspects every person who intends to emigrate. It's the Government's business. How's Barrows even going to get them off Earth?'

Maury said, 'Listen. It's none of our business how sound this scheme of his is. We're not in a position to judge. Only time will tell and if we don't do business with him even time won't tell.'

'I agree,' Pris said. 'We should confine ourselves to deciding what's in it for us.'

'Nothing's in it for us if he's caught and goes to prison,' I said. 'Which he will. Which he deserves to be. I say we've got to disengage, not do business with this man of any kind. It's shaky, risky, dishonest, and downright stupid. Our own ideas are nutty enough.'

The Lincoln said, 'Could Mr Stanton be here?'

'What?' Maury said.

'I think we would be advantaged if Mr Stanton were here and not in Seattle, as you tell me he is.'

We all looked at one another.

'He's right,' Pris said. 'We ought to get the Edwin M. Stanton back. He'd be of use to us; he's so inflexible.'

'We need iron,' I agreed. 'Backbone. We're bending too much.'

'Well, we can get it back,' Maury said. 'Tonight, even. We can charter a private plane, fly to the Sea-Tac Airfield outside Seattle, drive into Seattle and search until we find it and then come back here. Have it tomorrow morning when we confront Barrows.'

'But we'd be dead on our feet,' I pointed out, 'at best. And it might take us days to find it. It may not even be in Seattle, by now; it may have flown on to Alaska or to Japan – even taken off for one of Barrows' subdivisions on the Moon.'

We sipped our Dixie cups of bourbon morosely, all but the Lincoln; it had put its aside.

'Have you ever had any kangaroo tail soup?' Maury said.

We all looked at him, including the simulacrum.

'I have a can around here somewhere,' Maury said. 'We can heat it up on the hotplate; it's terrific. I'll make it.'

'Let me out,' I said.

'No thanks,' said Pris.

The simulacrum smiled its gentle, wan smile.

'I'll tell you how I happened to get it,' Maury said. 'I was in the supermarket, in Boise, waiting in line. The checker was saying to some guy, "No, we're not going to stock any kangaroo tail soup anymore." All of a sudden from the other side of the display – it was boxes of cereal or something – this hollow voice issues: "No more kangaroo tail soup? *Ever*?" and this guy comes hurrying around with his cart to buy up the last cans. So I got a couple. Try it, it'll make you all feel better.'

I said, 'Notice how Barrows worked us down. He calls the simulacra automatons first and then he calls them gimmicks and then he winds up calling them dolls.'

'It's a technique,' Pris said, 'a sales technique. He's cutting the ground out from under us.'

'Words,' the simulacrum said, 'are weapons.'

'Can't you say anything to him?' I asked the simulacrum. 'All you did was debate with him.'

The simulacrum shook its head no.

'Of course it can't do anything,' Pris said. 'Because it argues fair, like we did in school. That's the way they debated back in the middle of the last century. Barrows doesn't argue fair, and there's no audience to catch him. Right, Mr Lincoln?'

The simulacrum did not respond, but its smile seemed – to me – to become even sadder, and its face longer and more lined with care.

'Things are worse now than they used to be,' Maury said.

But, I thought, we still have to do something. 'He may have the Stanton under lock and key, for all we know. He may have it torn down on a bench somewhere, and his engineers are making one of their own slightly redesigned so as not to infringe on our patents.' I turned to Maury. 'Do we actually have patents?'

'Pending,' Maury said. 'You know how it works.' He did not sound encouraging. 'I don't doubt he can steal what we have, now that he's seen our idea. It's the kind

123

of thing that if you know it can be done, you can do it yourself, given enough time.'

'Okay,' I said, 'so it's like the internal combustion engine. But we've got a headstart; let's start manufacturing them at the Rosen factory as soon as possible. Let's get ours on the market before Barrows does.'

They all looked at me wide-eyed.

'I think you've got something there,' Maury said, chewing his thumb. 'What else can we do anyhow? You think your dad could get the assembly line going right away? Is he pretty fast on converting over, like this?'

'Fast as a snake,' I said.

Pris said derisively, 'Don't put us on. Old Jerome? It'll be a year before he can make dies to stamp the parts out with, and the wiring'll have to be done in Japan – he'll have to fly to Japan to arrange for that, and he'll want to take a boat, like before.'

'Oh,' I said, 'you've thought about it, I see.'

'Sure,' Pris said sneeringly. 'I actually considered it seriously.'

'In any case,' I said, 'it's our only hope; we've got to get the goddam things on the retail market – we've wasted enough time as it is.'

'Agreed,' Maury said. 'What we'll do is, tomorrow we'll go to Boise and commission old Jerome and your funny brother Chester to start work. Start making die stampers and flying to Japan – but what'll we tell Barrows?'

That stumped us. Again we were all silent.

'We'll tell him,' I announced, 'that the Lincoln busted. That it broke down and we've withdrawn it from market. And then he won't want the thing so he'll go back home to Seattle.'

Maury, coming over beside me, said in a low voice, 'You mean cut the switch on it. Shut it off.'

I nodded.

'I hate to do that,' Maury said. We both glanced at the Lincoln, which was regarding us with melancholy eyes.

'He'll insist on seeing it for himself,' Pris pointed out. 'Let him back on it a couple of times, if he wants to. Let him shake it like a gum machine; if we have it cut off it won't do a thing.'

'Okay,' Maury agreed.

'Good,' I said. 'Then we've decided.'

We shut off the Lincoln then and there. Maury, as soon as the deed was done, went downstairs and out to his car and drove home, saying he was going to bed. Pris offered to drive me to my motel in the Chevvy, taking it home herself and picking me up the next morning. I was so tired that I accepted her offer.

As she drove me through closed-up Ontario she said, 'I wonder if all wealthy, powerful men are like that.'

'Sure. All those who made their own money – not the ones who inherit it, maybe.'

'It was dreadful,' Pris said. 'Shutting the Lincoln off. To see it – stop living, as if we had killed it again. Don't you think?'

'Yes.'

Later, when she drew up before my motel, she said, 'Do you think that's the only way to make a lot of money? To be like him?' Sam K. Barrows had changed her; no doubt of that. She was a sobered young woman.

I said, 'Don't ask me. I draw seven-fifty a month, at best.'

'But one has to admire him.'

'I knew you'd say that, sooner or later. As soon as you said *but* I knew what was going to follow.'

Pris sighed. 'So I'm an open book to you.'

'No, you're the greatest enigma I've ever run up against. It's just in this one case I said to myself, "Pris is going to say but one has to admire him" and you did say it.'

'And I'll bet you also believe I'll gradually go back to the way I used to feel until I leave off the "but" and just admire him, period.'

I said nothing. But it was so.

'Did you notice,' Pris said, 'that I was able to endure the shutting down of the Lincoln? If I can stand that I can stand anything. I even enjoyed it although I didn't let it show, of course.'

'You're lying to beat hell.'

'I got a very enjoyable sense of power, an ultimate power. We gave it life and then we took the life right back – snap! As easy as that. But the moral burden doesn't rest on us anyhow; it rests on Sam Barrows, and he wouldn't have had a twinge, he would have gotten a big kick out of it. Look at the strength there, Louis. We really wish we were the same way. I don't regret turning it off. I regret being emotionally upset. I disgust myself for being what I am. No wonder I'm down here with the rest of you and Sam Barrows is up at the top. You can see the difference between him and us; it's so clear.'

She was quiet for a time, lighting a cigarette and sitting with it.

'What about sex?' she said presently.

'Sex is worse yet, even than turning off nice simulacra.'

'I mean sex changes you. The experience of intercourse.'

It froze my blood, to hear her talk like that.

'What's wrong?' she said.

'You scare me.'

'Why?'

'You talk as if – '

Pris finished for me, 'As if I was up there looking down even on my own body. I am. It's not me. I'm a soul.'

'Like Blunk said, "Show me."'

'I can't, Louis, but it's still true. I'm not a physical body in time and space. Plato was right.'

'What about the rest of us?'

126

'Well, that's your business. I perceive you as bodies, so maybe you are; maybe that's all you are. Don't you know? If you don't know I can't tell you.' She put out her cigarette. 'I better go home, Louis.'

'Okay,' I said, opening the car door. The motel, with all its rooms, was dark; even the big neon sign had been shut off for the night. The middle-aged couple who ran the place were no doubt tucked safely in their beds.

Pris said, 'Louis, I carry a diaphragm around in my purse.'

'The kind you put inside you? Or the kind that's in the chest and you breathe in and out by.'

'Don't kid. This is very serious for me, Louis. Sex, I mean.'

I said, 'Well, then give me funny sex.'

'Meaning what?'

'Nothing. Just nothing.' I started to shut the car door after me.

'I'm going to say something corny,' Pris said, rolling down the window on my side.

'No you're not, because I'm not going to listen. I hate corny statements by deadly serious people. Better you should stay a remote soul that sneers at suffering animals; at least – ' I hesitated. But what the hell. 'At least I can honestly soberly hate you and fear you.'

'How will you feel after you hear the corny statement?'

I said, 'I'll make an appointment with the hospital tomorrow and have myself castrated or whatever they call it.'

'You mean,' she said slowly, 'that I'm sexually desirable when I'm cruel and schizoid, but if I become MAUDLIN, THEN I'm not even that.'

'Don't say "even." That's a hell of a lot.'

'Take me into your motel room,' Pris said, 'and screw me.'

'There is, somehow, in your language, something,

127

which I can't put my finger on, that somehow leaves something to be desired.'

'You're just chicken.'

'No,' I said.

'Yes.'

'No, and I'm not going to prove it by doing so. I really am not chicken; I've slept with all sorts of women in my time. Honest. There isn't a thing about sex that could scare me; I'm too old. You're talking about college-boy stuff, first box of contraceptives stuff.'

'But you still won't screw me?'

'No,' I agreed, 'because you're not only detached, you're brutal. And not with just me but with yourself, with the physical body you despise and claim isn't you. Don't you remember that discussion between Lincoln – the Lincoln simulacrum, I mean – and Barrows and Blunk? An animal is close to being man and both are made out of flesh and blood. That's what you're trying not to be.'

'Not *trying* – am not.'

'What does that make you? A machine?'

'But a machine has wires. I have no wires.'

'Then what?' I said. 'What do you think you are?'

Pris said, 'I know what I am. The schizoid is very common in this century, like hysteria was in the nine-teenth. It's a form of deep, pervasive, subtle psychic alienation. I wish I wasn't, but I am . . . you're lucky, Louis Rosen; you're old-fashioned. I'd trade with you. I'm worried that my language regarding sex is crude. I scared you off with it. I'm very sorry about that.'

'Not crude. Worse. Inhuman. You'd – I know what you'd do. If you had intercourse with someone – if you've had.' I felt confused and tired. 'You'd observe, the whole goddam time; mentally, spiritually, in every way. Always be conscious.'

'Is that wrong? I thought everyone did.'

'Goodnight.' I started away from the car.

'Goodnight, coward.'

'Up yours,' I said.

'Oh, Louis,' she said, with a shiver of anguish.

'Forgive me,' I said.

Sniffling she said, 'What an awful thing to say.'

'For christ's sake, forgive me,' I said, 'you have to forgive me. I'm the sick one, for saying that to you; it's like something took hold of my tongue.'

Still sniffling, she nodded mutely. She started up the motor of the car and turned its lights on.

'Don't go,' I said. 'Listen, you can chalk it up to a demented subrational attempt on my part to reach you, don't you see? All your talk, your making yourself admire Sam Barrows even more than ever, that drove me out of my mind. I'm very fond of you, I really am; seeing you open up for a minute to a warm, human view, and then going back – '

'Thanks,' she said in a near whisper, 'for trying to make me feel better.' She shot me a tiny smile.

'Don't let this make you worse,' I said, holding onto the door of the car, afraid she would leave.

'I won't. In fact it barely touched me.'

'Come on inside,' I said. 'Sit for a moment, okay?'

'No. Don't worry – it's just the strain on us all. I know it upset you. The reason I use such crude words is that I don't know any better, nobody taught me how to talk about the unspeakable things.'

'It just takes experience. But listen, Pris, promise me something, promise me you won't deny to yourself that I hurt you. It's good to be able to feel what you felt just now, good to – '

'Good to be hurt.'

'No, I don't mean that; I mean it's encouraging. I'm not trying merely to make up for what I did. Look, Pris, the fact that you suffered so acutely just now because of what I – '

'The hell I did.'

129

'You did,' I said. 'Don't lie.'

'All right, Louis, I did; I won't lie.' She hung her head.

Opening the car door I said, 'Come with me, Pris.'

She shut off the motor and car lights and slid out; I took hold of her by the arm.

'Is this the first step in delicious intimacy?' she asked.

'I'm acquainting you with the unspeakable.'

'I just want to be able to talk about it, I don't want to have to do it. Of course you're joking; we're going to sit side by side and then I'll go home. That's best for both of us, in fact it's the only course open.'

We entered the dark little motel room and I switched on the light and then the heat and then the TV set.

'Is that so no one will hear us panting?' She shut off the TV set. 'I pant very lightly; it isn't necessary.' Removing her coat she stood holding it until I took it and hung it in the closet. 'Now tell me where to sit and how. In that chair?' She seated herself in a straight chair, folded her hands in her lap and regarded me solemnly. 'How's this? What else should I take off? Shoes? All my clothes? Or do you like to do it? If you do, my skirt doesn't unzip; it unbuttons, and be careful you don't pull too hard or the top button will come off and then I'll have to sew it back.' She twisted around to show me. 'There the buttons are, on the side.'

'All this is educational,' I said, 'but not illuminating.'

'Do you know what I'd like?' Her face lit up. 'I want you to drive out somewhere and come back with some kosher corned beef and Jewish bread and ale and some halvah for dessert. That wonderful thin-sliced corned beef that's two-fifty a pound.'

'I'd like to,' I said, 'but there's no place within hundreds of miles to get it.'

'Can't you get it in Boise?'

'No.' I hung up my coat. 'It's too late for kosher corned beef anyhow. I don't mean too late in the evening. I mean too late in our lives.' Seating myself across from her I drew my chair close and took hold of her hands. They were dry, small and quite hard. From all her tile-cutting she had developed sinewy arms, strong fingers. 'Let's run off. Let's drive south and never come back, never see the simulacra again or Sam Barrows or Ontario, Oregon.'

'No,' Pris said. 'We're compelled to tangle with Sam; can't you feel it around us, in the air? I'm surprised at you, imagining that you can hop in the car and drive off. It can't be evaded.'

'Forgive me,' I said.

'I forgive you but I can't understand you; sometimes you seem like a baby, unexposed to life.'

'What I've done,' I said, 'is I've hacked out little portions of reality here and there and familiarized myself with them, somewhat on the model of a sheep who's learned a route across a pasture and never deviates from that route.'

'You feel safe by doing that?'

'I feel safe *mostly*, but never around you.'

She nodded. 'I'm the pasture itself, to you.'

'That expresses it.'

With a sudden laugh she said, 'It's just like being made love to by Shakespeare. Louis, you can tell me you're going to crop, browse, graze among my lovely hills and valleys and in particular my divinely-wooded meadows, you know, where the fragrant wild ferns and grasses wave in profusion. I don't need to spell it out, do I?' Her eyes flashed. 'Now for christ's sake, take off my clothes or at least make the attempt to.' She began to pull off her shoes.

'No,' I said.

'Haven't we gotten through the poetry stage long ago? Can't we dispense with more of that and get down to the real thing?' She started to unfasten her skirt, but I took hold of her hands and stopped her.

'I'm too ignorant to proceed,' I said. 'I just don't have

131

it, Pris. Too ignorant and too awkward and too cowardly. Things have already gone far beyond my limited comprehension. I'm lost in a realm I don't understand.' I held on tightly to her hands. 'The best I can think of to do, the best I can manage at this time, would be to kiss you. Maybe on the cheek, if it's okay.'

'You're old,' Pris said. 'That's it. You're part of a dying world of the past.' She turned her head and leaned toward me. 'As a favor to you I'll let you kiss me.'

I kissed her on the cheek.

'Actually,' Pris said, 'if you want to know the facts, the fragrant wild ferns and grasses don't wave in profusion; there's a couple of wild ferns and about four grasses and that's it. I'm hardly grown, Louis. I only started wearing a bra a year ago and sometimes I forget it even now; I hardly need it.'

'Can't I kiss you on the mouth?'

'No,' Pris said, 'that's too intimate.'

'You can shut your eyes.'

'Instead, you turn off the lights.' She drew her hands away, rose and went to the wall switch. 'I'll do it.'

'Stop,' I said. 'I have an overwhelming sense of foreboding.'

At the wall switch she stood hesitating. 'It's not like me to be indecisive. You're undermining me, Louis. I'm sorry. I have to go on.' She switched off the light, the room disappeared into darkness. I could see nothing at all.

'Pris,' I said, 'I'm going to drive to Portland, Oregon and get the kosher corned beef.'

'Where can I put my skirt?' Pris said from the darkness. 'So it won't get wrinkled.'

'This is all some crazed dream.'

'No,' Pris said, 'it's bliss. Don't you know bliss when it runs into you and butts you in the face? Help me hang up my clothes. I have to go in fifteen minutes. Can you talk and make love at the same time or do you devolve to

132

animal gruntings?' I could hear her rustling around in the darkness, disposing of her clothes, groping about for the bed.

'There is no bed,' I said.

'Then the floor.'

'It scrapes your knees.'

'Not my knees; yours.'

'I have a phobia,' I said. 'I have to have the lights on or I get the fear I'm having intercourse with a thing made out of strings and piano wire and my grandmother's old orange quilt.'

Pris laughed. 'That's me,' she said from close by. 'That perfectly describes my essence. I almost have you,' she said, banging against something. 'You won't escape.'

'Stop it,' I said. 'I'm turning on the light.' I managed to find the switch; I pressed it and the room burst back into being, blinding me, and there stood a fully-dressed girl. She had not taken off her clothes at all, and I stared at her in astonishment while she laughed silently to see my expression.

'It's an illusion,' she said. 'I was going to defeat you at the final moment, I just wanted to drive you to a pitch of sexual desire and then – ' She snapped her fingers, 'Gooooodnight.'

I tried to smile.

'Don't take me seriously,' Pris said. 'Don't become emotionally involved with me. I'll break your heart.'

'So who's involved?' I said, hearing my voice choke. 'It's a game people play in the dark. I just wanted to tear off a piece, as they say.'

'I don't know that phrase.' She was no longer laughing; her eyes were no longer bright. She regarded me coolly. 'But I get the idea.'

'I'll tell you something else. Get ready. They do have kosher corned beef in Boise. I could have picked it up any time with no trouble.'

'You bastard,' she said. Seating herself she picked up her shoes and put them on.

'There's sand coming in the door.'

'What?' She glanced around. 'What are you talking about?'

'We're trapped down here. Somebody's got a mound going above us, we'll never get out.'

Sharply she said, 'Stop it.'

'You never should have confided in me.'

'Yes, you'll use it against me to torment me.' She went to the closet for her coat.

'Wasn't I tormented?' I said, following after her.

'Just now, you mean? Oh heck, I might not have run out, I might have stayed.'

'If I had done just right.'

'I hadn't made up my mind. It depended on you, on your ability. I expect a lot. I'm very idealistic.' Having found her coat she began putting it on; reflexively I assisted her.

'We're putting clothes back on,' I said, 'without having taken them off.'

'Now you regret it,' Pris said. 'Regrets – that's all you're good for.' She gave me a look of such loathing that I shrank back.

'I could say a few mean things about you,' I said.

'You won't, though, because you know if you do I'll come back so hard with a reply that you'll drop dead on the spot.'

I shrugged, unable to speak.

'It was fear,' Pris said. She walked slowly down the path, toward her parked car.

'Fear, right,' I said, accompanying her. 'Fear based on the knowledge that a thing like that has to come out of the mutual understanding and agreement of two people. It can't be forced on one by the other.'

'Fear of jail, you mean.' She opened the car door and got in, to sit behind the wheel. 'What you ought to have done, what a real man would have done, would be to grab me by the wrist, carry me to the bed and without paying any attention to what I had to say – '

'If I had done that, you would never have stopped complaining, first to me, then to Maury, then to a lawyer, then to the police, then in a court of law to the world at large.'

We were both silent, then.

'Anyhow,' I said, 'I got to kiss you.'

'Only on the cheek.'

'On the mouth,' I said.

'That's a lie.'

'I remember it as on the mouth,' I said, and shut the car door after her.

Rolling down her window she said, 'So, that's going to be your story, that you got to take liberties with me.'

'I'll remember it and treasure it, too,' I said. 'In my heart.' I put my hand to my chest.

Pris started up the motor, switched on the lights and drove away.

I stood for a moment and then I walked back down the path to my motel room. We're cracking up, I said to myself. We're so tired, so demoralized, that we're at the end. Tomorrow we've got to get rid of Barrows. Pris – poor Pris is getting it the worst. And it was shutting off the Lincoln that did it. The turning point came there.

Hands in my pockets I stumbled back to my open door.

The next morning there was plenty of warm sunlight, and I felt a good deal better without even getting up from my bed. And then, after I had gotten up and shaved, had breakfast at the motel cafe of hotcakes and bacon and coffee and orange juice and had read the newspaper, I felt as good as new. Really recovered.

It shows what breakfast does, I said to myself. Healed, maybe? I'm back in there a whole, well man again?

No. We're better but not healed. Because we weren't well in the first place, and you can't restore health where there wasn't any health to begin with. *What is this sickness*?

Pris has had it almost to the point of death. And it has touched me, moved into me and lodged there. And Maury and Barrows and after him all the rest of us until my father; my father has it the least.

Dad! I had forgotten; he was coming over.

Hurrying outside, I hailed a taxi.

I was the first to reach the office of MASA ASSOCIATES. A moment later, from the office window, I saw my Chevrolet Magic Fire parking. Out stepped Pris. Today she wore a blue cotton skirt and a long-sleeved blouse; her hair was tied up and her face was scrubbed and shiny.

As she entered the office she smiled at me. 'I'm sorry I used the wrong word last night. Maybe next time. No harm done.'

'No harm done,' I said.

'Do you mean that, Louis?'

'No,' I said, returning her smile.

The office door opened and Maury entered. 'I got a good night's rest. By god, buddy boy, we'll take this nogoodnik Barrows for every last cent he's got.'

Behind him came my dad, in his dark, striped, train-conductor's suit. He greeted Pris gravely, then turned to Maury and me. 'Is he here, yet?'

'No, Dad,' I said. 'Any time now.'

Pris said, 'I think we should turn the Lincoln back on. We shouldn't be afraid of Barrows.'

'I agree,' I said.

'No,' Maury said, 'and I'll tell you why. It whets Barrows' appetite. Isn't that so? Think about it.'

After a time I said, 'Maury's right. We'll leave it off. Barrows can kick it and pound it, but let's not turn it back on. It's greed that motivates him.' And, I thought, it's fear that motivates us; so much of what we've done of late has been inspired by fear, not by common sense . . .

There was a knock at the door.

'He's here,' Maury said, and cast a flickering glance at me.

The door opened. There stood Sam K. Barrows, David Blunk, Mrs Nild, and with them stood the somber, dark figure of Edwin M. Stanton.

'We met it down the street,' Dave Blunk boomed cheerfully. 'It was coming here and we gave it a lift in our cab.'

The Stanton simulacrum looked sourly at all of us.

Good lord, I said to myself. We hadn't expected this – does this make a difference? Are we hurt and if so how bad?

I did not know. But in any case we had to go on, and this time to a showdown. One way or the other.

11

Barrows said amiably, 'We parked down a little ways and had a talk with Stanton here, We've come to what we seem to feel is an understanding, at least of sorts.'

'Oh?' I said. Beside me, Maury had assumed a set, harsh expression. Pris shuddered visibly.

Holding out his hand my dad said, 'I am Jerome Rosen, owner of the Rosen spinet and electronic organ plant of Boise, Idaho. Do I have the honor of meeting Mr Samuel Barrows?'

So we each have a surprise for the other side, I said to myself. You managed, sometime during the night, to round up the Stanton; we for our part – if it's roughly equivalent – managed to obtain my dad.

That Stanton. As the Britannica had said: he had connived with the enemy for his own personal advantage. The skunk! And the idea swept over me: *probably he was with Barrows the entire time in Seattle; he had not gone off at all to open a law office or see the sights.* They had no doubt been talking terms from the start.

We had been sold out – by our first simulacrum.

A shocking omen it was.

At any rate, the Lincoln would never do that. And, realizing that, I felt a good deal better.

We had better get the Lincoln back on again, I said to myself.

To Maury I said, 'Go ask Lincoln to come up here, will you?'

He raised his eyebrow.

'We need him,' I said.

'We do,' Pris agreed.

'Okay.' Nodding, Maury went off.

138

We had begun. But begun what?

Barrows said, 'When we first ran into Stanton, here, we treated it as a mechanical contraption. But then Mr Blunk reminded me that you maintain it to be alive. I'd be curious to know what you pay the Stanton fellow, here.'

Pay, I thought wildly.

'There are peonage laws,' Blunk said.

I gaped at him.

'Do you have a work contract with Mr Stanton?' Blunk asked. 'And if you do I hope it meets the Minimum Wage law's requirements. Actually we've been discussing this with Stanton and he doesn't recall signing any contract. I therefore see no objection to Mr Barrows hiring him at say six dollars an hour. That's a more than fair wage, you'll agree. On that basis Mr Stanton has agreed to return with us to Seattle.'

We remained silent.

The door opened and Maury entered. With him shambled the tall, hunched, dark-bearded figure of the Lincoln simulacrum.

Pris said, 'I think we should accept his offer.'

'What offer?' Maury said. 'I haven't heard any offer.' To me he said, 'Have you heard any offer?'

I shook my head.

'Pris,' Maury said, 'have you been talking with Barrows?'

Barrows said, 'Here's my offer. We'll let MASA be assessed at a worth of seventy-five thousand dollars. I'll put up – '

'Have you two been talking?' Maury interrupted.

Neither Pris nor Barrows said anything. But it was clear to me and to Maury, clear to all of us.

'I'll put up one hundred and fifty thousand,' Barrows said. 'And I'll naturally have a controlling interest.'

Maury shook his head no.

'May we discuss this among ourselves?' Pris said to Barrows.

'Surely,' Barrows said.

We withdrew to a small supply room across the hall.

'We're lost,' Maury said, his face gray. 'Ruined.'

Pris said nothing. But her face was tight.

After a long time my father said, 'Avoid this Barrows. Don't be part of a corporation in which he holds control; this I know.'

I turned to the Lincoln, who stood there quietly listening to us. 'You're an attorney – in the name of God, help us.'

The Lincoln said, 'Louis, Mr Barrows and his compatriots hold a position of strength. No deception lies in his acts . . . he is the stronger party.' The simulacrum reflected, then it turned and walked to the window to look out at the street below. All at once it swung back toward us; the heavy lips twisted and it said, with pain in its face but a spark glowing in its eyes, 'Sam Barrows is a businessman but so are you. Sell MASA ASSOCIATES, your small firm, to Mr Jerome Rosen, here, for a dollar. Thereby it becomes the property of the Rosen spinet and organ factory, which has great assets. To obtain it, Sam Barrows must buy the entire establishment, including the factory, and he is not prepared to do that. As to Stanton, I can tell you this; Stanton will not cooperate with them much further. I can speak to him, and he will be persuaded to return. Stanton is temperamental, but a good man. I have known him for many years; he was in the Buchanan Administration, and against much protest I elected to keep him on, despite his machinations. Although quick-tempered and concerned with his own position, he is honest. He will not, in the end, consort with rascals. He does not want to open a law office and return to his law practice; he wishes a position of public power, and in that he is responsible – he makes a good public servant. I will tell him that you wish to make him Chairman of your Board of Directors, and he will stay.'

Presently Maury said softly, 'I never would have thought of that.'

Pris said, 'I – don't agree. MASA shouldn't be turned over to the Rosen family; that's out of the question. And Stanton won't buy an offer like that.'

'Yes he will,' Maury said. My father was nodding and I nodded, too. 'We'll make him a big man in our organization – why not? He has the ability. My good god, he can probably turn us into a million-dollar business inside a year.'

The Lincoln said gently,' You will not regret placing your trust, and your business, in Mr Stanton's hands.'

We filed back into the office. Barrows and his people awaited us expectantly.

'Here is what we have to say,' Maury said, clearing his throat. 'Uh, we've sold MASA to Mr Jerome Rosen.' He indicated my father. 'For one dollar.'

Blinking, Barrows said, 'Have you? Interesting.' He glanced at Blunk, who threw up his hands in a gesture of rueful, wry resignation.

The Lincoln said to the Stanton, 'Edwin, Mr Rock and the two Mr Rosens wish you to join their newly-formed corporation as Chairman of its Board of Directors.'

The sour, embittered, harsh features of the Stanton simulacrum faltered; emotions appeared, disappeared. 'Is that the actual fact of the matter?' it said questioningly to the group of us.

'Yes sir,' Maury said. 'That's a firm offer. We can use a man of your ability; we're willing to step down to make way for you.'

'Right,' I said.

My father said, 'This I agree to, Mr Stanton. And I can speak for my other son, Chester. We are sincere.'

Seating himself at one of MASA's old Underwood

electric typewriters, Maury inserted a sheet of paper and began to type. 'We'll put it in writing; we can sign it right now and get the barge towed out into the river.'

Pris said in a low, cold voice, 'I consider this a deceitful betrayal of not only Mr Barrows but everything we've strived for.'

Staring at her, Maury said in a shocked voice, 'Shut up.'

'I won't go along with this because it's wrong,' Pris said. Her voice was absolutely under control; she might have been ordering clothes over the telephone from Macy's. 'Mr Barrows and Mr Blunk, if you want me to come along with you, I will.'

We – including Barrows and Blunk – could not believe our ears.

However, Barrows recovered quickly. 'You, ah, helped build the two simulacra. You could build another, then?' He eyed her.

'No she couldn't,' Maury said. 'All she did was draw the face. What does she know about the electronic part? Nothing!' He continued to stare at his daughter.

Pris said, 'Bob Bundy will go with me.'

'Why?' I said. My voice wavered. 'Him, too?' I said. 'You and Bundy have been – ' I couldn't finish.

'Bob is fond of me,' Pris said remotely.

Reaching into his coat pocket, Barrows brought out his billfold. 'I'll give you money for the flight,' he said to Pris. 'You can follow us. So there won't be any legal complications . . . we'll travel separately.'

'Good enough,' Pris said. 'I'll be in Seattle in a day or so. But keep the money; I have my own.'

Nodding to Dave Blunk, Barrows said, 'Well, we've concluded our business here. We might as well get started back.' To Stanton, he said, 'We'll leave you here, Stanton; is that your decision?'

In a grating voice the Stanton simulacrum said, 'It is, sir.'

'Good day,' Barrows said to all of us. Blunk waved at us in a cordial fashion. Mrs Nild turned to follow Barrows – and they were gone.

'Pris,' I said, 'you're insane.'

'That's a value judgment,' Pris said in a faraway voice.

'Did you mean that?' Maury asked her, ashen-faced. 'About going over to Barrows? Flying to Seattle to join him?'

'Yes.'

'I'll get the cops,' Maury said, 'and restrain you. You're just a minor. Nothing but a child. I'll get the mental health people in on this; I'll get them to put you back in Kasanin.'

'No, you won't,' Pris said. 'I can do it, and the Barrows organization will help me. The mental health people can't hold me unless I go back in voluntarily, which I won't, or unless I'm psychotic, which I'm not. I'm managing my affairs very ably. So don't go into one of your emotional tantrums; it won't do any good.'

Maury licked his lip, stammered, then became mute. No doubt she was right; it could all be successfully arranged. And the Barrows people would see that there were no legal loopholes; they had the know-how and they had a lot to gain.

'I don't believe Bob Bundy will leave us on your account,' I said to her. But I could tell by her expression that he would. She knew. It was one of those things. How long had it been that way between them? No way to tell. It was Pris' secret; we had to believe it. To the Lincoln I said, 'You didn't expect this, did you?'

It shook its head no.

Maury said brokenly, 'Anyhow we got rid of them. We kept MASA ASSOCIATES. We kept the Stanton. They won't be back. I don't give a damn about Pris and Bob Bundy; if the two of them want to go to join him, good luck to them.' He glared at her wretchedly. Pris returned his glare with the same dispassion as before; nothing ruffled her. In a crisis she was even colder, more efficient, more in command, than ever.

Maybe, I said bitterly to myself, we're lucky she's leaving. We would not have been able to cope with her, finally – at least not me. Can Barrows? Perhaps he may be able to use her, exploit her . . . or she may damage, even destroy him. Or both. But then they also have Bundy. And between Pris and Bundy they can build a simulacrum with no trouble. They don't need Maury and they certainly don't need me.

Leaning toward me the Lincoln said in a sympathetic voice, 'You will benefit from Mr Stanton's ability to make firm decisions. He, with his enormous energy, will assist your enterprise almost at once.'

The Stanton grumbled, 'My health isn't as good as it ought to be.' But it looked confident and pleased nonetheless. 'I'll do what I can.'

'Sorry about your daughter,' I said to my partner.

'Christ,' he muttered, 'how could she do it?'

'She will come back,' my dad said, patting him on the arm. 'They do; the Kindern always do.'

'I don't want her back,' Maury said. But obviously he did.

I said, 'Let's go downstairs and across the street and have a cup of coffee.' There was a good breakfast type cafe, there.

'You go ahead,' Pris said. 'I think I'll drive on home; I have a good deal to get done. Can I take the Jaguar?'

'No,' Maury said.

She shrugged, picked up her purse, and left the office. The door closed after her. She was gone, then and there.

As we sat in the cafe having our coffee I thought to myself, The Lincoln did us plenty of good, back there with Barrows. It found a way to get us off the hook. And after all, it wasn't its fault that events wound up as they did . . . there was no way for it to know how Pris would jump. Nor could it know about her and Bundy, that she had our engineer in the palm of her hand by the use of her age-old equipment. I hadn't guessed and Maury hadn't either.

The waitress had been gazing at us and now she came over. 'This is that window dummy of Abraham Lincoln, isn't it?'

'No, actually it's a window dummy of W.C. Fields,' I said. 'But it has a costume on, a Lincoln costume.'

'We, my boyfriend and I, saw it demonstrating the other day. It's sure real-looking. Can I touch it?'

'Sure,' I said.

She reached out cautiously and touched the Lincoln's hand. Ooh, it's even warm!' she exclaimed. 'And jeez, it's drinking coffee!'

We got her to go off, finally, and were able to resume our melancholy discussion. I said to the simulacrum, 'You certainly have made a profound adjustment to this society. Better than some of us.'

In a brusque tone the Stanton spoke up. 'Mr Lincoln has always been able to come to terms with everyone and everything – by the one stale method of telling a joke.'

The Lincoln smiled as it sipped its coffee.

'I wonder what Pris is doing now,' Maury said. 'Packing, maybe. It seems awful, her not here with us. Part of the team.'

We lost a lot of people back there in the office, I realized. We got rid of Barrows, Dave Blunk, Mrs Nild, and to our surprise, Pris Frauenzimmer and our vital sole engineer, Bob Bundy. I wonder if we'll ever see Barrows again. I wonder if we'll ever see Bob Bundy again. I wonder if we'll ever see Pris again, and if we do, will she be changed?

'How could she sell us out like that?' Maury wondered aloud. 'Going over to the other side – that clinic and that Doctor Horstowski did nothing, exactly nothing, for all that time and money. What loyalty did she show? I mean,

I want all that money back I've shelled out. But her; I don't care if I ever see her again – I'm through with her. I mean it.'

To change the subject I said to the Lincoln, 'Do you have any other advice for us, sir? As to what we should do?'

'I fear I did not help you as much as I had hoped to,' the Lincoln said. 'With a woman there is no prediction; fate enters in a capricious form . . . however, I suggest you retain me as your legal counsel. As they retain Mr Blunk.'

'A terrific idea,' I said, getting out my checkbook. 'How much do you require as a retainer?'

'Ten dollars is sufficient,' the Lincoln said. So I wrote the check out for that amount; he accepted it and thanked me.

Maury, deep in his brooding, glanced up to say, 'The going retainer is at least two hundred these days; the dollar isn't worth what it used to be.'

'Ten will do,' the Lincoln said. 'And I will begin to draw up the papers of sale of MASA ASSOCIATES to your piano factory at Boise. As to ownership, I suggest that a limited corporation be formed, much like Mr Barrows suggested, and I will look into the law these days to see how the stock should be distributed. It will take me time to do research, I fear, so you must be patient.'

'That's okay,' I said. The loss of Pris had certainly deeply affected us, especially Maury. Loss instead of gain; that was how we had fared at Barrows' hands. And yet – was there any way we could have escaped? The Lincoln was right. It was the unpredictable at work in our lives; Barrows had been as surprised as we were.

'Can we build simulacra without her?' I asked Maury.

'Yeah. But not without Bob Bundy.'

'You can get somebody to replace him,' I said.

But Maury did not care about Bundy; he was still

thinking only about his daughter. 'I'll tell you what wrecked her,' he said. 'That goddam book *Marjorie Morningstar*.'

'Why?' I said. It was terrible to see Maury slipping away like this, into these random, pointless expostulations. It resembled senility. The shock had been that great.

'That book,' Maury said, 'gave Pris the idea she could meet someone rich and famous and handsome. Like you know who. Like Sam K. Barrows. It's an old-country idea about marriage. Cold-blooded, marrying because it's to your advantage. The kids in this country marry for love, and maybe that's sappy, but at least it's not calculating. When she read that book she began to get calculating about love. The only thing that could have saved Pris – if she had fallen head over heels in love with some boy. And now she's gone.' His voice broke. 'Let's face it; this isn't a business only. I mean, it's a business all right. But not the simulacrum business. She wants to sell herself to him, and get something back; you know what I mean, Louis.' He shook his head, gazing at me hopelessly. 'And he can give her what she wants. And she knows it.'

'Yeah,' I said.

'I should never have let him come near her. But I don't blame him; it's her fault. Anything that happens to her now is her fault. Whatever she does and becomes around him. We better watch the newspapers, Louis. You know how they always write up what Barrows does. We can find out about Pris from the goddam newspapers.' He turned his head away and drank noisily from his coffee cup, not letting us see his face.

We were all embarrassed. We all hung our heads.

After a time the Stanton simulacrum said, 'When do I assume my new duties as Chairman of the Board?'

'Any time you want,' Maury said.

'Is that agreeable with you other gentlemen?' the Stanton asked us. My dad and I nodded; so did the Lincoln. 'Then I will take it that I hold that post now,

147

gentlemen.' It cleared its throat, blew its nose, fussed for a time with its whiskers. 'We must begin the work ahead of us. A merger of the two companies will bring about a new period of activity. I have given thought to the product which we shall manufacture. I do not believe it would be wise to bring into existence more Lincoln simulacra, nor more – ' It reflected, and a caustic, sardonic grimace passed over its features. 'More Stantons, for that matter. One of each is enough. For the future let us bring forth something more simple. It will ameliorate our mechanical problems, as well; will it not? I must examine the work-men and equipment and see if all is as it ought to be . . . nevertheless, even now I am confident that our enterprise can produce some simple, worthy product desired by all, some simulacra not unique or complex and yet needed. Perhaps workers who can themselves produce more simulacra.'

It was a good – but frightening – idea, I thought.

'In my opinion,' the Stanton said, 'we should design, execute, and begin to build at once a standard, uniform item. It will be the first official simulacrum produced by our enterprise, and long before Mr Barrows has made use of Miss Frauenzimmer's knowledge and talents we will have it on the market and fully advertised.'

We all nodded.

'I suggest specifically,' the Stanton said, 'a simulacrum which does one simple task for the home, and on that basis sell it: a babysitter. And we should relieve the complexity of it so that it may sell for as low a figure as possible. For example, forty dollars.'

We glanced at each other; it wasn't a bad idea at all.

'I have had the opportunity of seeing this need,' the Stanton continued, 'and I know that if it were adequate to mind the children of a family at all times, it would be an instantly salable item and we would have in the future no problems of a financial nature. So I shall ask for a vote as to that proposal. All those favoring it say "Aye".'

148

I said, 'Aye.'

Maury said, 'Aye.'

After a moment of consideration my father said, 'I, too.'

'Then the motion has been carried,' the Stanton declared. It sipped its coffee for a moment, and then, putting the cup down on the counter, it said in a stern, confident voice, 'The enterprise needs a name, a new name. I propose we call the enterprise R AND R ASSOCIATES OF BOISE, IDAHO; is that satisfactory?' It glanced around at us. We were nodding. 'Good.' It patted its mouth with its paper napkin. 'Then let us begin at once; Mr Lincoln, as our solicitor, will you be good enough as to see to it that our legal papers are in order? If necessary, you may obtain a younger lawyer more experienced in the current legalities; I authorize you to do that. We shall begin our work at once; our future is full of honest, active endeavour, and we shall not dwell on the past, on the unpleasantness and setbacks which we have experienced so recently. It is essential, gentlemen, that we look ahead, not back – can we do that, Mr Rock? Despite all temptation?'

'Yeah,' Maury said. 'You're right, Stanton.' From his coat pocket he got matches; stepping from his stool he went up to the cash register at the counter and fished about in the cigar boxes there. He returned, with two long gold-wrapped cigars, one of which he gave to my dad. 'Elconde de Guell,' he said. 'Made in the Philippines.' He unwrapped his and lit up; my father did the same.

'We will do well,' my father said, puffing away.

'Right,' Maury said, also puffing.

The others of us finished our coffee.

12

I had been afraid that Pris' going over to Barrows would weigh Maury down so much that he would no longer be worth much as a partner. But I was wrong. In fact he seemed to redouble his efforts: he answered letters about organs and spinets, arranged shipments from the factory to every point in the Pacific Northwest and down into California and Nevada and New Mexico and Arizona – and in addition he threw himself into the new task of designing and beginning production of the simulacra babysitters.

Without Bob Bundy we could develop no new circuits; Maury found himself in the position of having to modify the old. Our babysitters would be an evolution – an offspring, so to speak – of the Lincoln.

Years ago in a bus Maury had picked up a science fiction magazine called *Thrilling Wonder Stories* and in it was a story about robot attendants who protected children like huge mechanical dogs; they were called 'Nannies', no doubt after the pooch in Peter Pan. Maury liked the name and when our Board of Directors met – Stanton presiding, plus myself, Maury, Jerome and Chester, with our attorney Abraham Lincoln – he advanced the idea of using it.

'Suppose the magazine or the author sues,' I said.

'It was so long ago,' Maury said. 'The magazine doesn't exist anymore and probably the author's dead.'

'Ask our attorney.'

After careful consideration Mr Lincoln decided that the notion of titling a mechanical children's attendant Nanny was now public domain. 'For I notice,' he pointed out, 'that the group of you know without having read the story from whence comes this name.'

So we called our simulacra babysitters Nannies. But the decision cost us several valuable weeks, since to make his decision, the Lincoln had to read the Peter Pan book. He enjoyed it so much that he brought it to board meetings and read it aloud, with many chuckles, particularly the parts which especially amused him. We had no choice; we had to endure the readings.

'I warned you,' the Stanton told us, after one lengthy reading had sent us to the men's room for a smoke.

'What gets me,' Maury said, 'is that it's a goddam kids' book; if he has to read aloud, why doesn't he read something useful like the New York *Times*?'

Meanwhile, Maury had subscribed to the Seattle newspapers, hoping to find out about Pris. He was positive that an item would appear shortly. She was there, all right, because a moving van had arrived at the house and picked up the rest of her possessions, and the driver had told Maury that he was instructed to transport it all to Seattle. Obviously Sam K. Barrows was paying the bill; Pris did not have that kind of money.

'You could still get the cops,' I pointed out to Maury.

Gloomily he said, 'I have faith in Pris. I know that of her own accord she'll find the right path and return to me and her mother. And anyhow let's face it; she's a ward of the Government – I'm no longer legally her guardian.'

For my part I still hoped that she would *not* return; in her absence I had felt a good deal more relaxed and at good terms with the world. And it seemed to me that despite his appearance of gloom Maury was getting more out of his work. He no longer had the bundle of worries at home to gnaw at him. And also he did not have Doctor Horstowski's staggering bill each month.

'You suppose Sam Barrows has found her a better out-patient analyst?' he asked me, one evening. 'I wonder how much it's costing him. Three days a week at forty

151

dollars a visit is a hundred and twenty a week; that's almost five hundred a month. Just to cure her fouled-up psyche!' He shook his head.

I was reminded of that mental health slogan which the authorities had pasted up in every post office in the US, a year or so ago.

LEAD THE WAY TO MENTAL HEALTH –
BE THE FIRST IN YOUR FAMILY TO ENTER A MENTAL HEALTH CLINIC!

And school kids wearing bright badges had rung doorbells in the evenings to collect funds for mental health research; they had overpowered the public, wrung a fortune from them, all for the good cause of our age.

'I feel sorry for Barrows,' Maury said. 'I hope for his sake she's got her back in it, designing a simulacrum body for him, but I doubt it. Without me she's just a dabbler; she'll fool around, make pretty drawings. That bathroom mural – that was one of the few things she's ever brought to completion. And she's got hundreds of bucks worth of material left over.'

'Wow,' I said, once more congratulating myself and the rest of us on our good luck: that Pris was no longer with us.

'Those creative projects of hers,' Maury said, 'she really throws herself into them, at least at the start.' Admonishingly he said, 'Don't ever sell her short, buddy boy. Like look how well she designed the Stanton and Lincoln bodies. You have to admit she's good.'

'She's good,' I agreed.

'And who's going to design the Nanny package for us, now that Pris has gone? Not you; you don't have a shred of artistic ability. Not me. Not that thing that crept up out of the ground which you call your brother.'

I was preoccupied. 'Listen, Maury,' I said suddenly, *what about Civil War mechanical babysitters?*'

He stared at me uncertainly.

'We already have the design,' I went on. 'We'll make

two models, one a babysitter in Yankee blue, the other in Rebel gray. Pickets, doing their duty. What do you say?'

'I say what's a picket?'

'Like a sentry, only there're a lot of them.'

After a long pause Maury said, 'Yes, the soldier suggests devotion to duty. And it would appeal to the kids. It'd get away from that robot type design; it wouldn't be cold and impersonal.' He nodded. 'It's a good idea, Louis. Let's call a meeting of the Board and lay our idea, or rather your idea, right out, so we can start work on it. Okay?' He hurried to the door, full of eagerness. 'I'll call Jerome and Chester and I'll run downstairs and tell Lincoln and Stanton.' The two simulacra had separate quarters on the bottom floor of Maury's house; originally he had rented the units out, but now he kept them for this use. 'You don't think they'll object, do you? Especially Stanton; he's so hardheaded. Suppose he thinks it's – blasphemy? Well, we'll just have to set fire to the idea and push it out in the river.'

'If they object,' I said, 'we'll keep plugging for our idea. In the end we'll be able to get it because what could there possibly be against it? Except some weird puritanical notion on Stanton's part.'

And yet, even though it was my own idea, I felt a strange weary sensation, as if in my moment of creativity, my last burst of inspiration, I had defeated us all and everything we were trying for. Why was that? Was it too easy, this idea? After all, it was simply an adaptation of what we – or rather Maury and his daughter – had originally started out with. In the beginning they had dreamed their dream of refighting the entire Civil War, with all the millions of participants; now we were enthusiastic merely at the notion of a Civil War type mechanical servant to relieve the housewife of her deadly daily chores. Somewhere along the line we had lost the most valuable portion of our ideas.

Once more we were just a little firm out to make money; we had no grand vision, only a scheme to get rich. We were another Barrows but on a tiny, wretched scale; we had his greed but not his size. We would soon, if possible, commence a schlock Nanny operation; probably we would market our product by some phony sales pitch, some gimmick comparable to the classified 'repossession' ad which we had been using.

'No,' I said to Maury. 'It's terrible. Forget it.'

Pausing at the door he yelled, 'WHY? It's terrific.'

'Because,' I said, 'it's – ' I could not express it. I felt worn out and despairing – and, even more than that, lonely. For who or what? For Pris Frauenzimmer? For Barrows . . . for the entire gang of them, Barrows and Blunk and Colleen Nild and Bob Bundy and Pris; what were they doing, right now? What crazy, wild, impractical scheme were they hatching out? I longed to know. We, Maury and I and Jerome and my brother Chester, we had been left behind.

'Say it,' Maury said, dancing about with exasperation.

'Why?'

I said, 'It's – corny.'

'Corny! The hell it is.' He glared at me, baffled.

'Forget the idea. What do you suppose Barrows is up to, right this minute? You think they're building the Edwards family? Or are they stealing our Centennial idea? Or hatching out something entirely new? Maury, we don't have any vision. That's what's wrong. No vision.'

'Sure we do.'

'No,' I said. '*Because we're not crazy*. We're sober and sane. We're not like your daughter, we're not like Barrows. Isn't that a fact? You mean you can't feel it? The lack of that, here in this house? Some lunatic clack-clacking away at some monstrous nutty project until all hours, maybe leaving it half done right in the middle and going on to something else, something equally nutty?'

'Maybe so,' Maury said. 'But god almighty, Louis; we

can't just lie down and die because Pris went over to the other side. Don't you imagine I've had thoughts of this kind? I knew her a lot better than you, buddy, a hell of a lot better. I've been tormented every night, thinking about them all together, but we have to go on and do the best we can. This idea of yours; it may not be equal to the electric light or the match, but it's good. It's small and it's salable. It'll work. And what do we have that's better? At least it'll save us money, save us having to hire some outside designer to fly out here and design the body of the Nanny, and an engineer to take Bundy's place – assuming we could get one. Right, buddy?'

Save us money, I thought. Pris and Barrows wouldn't have bothered to worry about that; look at them sending that van to carry her things all the way from Boise to Seattle. We're small-time. We're little.

We're beetles.

Without Pris – without her.

What did I do? I asked myself. Fall in love with her? A woman with eyes of ice, a calculating, ambitious schizoid type, a ward of the Federal Government's Mental Health Bureau who will need psychotherapy the rest of her life, an ex-psychotic who engages in catatonic-excitement hare-brained projects, who vilifies and attacks everyone in sight who doesn't give her exactly what she wants when she wants it? What a woman, what a *thing* to fall in love with. What terrible fate is in store for me now?

It was as if Pris, to me, were both life itself – and anti-life, the dead, the cruel, the cutting and rending, and yet also the spirit of existence itself. Movement: she was motion itself. Life in its growing, planning, calculating, harsh, thoughtless actuality. I could not stand having her around me; I could not stand being without her. Without Pris I dwindled away until I became nothing and eventually died like a bug in the backyard, unnoticed and unimportant; around her I was slashed, goaded, cut to pieces, stepped on – yet somehow I lived: in that, I was real. Did I enjoy suffering? No. It was that it seemed as if suffering was part of life, part of being with Pris. Without Pris there was no suffering, nothing erratic, unfair, unbalanced. But also, there was nothing alive, only small-time schlock schemes, a dusty little office with two or three men scrabbling in the sand . . .

God knew I didn't want to suffer at Pris' hands or at anyone else's. But suffering was an indication that reality was close by. In a dream there is fright, but not literal, slow, bodily pain, the daily torment that Pris made us endure by her very presence. It was not something which she did to us deliberately; it was a natural outgrowth of what she *was*.

We could evade it only by getting rid of her, and that was what we had done: we had lost her. And with her went reality itself, with all its contradictions and peculiarities; life now would be predictable: we would produce the Civil War Soldier Nannies, we would have a certain amount of money, and so forth. But what did it mean? What did it matter?

'Listen,' Maury was saying to me. 'We have to go on.'

I nodded.

'I mean it,' Maury said loudly in my ear. 'We can't give up. We'll call a meeting of the Board, like we were going to do; you tell them your idea, fight for your idea like you really believed in it. Okay? You promise?' He whacked me on the back. 'Come on, goddam you, or I'll give you a crack in the eye that'll send you to the hospital. Buddy, come on!'

'Okay,' I said, 'but I feel you're talking to someone on the other side of the grave.'

'Yeah, and you look like it, too. But come on anyhow and let's get going; you go downstairs and talk Stanton into it; I know Lincoln won't give us any trouble – all he does is sit there in his room and chuckle over *Winnie the Pooh*.'

'What the hell is that? Another kids' book?'

'That's right, buddy,' Maury said. 'So go on down there.'

I did so, feeling a little cheered up. But nothing would bring me back to life, not really, except for Pris. I had to deal with that fact and face it with greater force every moment of the day.

The first item which we found in the Seattle papers having to do with Pris almost got by us, because it did not seem to be about Pris at all. We had to read the item again and again until we were certain.

It told about Sam K. Barrows – that was what had caught our eye. And a stunning young artist he had been seen at nightclubs with. The girl's name, according to the columnist, was Pristine Womankind.

'Jeezus!' Maury screeched, his face black. 'That's her name; that's a translation of Frauenzimmer. But it isn't. Listen, buddy, I always put everybody on about that, you and Pris and my ex-wife. Frauenzimmer doesn't mean womankind; it means ladies of pleasure. You know. Street-walkers.' He reread the item incredulously. 'She's changed her name but she doesn't know; hell, it ought to be Pristine Streetwalkers. What a farce, I mean, it's insane. You know what it is? That *Marjorie Morningstar*; her name was Morgenstern, and it meant Morningstar; Pris got the idea from that, too. And Priscilla to Pristine. I'm going mad.' He paced frantically around the office, rereading the newspaper item again and again. 'I know it's Pris; it has to be. Listen to the description. You tell me if this isn't Pris:

'Seen at Swami's: None other than Sam (The Big Man) Barrows, escorting what for the kiddies who stay up late we like to call his "new protégé," a sharper-than-a-sixth-grade-teacher's-grading-pencil chick, name of – if you can swallow this – Pristine Womankind, with a better-than-this-world expression, like she doesn't dig us ordinary mortals, black hair, and a figure that

157

*would make those old wooden fronts of ships (y'know the kind?)
green with envy. Also in the company, Dave Blunk, the attorney,
tells us that Pris is an artist, with other talents which you can't see
. . . and, Dave grins, maybe going to show up on TV one of
these years, as an actress, no less! . . .'*

'God, what rubbish,' Maury said, tossing the paper
down. 'How can those gossip columnists write like that?
They're demented. But you can tell it's Pris anyhow.
What's that mean about her going to turn up as a TV
actress?'

I said, 'Barrows must own a TV station or a piece of
one.'

'He owns a dogfood company that cans whale blubber,'
Maury said. 'And it sponsors a TV show once a week, a
sort of circus and variety piece of business. He's probably
putting the bite on them to give Pris a couple of minutes.
But doing what? She can't act! She has no talents! I think
I will call the police. Get Lincoln here; I want an
attorney's advice!'

I tried to calm him down; he was in a state of wild
agitation.

'He's sleeping with her! That beast is sleeping with my
daughter Pris! He's corruption itself!' Maury began calling
the airfield at Boise, trying to get a rocket flight to
Seattle. 'I'm going down there and arrest him,' he told
me between calls. 'I'm taking a gun along; the hell with
going to the police. That girl's only eighteen; it's a felony.
We've got a prima facie case against him – I'll wreck his
life. He'll be in the can for twenty-five years.'

'Listen,' I said. 'Barrows has absolutely thought it
through, as we've said time and again; he's got that
lawyer Blunk tagging along. They're covered; don't ask
me how, but they've thought of everything there is. Just
because some gossip columnist chose to write that your
daughter is – '

'I'll kill her, then,' Maury said.

158

'Wait. For god's sake shut up and listen. Whether she's sleeping, as you put it, with him or not I don't know. Probably she is his mistress. I think you're right. But proving it is another matter altogether. Now, you can force her to return here to Ontario, but there's even a way he can eventually get around that.'

'I wish she was back in Kansas City; I wish she had never left the mental health clinic. She's just a poor ex-psychotic child!' He calmed a little. 'How could he get her back?'

'Barrows can have some punk in his organization marry her. And once that happens no one has authority over her. Do you want that?' I had talked to the Lincoln and I knew; the Lincoln had already shown me how difficult it was to force a man like Barrows who knew the law to do *anything*. Barrows could bend the law like a pipe-cleaner. For him it was not a rule or a hindrance; it was a convenience.

'That would be terrible,' Maury said. 'I see what you mean. As a legal pretext to permit him to keep her in Seattle.' His face was gray.

'And then you'll never get her back.'

'And she'll be sleeping with two men, her punk husband, some goddam messenger boy from some factory Barrows owns, and – Barrows, too.' He stared at me wild-eyed.

'Maury,' I said, 'we have to face facts Pris probably slept with boys already, for instance in school.'

His expression became more distorted.

'I hate to tell you this,' I said, 'but the way she talked to me one night – '

'Okay,' Maury said. 'We'll let it go.'

'Sleeping with Barrows won't kill her, and it won't kill you. At least she won't become pregnant, he's smart enough to make sure of that. He'll see she takes her shots.'

Maury nodded. 'I wish I was dead,' he said.

'I feel the same way. But remember what you told me not more than two days ago? That we had to go on, no matter how badly we felt? Now I'm telling you the same thing. No matter how much Pris meant to either of us – isn't that so?'

'Yeah,' he said at last.

We went ahead, then, and picked up where we had left off. At the Board meeting the Stanton had objected to any of the Nannies wearing the Rebel gray; it was willing to go along with the Civil War theme, but the soldiers had to be loyal Union lads. Who, the Stanton demanded, would trust their child with a Reb? We gave in, and Jerome was told to begin tooling up the Rosen factory; meanwhile we at Ontario, at the R & R ASSOCIATES business office, began making the layouts, conferring with a Japanese electronics engineer whom we had called in on a part-time basis.

Several days later a second item appeared in a Seattle newspaper. This one I saw before Maury did.

Miss Pristine Womankind, scintillating raven-haired young starlet discovered by the Barrows organization, will be on hand to award a gold baseball to the Little League champions, Irving Kahn, press secretary for Mr Barrows, told representatives of the wire services today. Since one game of the Little League play-offs remains yet to be played, it is still

So Sam K. Barrows had a press agent at work, as well as Dave Blunk and all the others. Barrows was giving Pris what she had long wanted; he was keeping his end of whatever bargain they had made – no doubt of that. And I had no doubt that she was keeping her end as well.

She's in good hands, I said to myself. Probably there isn't a human being in North America more qualified to give Pris what she wants out of life.

The article was titled BIG LEAGUE AWARDS GOLD BASEBALL TO LITTLE LEAGUERS, Pris being 'big league', now. A further study of it told me that Mr Sam K. Barrows had paid for the uniforms of the Little League club expected to win the gold baseball – needless to say, Barrows was providing the gold baseball – and on their backs appeared the words:

BARROWS ORGANIZATION

On the front, of course, appeared the name of their team, whatever area or school it was the boys came from.

I had no doubt that she was very happy. After all Jayne Mansfield had begun by being Miss Straight Spine, picked by the chiropractors of America back in the 'fifties; that had been her first publicity break. She had been one of those health food addicts in those days.

So look what may lie ahead for Pris, I said to myself. First she hands out a gold baseball to a kids' ballteam and from there she goes rapidly to the top. Maybe Barrows can get a spread of nude shots of her into *Life*; it's not out of the question, they do have their nude spread each week. That way her fame would be great. All she would have to do is take off her clothes in public, before an expert color photographer, instead of merely in private before the eyes of Sam K. Barrows.

Then she can briefly marry President Mendoza. He's been married, what is it, forty-one times already, sometimes for no longer than a week. Or at least get invited to one of the stag gatherings at the White House or out on the high seas in the Presidential yacht, or for a weekend at the President's luxurious vacation satellite. Especially those stag gatherings; the girls who are invited to perform there are never the same again – their fame is assured and all sorts of careers are open to them, especially in the entertainment field. For if President Mendoza wants them, every man in the US wants them, too, because as everybody knows the President of the United States has incredibly high taste as well as having the first choice of –

I was driving myself insane with these thoughts.

How long will it take? I wondered. Weeks? Months? Can he do this right away or does it take a lot of time?

A week later, while browsing through the TV guide, I discovered Pris listed in the weekly show sponsored by Barrows' dogfood company. According to the ad and the listing she played the girl in a knife-throwing act; flaming knives were thrown at her while she danced the Lunar Fling wearing one of the new transparent bathing suits. The scene had been shot in Sweden, such a bathing suit still being illegal at beaches in the United States.

I did not show the listing to Maury, but he came across it on his own anyhow. A day before the program he called me over to his place and showed me the listing. In the magazine there was a small shot of Pris, too, just her head and shoulders. It had, however, been taken in such a way as to indicate that she wore nothing at all. We both gazed at it with ferocity and despair. And yet, she certainly looked happy. Probably she was.

Behind her in the picture one could see green hills and water. The natural, healthy wonders of Earth. And against that this laughing black-haired slender girl, full of life and excitement and vitality. Full of – the future.

The future belongs to her, I realized as I examined the picture. Whether she appears nude on a goat-hair, vegetable-dye rug in *Life* or becomes the President's mistress for a weekend or dances madly, naked from the waist up, while flaming knives are hurled at her during a kiddies' TV program – she is still real, still beautiful and wonderful, like the hills and the ocean, and no one can destroy that or spoil that, however angry and wretched they feel. What do Maury and I have? What can we offer her? Only something moldy. Something that reeks – not of tomorrow – but of yesterday, the past. Of age, sorrow, and old death.

'Buddy,' I said to Maury, 'I think I'm going to Seattle.'

162

He said nothing; he continued reading the text in the TV guide.

'I frankly don't care any more about simulacra,' I said. 'I'm sorry to say it but it's the truth; I just want to go to Seattle and see how she is. Maybe afterward – '

'You won't come back. Either of you.'

'Maybe we will.'

'Want to bet?'

I bet him ten bucks. That was all I could do; there was no use making him a promise which I probably could not – and would not – keep.

'It'll wreck R & R ASSOCIATES,' Maury said.

'Maybe so, but I still have to go.'

That night I began packing my clothes. I made a reservation on a TWA Boeing 900 rocket flight for Seattle; it left the following morning at ten-forty. Now there was no stopping me; I did not even bother to telephone Maury and tell him anything more. Why waste my time? He could do nothing. Could I? That remained to be seen.

My Service .45 was too large, so instead of it I packed a smaller pistol, a .38, wrapped in a towel with a box of shells. I had never been much of a shot but I could hit another human being within the confines of an ordinary-sized room, and possibly across the space of a public hall such as a nightclub or theater. And if worst came to worst I could use it on myself; surely I could hit that – my own head.

There being nothing else to do until the next morning I settled down with a copy of *Marjorie Morningstar* which Maury had loaned me. It was his own, and quite possibly it was the identical copy which Pris had read years ago. By reading it I hoped to get more of an insight into Pris; I was not reading it for pleasure.

The next morning I rose early, shaved and washed, ate a light breakfast, and started for Boise and the airfield.

13

If you wonder what San Francisco would have looked like had there been no earthquake and fire, you can find out by going to Seattle. It's an old seaport town built on hills, with windy, canyon type streets; nothing is modern except the public library, and in the slum part you'll see cobblestone and red brick, like parts of Pocatello, Idaho. The slums extend for miles and are rat-infested. In the center of Seattle there is a prosperous genuine city-like shopping area built near one or two great old hotels such as the Olympus. The wind blows in from Canada, and when the Boeing 900 sets down at the Sea-Tac Airfield you catch a glimpse of the mountains of origin. They're frightening.

I took a limousine into Seattle proper from the airport, since it cost only five dollars. The lady driver crept at snail's pace through traffic for miles until at last we had reached the Olympus Hotel. It's much like any good big-city hotel, with its arcade of shops below ground level; it has all services which a hotel must have, and the service is excellent. There're several dining rooms; in fact you're in a dark, yellow-lit world of your own at a big city hotel, a world made up of carpets and ancient varnished wood, people well-dressed and always talking, corridors and elevators, plus maids cleaning constantly.

In my room I turned on the wired music in preference to the TV set, peeped out the window at the street far below, adjusted the ventilation and the heat, took off my shoes and padded about on the wall-to-wall carpeting, then opened my suitcase and began to unpack. Only an hour ago I had been in Boise; now here I was on the West Coast almost at the Canadian border. It beat driving. I had gone from one large city directly to another without having to endure the countryside in between. Nothing could have pleased me more.

You can tell a good hotel by the fact that when you have any sort of room service the hotel employee when he enters never looks at you. He looks down, through and beyond; you stay invisible, which is what you want, even if you're in your shorts or naked. The employee comes in very quietly, leaves your pressed shirt or your tray of food or newspaper or drink; you hand him the money, he makes a murmuring thank you noise, and he goes. It is almost Japanese, the way they don't stare. You feel as if no one had been in your room ever, even the previous guest; it is absolutely yours, even when you meet up with cleaning women in the hall outside. They – the hotel people – have such absolute respect for your privacy it's uncanny. Of course when it's time to settle up at the desk at the end, you pay for all that. It costs you fifty dollars instead of twenty. But don't ever let anyone tell you it isn't worth it. A person on the brink of a psychotic breakdown could be restored by a few days in an authentic first-class hotel, with its twenty-four hour room service and shops; believe me.

By the time I had been in my room at the Olympus for a couple of hours I wondered why I had ever felt agitated enough to make the trip in the first place. I felt as if I were on a well-deserved vacation and rest. I could have lived there, eating the hotel food, shaving and showering in my private bathroom, reading the paper, shopping in the shops, until my money ran out. But nonetheless I had come on business. That's what's so hard, to leave the hotel, to get out on those drafty, windy, cold, gray sidewalks and hobble along on your errand. That's where the pain enters. You're back in a world where no one holds the door for you; you stand on the corner with other people equal to yourself, all good as you, waiting for the lights to change, and once again you're an ordinary suffering individual, prey to any passing ailment. It's a sort of birth trauma all over again, but at least you can finally scuttle back to the hotel, once your business is done.

And, by using the phone in the hotel room, you can conduct some of your business without stirring outside at all. You do as much as you can that way; it's instinct to do that. In fact you try to get people to come and see you there, rather than the other way.

This time my business could not be conducted within the hotel, however; I did not bother to make the try. I simply put it off as long as I could: I spent the rest of the day in my room and at nightfall I went downstairs to the bar and then one of the dining rooms, and after that I strolled about the arcade and into the lobby and then back among the shops once more. I loitered wherever I could loiter without having to step outdoors into the cold, brisk, Canadian type night.

All this time I had the .38 in my inside coat pocket.

It was strange, coming on an illegal errand. Perhaps I could have done it all legally, through Lincoln found a way of getting Pris out of Barrows' hands. But on some deep level I enjoyed this, coming up here to Seattle with the gun in my suitcase and now in my coat. I liked the feeling of being alone, knowing no one, about to go out and confront Mr Sam Barrows with no one to help me. It was like an epic or an old western TV play. I was the stranger in town, armed, and with a mission.

Meanwhile, I drank at the bar, went back up to my room, lay on the bed, read the newspapers, looked at TV, ordered hot coffee from the room service at midnight. I was on top of the world. If only it could last.

Tomorrow morning I'll go look up Barrows, I said to myself. This must end. But not quite yet.

And then – it was about twelve-thirty at night and I was getting ready to go to bed – it occurred to me. Why don't I phone Barrows right now? Wake him up, like the

Gestapo used to? Not tell him where I am, just say *I'm coming, Sam*. Put a real scare in him; he'll be able to tell by the nearness of my voice that I'm somewhere in town.

Neat!

I had had a couple of drinks; heck, I had had six or seven. I dialed and told the operator, 'Get me Sam K. Barrows. I don't know the number.' It was the hotel operator, and she did so.

Presently I heard Sam's phone ringing.

To myself, I practiced what I was going to say. 'Give Pris back to R & R ASSOCIATES.' I would tell him. 'I hate her, but she belongs with us. She's life itself, as far as we're concerned.' The phone rang on and on; obviously no one was home, or no one was up and going to answer. Finally I hung up the receiver.

What a hell of a situation for grown men to be in, I said to myself as I roamed aimlessly around my hotel room. How could something on the order of Pris begin to represent life itself to us, as I was going to tell Sam Barrows? Are we that warped? Are we warped at all? Isn't that nothing but an indication of the nature of life, not of ourselves? Yes, it's not our fault life's like that; we didn't invent it. Or did we?

And so on. I must have spent a couple of hours roaming about, with nothing more on my mind than such indistinct preoccupations. I was in a terrible state. It was like a virus flu, a kind that attacks the metabolism of the brain, the next state from death. Or anyhow, so it seemed to me during that interval. I had lost all contact with healthy normal reality, even that of the hotel; I had forgotten room service, the arcade of shops, the bars and the dining rooms – I even gave up, for a while, stopping by the window of the room to look out at the lights and deep, illuminated streets. That's a form of dying, that losing contact with the city like that.

At one o'clock – while I was still pacing around the room – the phone rang.

167

'Hello,' I said into it.

It was not Sam K. Barrows. It was Maury, calling me from Ontario.

'How did you know I'd be at the Olympus?' I asked. I was totally baffled; it was as if he had used some occult power to track me down.

'I knew you were in Seattle, you moron. How many big hotels are there? I knew you'd want the best; I bet you've got the bridal suite and some dame there with you and you're going at it like mad.'

'Listen, I came here to kill Sam K. Barrows.'

'With what? Your hard head? You're going to run at him and butt him in the stomach and rupture him to death?'

I told Maury about the .38 pistol.

'Listen, buddy,' Maury said in a quiet voice. 'If you do that all of us are ruined.'

I said nothing.

'This call is costing us plenty,' Maury said, 'so I'm not going to spend an hour pleading with you like those pastors. You get some sleep and tomorrow call me back, you promise? Promise or I'll call the Seattle police department and have you arrested in your room, so help me god.'

'No,' I said.

'You have to promise.'

I said, 'Okay, Maury. I promise not to do anything tonight.' How could I? I had tried and failed already; I was just pacing around.

'Good enough. Listen, Louis. This won't get Pris back. I already thought about it. It'll only wreck her life if you go over there and blast away at the guy. Think about it and I know you'll see. Don't you imagine I'd do it if I thought it would work?'

I shook my head. 'I dunno.' My head ached and I felt bone-weary. 'I just want to go to bed.'

'Okay, buddy. You get your rest. Listen. I want you to

168

look around the room. You see if there isn't a table with drawers of some sort. Right? Look in the top drawer. Go on, Louis. Do it right now, while I'm on the phone. Look in it.'

'For what?'

'There's a Bible, there. That society puts it there.'

I slammed the phone down.

The bastard, I said to myself. Giving me advice like that.

I wished I had not come to Seattle at all. I was like the Stanton simulacrum, like a machine: propelling itself forward into a universe it did not comprehend, searching Seattle for a familiar corner in which it could perform its customary act. In the Stanton's case, opening a law office; in my case – what in my case? Trying somehow to re-establish a familiar environment, however unpleasant. I was used to Pris and her cruelty; I had even begun to get used – to expect to encounter – Sam K. Barrows and his doxie and his attorney. My instincts were propelling me from the unfamiliar back to the known. It was the only way I could operate. It was like a blind thing flopping along in order to spawn.

I know what I want! I said to myself. I want to join the Sam K. Barrows organization! I want to be a part of it, like Pris; I don't want to shoot him at all.

I'm going over to the other side.

There must be a place for me, I told myself. Maybe not doing the Lunar Fling; I'm not after that. I don't want to go on TV; I'm not interested in seeing my name in lights. I just want to be useful. I want to have my abilities made use of by the big cheese.

Picking up the phone I asked the operator for Ontario, Oregon. I got the operator at Ontario and gave her Maury's home phone number.

The phone rang, and then Maury sleepily answered.

'What did you do, go to bed?' I asked. 'Listen, Maury. I had to tell you this, it's right you should know. I'm

169

going over to the other side; I'm joining up with Barrows and the hell with you and my dad and Chester and the Stanton, which is a dictator anyhow and would make life unendurable for us. The only one I regret doing this to is Lincoln. But if he's so all-wise and understanding he'll understand and forgive, like Christ.'

'Pardon?' Maury said. He did not seem to comprehend me.

'I sold out,' I said.

'No,' Maury said, 'you're wrong.'

'How can I be wrong? What do you mean I'm wrong?'

'If you go over to Barrows, there won't be any R & R ASSOCIATES, so there won't be anything to sell out. We'll simply fold, buddy. You know that.' He sounded perfectly calm. 'Isn't that a fact?'

'I don't give a damn. I just know that Pris is right; you can't meet a man like Sam Barrows and then forget you met him. He's a star; he's a comet. You either tag along in his wake or you cease for all intents and purposes to exist. It's an emotional hunger inside me, irrational but it's real. It's an instinct. It'll hit you, too, one of these days. He's got magic. Without him we're snails. What's the purpose of life anyhow? To drag along in the dust? You don't live forever. If you can't raise yourself up to the stars you're dead. You know the .38 pistol I have with me? If I can't make it with the Barrows organization I'm going to blow my goddam brains out. I'm not going to be left behind. The instincts inside a person – instincts to live! – are too strong.'

Maury was silent. But I could hear him there at the other end.

'Listen,' I said, 'I'm sorry to wake you up but I had to tell you.'

'You're mentally ill,' Maury said. 'I'm going to – listen, buddy. I'm going to call Doctor Horstowski.'

'What for?'

'Have him call you there at your hotel.'

'Okay,' I said. 'I'll get off the line.' I hung up, then.

I sat on the bed waiting and sure enough, not twenty minutes later, at about one-thirty in the morning the phone rang once more.

'Hello,' I said into it.

A far-off voice. 'This is Milton Horstowski.'

'Louis Rosen, Doctor.'

'Mr Rock called me.' A long pause. 'How are you feeling, Mr Rosen? Mr Rock said you seemed upset about something.'

'Listen, you Government employee,' I said, 'this is no business of yours. I had a beef with my partner, Maury Rock, and that's it. I'm now in Seattle on my way to linking up with a much bigger and more progressive organization; you recall my mentioning Sam K. Barrows?'

'I know who he is.'

'Is that so crazy?'

'No,' Doctor Horstowski said. 'Not on the face of it.'

'I told that about the gun to Maury just to get his goat. It's late and I'm a little stewed. Sometimes when you break up a partnership it's hard psychologically.' I waited but Horstowski said nothing. 'I guess I'll turn in now. Maybe when I get back to Boise I'll drop in and see you; this is all very hard on me. Pris went and joined the Barrows organization, you know.'

'Yes I know. I'm still in touch with her.'

'She's quite a girl,' I said. 'I'm beginning to think I'm in love with her. Could that be? I mean, a person of my psychological type?'

'It's possible.'

'Well, I guess that's probably what's happened. I can't live without Pris, so that's why I'm in Seattle. But I still say I made up that about the gun; you can quote me to Maury to that effect if it'll calm him. I was just trying to show him I'm serious. You get it?'

'Yes, I think so,' Doctor Horstowski said.

We talked on to no point for a while longer, and then

171

he rang off. As soon as I had hung up I said to myself, The guy'll probably phone the Seattle police or the FBMH here. I can't take the chance; he just might.

So I began packing my things as fast as I could. I got everything into the suitcase and then I left the room; I took the elevator downstairs to the main floor, and, at the desk, I asked for my bill.

'You weren't displeased with anything, were you, Mr Rosen?' the night clerk asked me as the girl computed the charges.

'Naw,' I said. 'I managed to contact the person I came here to meet and he wants me to spend the night at his place.'

I paid the bill – it was quite moderate – and then called a taxi. The doorman carried my suitcase out and stuffed it in the trunk of the cab; I tipped him a couple of dollars and a moment later the cab shot out into the surprisingly dense traffic.

When we passed a likely-looking modern motel I took note of the location; I had the cab stop a few blocks beyond it, paid the driver, and then on foot walked back. I told the motel owner that my car had broken down – I was driving through Seattle on business – and I registered under the name James W. Byrd, a name I made up on the spot. I paid in advance – eighteen-fifty – and then, with the motel key in my hand, set off for room 6.

It was pleasant, clean and bright, just what I wanted; I at once turned in and was soon sound asleep. They won't get me now, I remember saying to myself as I drifted off. I'm safe. And tomorrow I'll get hold of Sam Barrows and give him the news that I'm coming over.

And then, I remember thinking, I'll be back with Pris again; I'll get in on her rise to fame. I'll be there to see the whole thing. Maybe we'll get married. I'll tell her how I feel about her, that I'm in love with her. She's probably twice as beautiful now as she was before, now that Barrows has gotten hold of her. And if Barrows

172

competes with me, I'll wipe him out of existence. I'll atomize him with methods hitherto unglimpsed. He won't stand in my way; I'm not kidding.

Thinking that, I drifted off.

The sun woke me at eight o'clock, shining in on me and the bed and the room. I had not pulled the curtains. Cars parked in a row outside gleamed and reflected the sun. It looked like a nice day.

What had I thought the night before? My thoughts while going to sleep came back to me. Nutty, wild thoughts, all about marrying Pris and killing Sam Barrows, kid's thoughts. When you're going to sleep you revert to childhood, no doubt of it. I felt ashamed.

And yet, basically I stuck to my position. I had come to get Pris and if Barrows tried to stand in my way – too bad for him.

I had run amok, but I did not intend to back down. Sanity prevailed, now that it was daylight; I padded into the bathroom and took a long cold shower, but even the light of day did not dispel my deep convictions. I just worked them about until they were more rational, more convincing, more practical.

First, I had to approach Barrows in the proper manner; I had to conceal my actual feelings, my real motive. I had to hide anything to do with Pris; I would tell him that I wanted to go to work for him, maybe help design the simulacrum – bring all the knowledge and experience I had built up from my years with Maury and Jerome. But no hint about Pris because if he caught even the slightest note, there –

You're shrewd, Sam K. Barrows, I said to myself. But you can't read my mind. And it won't show on my face; I'm too experienced, too much a professional, to give myself away.

As I dressed, tying my tie, I practiced in front of the mirror. My face was absolutely impassive; no one would have guessed that inside me my heart was being gnawed away, eaten at by the worm of desire: love for Pris Frauenzimmer or Womankind or whatever she called herself now.

That's what's meant by maturity, I said to myself as I sat on the bed shining my shoes. Being able to conceal your real feelings, being able to erect a mask. Being able even to fool a big man like Barrows. If you can do that, you've made it.

Otherwise, you're finished. The whole secret's there.

There was a phone in the motel room. I went out and had breakfast, ham and eggs, toast, coffee, everything including juice. Then, at nine-thirty I returned to my motel room and got out the Seattle phonebook. I spent a good long time examining the listings of Barrows' various enterprises, until I found the one at which I thought he would be. I then dialed.

'Northwest Electronics,' the girl said brightly. 'Good morning.'

'Is Mr Barrows in yet?'

'Yes sir, but he's on the other phone.'

'I'll wait.'

The girl said brightly, 'I'll give you his secretary.' A long pause and then another voice, also a woman's but much lower and older-sounding.

'Mr Barrows' office. Who is calling, please?'

I said, 'I'd like an appointment to see Mr Barrows. This is Louis Rosen, I flew into Seattle from Boise last night; Mr Barrows knows me.'

'Just a moment.' A long pause. Then the woman again. 'Mr Barrows will speak with you now; go ahead, sir.'

'Hello,' I said.

'Hello,' Barrows' voice came in my ear. 'How are you, Rosen? What can I do for you?' He sounded cheerful.

'How's Pris?' I said, taken by surprise to find myself actually speaking to him.

'Pris is fine. How're your father and brother?'

174

'Fine.'

'That must be interesting, to have a brother whose face is on upside down; I wish I could have met him. Why don't you drop by for a moment, while you're here in Seattle? Around one this afternoon?'

'Around one,' I said.

'Okay. Thanks and bye-bye.'

'Barrows,' I said, 'are you going to marry Pris?'

There was no answer.

'I'm going to shoot you,' I said.

'Aw, for god's sake!'

'Sam, I've got a Japanese-made all-transistorized encephalotropic floating antipersonnel mine in my possession.' That was how I was thinking of my .38 pistol. 'And I'm going to release it in the Seattle area. Do you know what that means?'

'Uh, no not exactly. Encephalotropic . . . doesn't that have something to do with the brain?'

'Yes, Sam. *Your* brain. Maury and I recorded your brain-pattern when you were at our office in Ontario. That was a mistake on your part to go there. The mine will seek you out and detonate. Once I release it there's no holding it back; it's curtains for you.'

'Awfrgawdsake!'

'Pris is in love with me,' I said. 'She told me one night when she drove me home. Get away from her or you're finished. You know how old she is? You want to know?'

'Eighteen.'

I slammed down the phone.

I'm going to kill him, I said to myself. I really am. He's got my girl. God knows what he's doing with her, and to her.

Dialing the phone once more I got the same bright-voiced switchboard operator. 'Northwest Electronics, good morning.'

'I was just talking to Mr Barrows.'

175

'Oh, were you cut off? I'll put you through again, sir; just a moment.'

'Tell Mr Barrows,' I said to her, 'that I'm coming to get him with my advanced technology. Will you tell him that? Goodbye.' Once more I hung up.

He'll get the message, I said to myself. Maybe I should have told him to bring Pris over here, or something like that. Would he do that, to save his hide? Goddam you, Barrows!

I know he would do that, I said to myself. He'd give her up to save himself; I could get her back any time. She didn't mean that much to him; she was just another pretty young woman to him. I was the only one really in love with her for what she actually, uniquely was.

Once more I dialed.

'Northwest Electronics, good morning.'

'Put me through to Mr Barrows again, please.'

A series of clicks.

'Miss Wallace, Mr Barrows' secretary. Who is calling?'

'This is Louis Rosen. Let me talk to Sam again.'

A pause. 'Just a moment, Mr Rosen.'

I waited.

'Hello, Louis.' Sam Barrows' voice. 'Well, you're really stirring things up, aren't you?' He chuckled. 'I called the Army arsenal down the Coast and there really is such a thing as an encephalotropic mine. How'd you get hold of one? I'll bet you don't have one really.'

'Turn Pris over to me,' I said, 'and I'll spare you.'

'Come on, Rosen.'

'I'm not spoofing.' My voice shook. 'You think this is a game? I'm at the end of my rope; I'm in love with her and nothing else matters to me.'

'Jesus Christ.'

'Will you do that?' I yelled. 'Or do I have to come and get you?' My voice broke; I was screeching. 'I've got all kinds of Service weapons here with me, from when I was overseas; I mean business!' In the back of my mind a calm part of me thought, The bastard will give her up; I know what a coward he is.

Barrows said, 'Calm down.'

'Okay, I'm coming to get you, and with all the technological improvements at my disposal.'

'Now listen, Rosen. I suppose Maury Rock egged you into this. I talked it over with Dave and he assured me that the statutory rape charge has no meaning if – '

'I'll kill you if you raped her,' I screamed into the phone. And, in the back of my mind, the calm, sardonic voice was smirking and saying, That's giving it to the bastard. The calm, sardonic voice laughed delightedly; it was having a grand time. 'You hear me?' I screamed.

Presently Barrows said, 'You're psychotic, Rosen. I'm going to call Maury; at least he's sane. Look, I'll call him and tell him Pris is flying back to Boise.'

'When?' I screamed.

'Today. But not with you. And I think you should see a Government psychiatrist, you're very ill.'

'Okay,' I said, more quietly. 'Today. But I'm staying here until Maury calls me and says she's in Boise.' I hung up, then.

Wow.

I tottered away from the phone, went into the bathroom and washed my face with cold water.

So behaving in an irrational and uncontrolled manner paid off! What a thing to learn at my age. I had gotten Pris back! I had scared him into believing I was a madman. And wasn't that actually the truth? I really was out of my head; look at my conduct. The loss of Pris had driven me insane.

After I had calmed down I returned to the phone and called Maury at the factory in Boise. 'Pris is coming back. You call me as soon as she arrives. I'll stay here. I scared Barrows; I'm stronger than he is.'

Maury said, 'I'll believe it when I see her.'

'The man's terrified of me. Petrified – he couldn't wait

to get her off his hands. You don't realize what a raving maniac I was turned into by the terrible stress of the situation.' I gave him the phone number of the motel.

'Did Horstowski call you last night?'

'Yes,' I said, 'but he's incompetent. You wasted all that money, as you said. I've got nothing but contempt for him and when I get back I'm going to tell him so.'

'I admire your cool poise,' Maury said.

'You're right to admire it; my cool poise, as you call it, got Pris back. Maury, I'm in love with her.'

After a long silence Maury said, 'Listen, she's a child.'

'I mean to marry her. I'm not another Sam Barrows.'

'I don't care who or what you are!' Now Maury was yelling. 'You can't marry her; she's a baby. She has to go back to school. Get away from my daughter, Louis!'

'We're in love. You can't come between us. Call me as soon as she sets foot in Boise; otherwise I'm going to give it to Sam K. Barrows and maybe her and myself, if I have to.'

'Louis,' Maury said in a slow, careful voice, 'you need Federal Bureau of Mental Health help, honest to god, you do. I wouldn't let Pris marry you for all the money on Earth or for any other reason. I wish you had let things lie. I wish you hadn't gone to Seattle. I wish she was staying with Barrows; yes, better Pris should be with Barrows than you. What can you give her? Look at all the things Sam Barrows can give a girl!'

'He made her into a prostitute, that's what he gave her.'

'I don't care!' Maury shouted. 'That's just talk, a word, nothing more. You get back here to Boise. Our partnership is off. You have to get out of R & R ASSOCIATES. I'm calling Sam Barrows and telling him I have nothing to do with you; I want him to keep Pris.'

'Goddam you,' I said.

'You as my son-in-law? You think I gave birth to her –

in a manner of speaking – so she could marry you? What a laugh. You're absolutely nothing! Get out of here!'

'Too bad,' I said. But I felt numb. 'I want to marry her,' I repeated.

'Did you *tell* Pris you're going to marry her?'

'No, not yet.'

'She'll spit in your face.'

'So what?'

'So what? So who wants you? Who needs you? Just your defective brother Chester and your senile father. I'm talking to Abraham Lincoln and finding out how to end our relationship forever.' The phone clicked; he had hung up on me.

I could not believe it. I sat on the unmade bed, staring at the floor. So Maury, like Pris, was after the big time, the big money. Bad blood, I said to myself. Carried by the genes.

I should have known. She had to get it somewhere.

What do I do now? I asked myself.

Blow my brains out and make everyone happy; they can do fine without me, like Maury said.

But I did not feel like doing that; the cold calm voice inside me, the instinctive voice, said no. *Fight them all*, it said. *Take them all on* . . . Pris and Maury, Sam Barrows, Stanton, the Lincoln; stand up and fight.

What a thing to find out about your partner; how he really feels about you, how he looks at you secretly. God, what a dreadful thing – the truth.

I'm glad I found out, I said to myself. No wonder he threw himself into the Civil War Soldier Babysitter simulacrum; he was *glad* his daughter had gone off to be Sam K. Barrows' mistress. He was proud. He read that *Marjorie Morningstar*, too.

Now I know what makes the world up, I said to myself. I know what people are like, what they prize in this life. It's enough to make you drop down dead right on the spot, or at least go and commit yourself.

179

But I won't give up, I said to myself. I want Pris and I'm going to get her away from Maury and Sam Barrows and all the rest of them. Pris is mine, she belongs to me. I don't care what she or they or anybody else thinks. I don't care what evil prize of this world they're busy hungering after; all I know is what my instinctive inner voice says. It says: Get Pris Frauenzimmer away from them and marry her. She was destined from the start to be Mrs Louis Rosen of Ontario, Oregon.

That was my vow.

Picking up the phone I once more dialed.

'Northwest Electronics, good morning.'

'Give me Mr Barrows again. This is Louis Rosen.'

A pause. Then the deeper-voiced woman. 'Miss Wallace.'

'Let me talk to Sam.'

'Mr Barrows has gone out. Who is calling?'

'This is Louis Rosen. Tell Mr Barrows to have Miss Frauenzimmer – '

'Who?'

'Miss Womankind, then. Tell Barrows to send her over to my motel in a taxi.' I gave her the address, reading it from the doorkey. 'Tell him not to put her on a plane for Boise. Tell him if he doesn't I'm coming in there and get her.'

There was silence. Then Miss Wallace said, 'I can't tell him anything because he's not here, he went home, he honestly did.'

'I'll call him at home, then. Give me his number.'

In a squeaky voice Miss Wallace gave me the phone number. I knew it already; I had called it the night before.

I jiggled the hook and called that number.

Pris answered the phone.

'This is Louis,' I said. 'Louis Rosen.'

'For goodness sakes,' Pris said, taken by surprise.

180

'Where are you? You sound so close.' She seemed nervous.

'I'm here in Seattle. I flew in by TWA last night; I'm here to rescue you from Sam Barrows.'

'Oh my god.'

'Listen, Pris. Stay where you are; I'm driving right on over. Okay? You understand?'

'Oh no,' Pris said. 'Louis – ' Her voice became hard. 'Wait just a second. I talked to Horstowski this morning; he told me about you and your catatonic rampage; he warned me about you.'

'Tell Sam to put you in a cab and send you over here,' I said.

'I thought you were Sam calling.'

'If you don't come with me,' I said, 'I'm going to kill you.'

'No you're not,' she said in a hard calm voice; she had regained her deadly cold poise. 'You just try. You low-class creep.'

I was stunned. 'Listen,' I began.

'You prole. You goofball. Drop dead, if you think you're going to horn in. I know all about what you're up to; you fat-assed fart-faces can't design your simulacrum without me, can you? So you want me back. Well go to hell. And if you try to come around here I'll scream you're raping me or killing me and you'll spend the rest of your life in jail. So think about that.' She ceased, then, but she did not hang up; I could hear her there. She was waiting, with relish, to hear what I had – if anything – to say.

'I'm in love with you,' I told her.

'Go take a flying fling. Oh, here's Sam at the door. Get off the phone. And don't call me Pris. My name's Pristine, Pristine Womankind. Go back to Boise and dabble with your poor little stunted second-rate simulacra, as a favor to me, please?' Again she waited and again I could think of nothing to say; nothing anyhow that was worth saying.

181

'Goodbye, you low-class poor ugly nothing,' Pris said in a matter-of-fact voice. 'And please don't annoy me with phone calls in the future. Save it for some greasy woman who wants you to paw her. If you can manage to find one that greasy, ugly and low-class.' This time the phone clicked; she had at last hung up, and I shook with relief. I trembled and quaked at having gotten off the phone and away from her, away from the calm, stinging, accusing, familiar voice.

Pris, I thought. I love you. Why? What have I done to be driven toward you? What twisted instinct is it?

I sat down on the bed and closed my eyes.

14

There was nothing to do but return to Boise.

I had been defeated – not by powerful, experienced Sam K. Barrows, not by my partner Maury Rock, either, but by eighteen-year-old Pris. There was no use hanging around Seattle.

What lay ahead for me? Back to R & R ASSOCIATES, make peace with Maury, resume where I had left off. Back to work on the Civil War Soldier Babysitter. Back to working for harsh, grim, bad-tempered Edwin M. Stanton. Back to having to put up with interminable readings-aloud by the Lincoln simulacrum from *Winnie the Pooh* and *Peter Pan*. Once more the smell of Corina Lark cigars, and now and then the sweeter smell of my father's A & Cs. The world I had left, the electronic organ and spinet factory at Boise, our office in Ontario . . .

And there was always the possibility that Maury would not let me come back, that he was serious about breaking up the partnership. So I might find myself without even the same drab world I had known and left; I might not even have that to look forward to.

Maybe now was the time. The moment to get out the .38 and blow off the top of my head. Instead of returning to Boise.

The metabolism of my body was speeding up and slowing down; I was breaking up due to centrifugal force and at the same time I groped out, trying to catch hold of everything near me. Pris had me, and yet in the instant of having me she flung me away, ejected me in a fit of cursing and retching. It was as if the magnet attracted particles which it simultaneously repelled; I was caught in a deadly oscillation.

Meanwhile Pris continued on without noticing.

The meaning of my life was at last clear to me. I was doomed to loving something beyond life itself, a cruel, cold and sterile thingthing – Pris Frauenzimmer. It would have been better to hate the entire world.

In view of the near-hopelessness of my situation I decided to try one final measure. Before I gave up I would try the Lincoln simulacrum. It had helped before; maybe it could help me now.

'This is Louis again,' I said when I had gotten hold of Maury. 'I want you to drive the Lincoln to the airfield and put it on a rocket flight to Seattle right now. I want the loan of it for about twenty-four hours.'

He put up a rapid, frantic argument; we fought it out for half an hour. But at last he gave in; when I hung up the phone I had his promise that the Lincoln would be on the Seattle Boeing 900 by nightfall.

Exhausted, I lay down to recover. If it can't find this motel, I decided, it probably wouldn't be of use anyhow . . . I'll lie here and rest.

The irony was that Pris had designed it.

Now we'll make back some of our investment, I said to myself. It cost us plenty to build and we didn't manage to make a deal with Barrows; all it does is sit around all day reading aloud and chuckling.

Somewhere in the back of my mind I recalled an anecdote having to do with Abe Lincoln and girls. Some particular girl he had had a crush on in his youth. Successful? For God's sake; I couldn't recall how he had come out. All I could dredge up was that he had suffered a good deal because of it.

Like me, I said to myself. Lincoln and I have a lot in common; women have given us a bad time. So he'd be sympathetic.

What should I do until the simulacrum arrived? It was risky to stay in my motel room . . . go to the Seattle public library and read up on Lincoln's courtship and his youth? I told the motel manager where I'd be if someone looking like Abraham Lincoln came by looking for me, and then I called a cab and started out. I had a large amount of time to kill; it was only ten o'clock in the morning.

There's hope yet, I told myself as the cab carried me through traffic to the library. I'm not giving up!

Not while I have the Lincoln to help bail me out of my problems. One of the finest presidents in American history, and a superb lawyer as well. Who could ask for more?

If anybody can help me, Abraham Lincoln can.

The reference books in the Seattle library did not do much to sustain my mood. According to them, Abe Lincoln had been turned down by the girl he loved. He had been so despondent that he had gone into a near-psychotic melancholia for months; he had almost done away with himself, and the incident had left emotional scars on him for the remainder of his life.

Great, I thought grimly as I closed the books. Just what I need: someone who's a bigger failure than I am.

But it was too late, the simulacrum was on its way from Boise.

Maybe we'll both kill ourselves, I said to myself as I left the library. We'll look over a few old love letters and then – blam, with the .38.

On the other hand, he had been successful afterward; he had become a President of the United States. To me, that meant that after nearly killing yourself with grief over a woman you could go on, rise above it, although of course never forget it. It would continue to shape the course of your life; you'd be a deeper, more thoughtful person. I had noticed that melancholy in the Lincoln. Probably I'd go to my grave the same sort of figure.

However, that would take years, and I had right now to consider.

185

I walked the streets of Seattle until I found a bookstore which sold paperbacks; there I bought a set of Carl Sandburg's version of Lincoln's life and carried it back to my motel room, where I made myself comfortable with a six-pack of beer and a big sack of potato chips.

In particular I scrutinized the part dealing with Lincoln's adolescence and the girl in question. Ann Rutledge. But something in Sandburg's way of writing kept blurring the point; he seemed to talk around the matter. So I left the books, the beer and the potato chips, and took a cab back to the library and the reference books there. It was now early in the afternoon.

The affair with Ann Rutledge. After her death from malaria in 1835 – at the age of nineteen – Lincoln had fallen into what the Britannica called 'a state of morbid depression which appeared to have given rise to the report that he had a streak of insanity. Apparently he himself felt a terror of this side of his make-up, a terror which is revealed in the most mysterious of his experiences, several years later.' That 'several years later' was the event in 1841.

In 1840 Lincoln got engaged to a good-looking girl named Mary Todd. He was then twenty-nine. But suddenly, on January first of 1841, he cut off the engagement. A date had been set for the wedding. The bride had on the usual costume; all was in readiness. Lincoln, however, did not show up. Friends went to see what had happened. They found him in a state of insanity. And his recovery from this state was very slow. On January twenty-third he wrote to his friend John T. Stuart:

I am now the most miserable man living. If what I feel were equally distributed to the whole human family, there would not be one cheerful face on the earth. Whether I shall ever be better I can not tell; I awfully forebode I shall not. To remain as I am is impossible; I must die or be better, it appears to me.

186

And in a previous letter to Stuart, dated January 20, Lincoln says:

I have, within the last few days, been making a most discreditable exhibition of myself in the way of hypochondriacism and thereby got an impression that Dr Henry is necessary to my existence. Unless he gets that place he leaves Springfield. You therefore see how much I am interested in the matter.

The 'matter' is getting Dr Henry appointed as Postmaster, at Springfield, so he can be around to keep tinkering with Lincoln in order to keep him alive. In other words, Lincoln, at that point in his life, was on the verge of suicide or insanity or both together.

Sitting there in the Seattle public library with all the reference books spread out around me, I came to the conclusion that Lincoln was what they now call a manic-depressive psychotic.

The most interesting comment is made by the Britannica, and goes as follows:

All his life long there was a certain remoteness in him, a something that made him not quite a realist, but which was so veiled by apparent realism that careless people did not perceive it. He did not care whether they perceived it or not, was willing to drift along, permitting circumstances to play the main part in determining his course and not stopping to split hairs as to whether his earthly attachments sprang from genuine realistic perceptions of affinity or from approximation more or less to the dreams of his spirit.

And then the Britannica comments on the part about Ann Rutledge. It also adds this:

They reveal the profound sensibility, also the vein of melancholy and unrestrained emotional reaction which came and went, in alternation with boisterous mirth, to the end of his days.

Later, in his political speeches, he engaged in biting sarcasm, a trait, I discovered after research, found in manic-depressives. And the alternation of 'boisterous mirth' with 'melancholy' is the basis of the manic-depressive classification.

But what undermines this diagnosis of mine is the following ominous note.

Reticence, degenerating at times into secretiveness, is one of his fixed characteristics.

And:

. . . His capacity for what Stevenson called 'a large and genial idleness' is worth considering.

But the most ominous part of all deals with his indecision. Because that isn't a symptom of manic-depression; that's a symptom – if it's a symptom at all – of the introverted psychosis. Of schizophrenia.

It was now five-thirty in the afternoon, time for dinner; I was stiff and my eyes and head ached. I put the reference books away, thanked the librarian, and made my way out onto the cold, wind-swept sidewalk, in search of a place to eat dinner.

Clearly, I had asked Maury for the use of one of the deepest, most complicated humans in history. As I sat in the restaurant that evening eating dinner – and it was a good dinner – I mulled it over in my mind.

Lincoln was exactly like me. I might have been reading my own biography, there in the library; psychologically we were as alike as two peas in a pod, and by understanding him I understood myself.

Lincoln had taken everything hard. He might have been remote, but he was not dead emotionally; quite the contrary. So he was the opposite of Pris, of the cold schizoid type. Grief, emotional empathy, were written on his face. He fully felt the sorrows of the war, every single death.

So it was hard to believe that what the Britannica called his 'remoteness' was a sign of schizophrenia. The same with his well-known indecision. And in addition, I had my own personal experience with him – or to be more exact, with his simulacrum. I didn't catch the *alienness*, the otherness, with the simulacrum that I had caught with Pris.

I had a natural trust and liking for Lincoln, and that was certainly the opposite to what I felt toward Pris. There was something innately good and warm and human about him, a vulnerability. And I knew, by my own experience with Pris, that the schizoid was not vulnerable; he was withdrawn to safety, to a point where he could observe other humans, could watch them in a scientific manner without jeopardizing himself. The essence of someone like Pris lay in the matter of distance. Her main fear, I could see, was of closeness to other people. And that fear bordered on suspicion of them, assigning motives to their actions which they didn't actually have. She and I were so different. I could see she might switch and become paranoid at any time; she had no knowledge of authentic human nature, none of the easy, day-to-day encounter with people that Lincoln had acquired in his youth. In the final analysis, that was what distinguished the two of them. Lincoln knew the paradoxes of the human soul, its great parts, its weak parts, its lusts, its nobility, all the odd-shaped pieces that went to make it up in its almost infinite variety. He had bummed around. Pris – she had an ironclad rigid schematic view, a blueprint, of mankind. An abstraction. And she lived in it.

No wonder she was impossible to reach.

I finished my dinner, left the tip, paid the bill, and walked back outside onto the dark evening sidewalk. Where now? To the motel once more. I attracted a cab and soon I was riding across town.

When I reached the motel I saw lights on in my room. The manager hurried out of his office and greeted me.

'You have a caller. My god, he sure does look like Lincoln, like you said. What is this, a gag or something? I let him in.'

'Thanks,' I said, and went on into the motel room.

There, in a chair, leaning back with his long legs stuck out before him, sat the Lincoln simulacrum. He was engrossed, unaware of me; he was reading the Carl Sandburg biography. Beside him on the floor rested a little cloth bag: his luggage.

'Mr Lincoln,' I said.

Presently he glanced up, smiled at me. 'Good evening, Louis.'

'What do you think of the Sandburg book?'

'I have not yet had time to form an opinion.' He marked his place in the book, closed it and put it aside. 'Maury told me that you are in grave difficulty and required my presence and advice. I hope I have not arrived too late on the scene.'

'No, you made good time. How did you like the flight from Boise?'

'I was taken with astonishment to observe the fast motion of the landscape beneath. We had hardly risen, when we were already here and landing; and the shepherdess told me that we had gone over a thousand miles.'

I was puzzled. 'Oh. Stewardess.'

'Yes. Forgive my stupidity.'

'Can I pour you a drink?' I indicated the beer, but the simulacrum shook its head no.

'I would prefer to decline. Why don't you present me with your problems, Louis, and we will see at once what is to be done.' With a sympathetic expression the simulacrum waited to hear.

I seated myself facing him. But I hesitated. After what I had read today I wondered if I wanted to consult him after all. Not because I did not have faith in his opinions – but because my problem might stir up his own buried

190

sorrows. My situation was too much like his own with Ann Rutledge.

'Go ahead, Louis.'

'Let me fix myself a beer, first.' With the opener I set to work on the can; I fooled with that for a time, wondering what to do.

'Perhaps I should speak, then. During my trip from Boise I had certain meditations on the situation with Mr Barrows.' Bending, he opened his overnight bag and brought out several lined pages on which he had written in pencil. 'Do you desire to put great force to bear against Mr Barrows? So that he will of his own will send back Miss Frauenzimmer, no matter how she may feel about it?'

I nodded.

'Then,' the simulacrum said, 'telephone this person.' He passed me a slip of paper; on it was a name.

SILVIA DEVORAC

I could not for the life of me place the name. I had heard it before but I couldn't make the connection.

'Tell her,' the simulacrum went on softly, 'that you would like to visit her in her home and discuss a matter of delicacy. A topic having to do with Mr Barrows . . . that will be enough; she will at once invite you over.'

'What then?'

'I will accompany you. There will be no problem, I think. You need not resort to any fictitious account with her; you need only describe your relationship with Miss Frauenzimmer, that you represent her father and that you have profound emotional attachments towards the girl yourself.'

I was mystified. 'Who is this Silvia Devorac?'

'She is the political antagonist of Mr Barrows; it is she who seeks to condemn the Green Peach Hat housing which he owns and from which he derives enormous rents. She is a socially-inclined lady, given to worthy

191

projects.' The simulacrum passed me a handful of newspaper cuttings from Seattle papers. 'I obtained these through Mr Stanton's assistance. As you can see from them, Mrs Devorac is tireless. And she is quite astute.'

'You mean,' I said, 'that this business about Pris being under the age of consent and a mentally-ill ward of the Federal Government – '

'I mean, Louis, that Mrs Devorac will know what to do with the information which you bring to her.'

After a moment I said, 'Is it worth it?' I felt weighed down. 'To do a thing like that . . .'

'Only God can be certain,' the simulacrum said.

'What's your opinion?'

'Pris is the woman whom you love. Is that not the actual fact of the matter? What is there in the world more important to you? Wouldn't you stake your life in this contest? I think you have already, and perhaps, if Maury is correct, the lives of others.'

'Hell,' I said, 'love is an American cult. We take it too seriously; it's practically a national religion.'

The simulacrum did not speak. It rocked back and forth instead.

'It's serious to me,' I said.

'Then that is what you must consider, not whether it is properly serious to others or not. I think it would be inhuman to retire to a world of rent-values, as Mr Barrows will do. Is it not the truth that he stands opposite you, Louis? You will succeed precisely on that point: *that to him his feeling for Miss Pris is not serious*. And is that good? Is that more moral or rational? If he felt as you do he would let Mrs Devorac obtain her condemnation notice; he would marry Pris, and he would, in his own opinion, have obtained the better bargain. But he does not, and that sets him apart from his humanity. You would not do that; you would – and are – staking all in this. To you, the person you love matters over everything else, and I do think you are right and he wrong.'

'Thank you,' I said. 'You know, you certainly have a deep understanding of what the proper values in life are; I have to hand it to you. I've met a lot of people but I mean, you go right to the core of things.'

The simulacrum reached out and patted me on the shoulder. 'I think there is a bond between us, Louis. You and I have much in common.'

'I know,' I said. 'We're alike.'

We were both deeply moved.

15

For some time the Lincoln simulacrum coached me as to exactly what I should say on the phone to Mrs Silvia Devorac. I practiced it again and again, but a dreadful foreboding filled me.

However at last I was ready. I got her number from the Seattle phonebook and dialed. Presently a melodious, cultivated, middle-aged type of woman's voice said in my ear:

'Yes?'

'Mrs Devorac? I'm sorry to bother you. I'm interested in Green Peach Hat and your project to have it torn down. My name is Louis Rosen and I'm from Ontario, Oregon.'

'I had no idea our committee had attracted notice that far away.'

'What I was wondering is, can I drop over with my attorney for a few minutes to your house and chat with you?'

'Your attorney! Oh goodness, is anything wrong?'

'There is something wrong,' I said, 'but not with your committee. It has to do – ' I glanced at the simulacrum; it nodded yes to me. 'Well,' I said heavily, 'it has to do with Sam K. Barrows.'

'I see.'

'I know Mr Barrows through an unfortunate business association which I had with him in Ontario. I thought possibly you could give me some assistance.'

'You do have an attorney, you say . . . I don't know what I could do for you that he can't.' Mrs Devorac's voice was measured and firm. 'But you're welcome to

194

drop by if we can keep it down to, say, half an hour; I have guests expected at eight.'

Thanking her, I rang off.

The Lincoln said, 'That was satisfactorily done, Louis.' It rose to its feet. 'We shall go at once, by cab.' It started toward the door.

'Wait,' I said.

At the door it glanced back at me.

'I can't do it.'

'Then,' the simulacrum said, 'let us go for a walk instead.' It held the door open for me. 'Let us enjoy the night air, it smells of mountains.'

Together the two of us walked up the dark sidewalk.

'What do you think will become of Miss Pris?' the simulacrum asked.

'She'll be okay. She'll stay with Barrows; he'll give her everything she wants out of life.'

At a service station the simulacrum halted. 'You will have to call Mrs Devorac back to tell her we are not coming.' There was an outdoor public phonebooth.

Shutting myself in the booth I dialed Mrs Devorac's number once more. I felt even worse than I had earlier; I could hardly get my finger into the proper slots.

'Yes?' the courteous voice came in my ear.

'This is Mr Rosen again. I'm sorry but I'm afraid I don't have my facts completely in order yet, Mrs Devorac.'

'And you want to put off seeing me until a later time?'

'Yeah.'

'That's perfectly all right. Any time that's convenient for you. Mr Rosen, before you ring off – have you ever been to Green Peach Hat?'

'No.'

'It is quite bad.'

'I'm not surprised.'

'Please try to visit it.'

'Okay, I will,' I told her.

She rang off. I stood holding the receiver and then at last I hung it up and walked out of the phonebooth.

The Lincoln was nowhere in sight.

Has he gone off? I asked myself. Am I alone, now? I peered into the darkness of the Seattle night.

The simulacrum sat inside the building of the service station, in a chair opposite the boy in the white uniform; rocking the chair back and forth it chatted amiably. I opened the door. 'Let's go,' I said. The simulacrum said goodnight to the boy and together the two of us walked on in silence.

'Why not drop by and visit Miss Pris?' the simulacrum said.

'Oh no,' I said horrified. 'There may be a flight back to Boise tonight; if so we should take it.'

'She frightens you. In any case we would not find her and Mr Barrows home; they no doubt are out enjoying themselves in the public eye. The lad in the fuel station tells me that world-famous people of the entertainment arts, some even from Europe, appear in Seattle and perform. I believe he said that Earl Grant is here now. Is he esteemed?'

'Very.'

'The lad said they generally appear but one night and then fly on. Since Mr Grant is here tonight I would suppose he was not here last night, and so possibly Mr Barrows and Miss Pris are attending his performance.'

'He sings,' I said, 'and very well.'

'Do we have enough money to go?'

'Yes.'

'Why not, then?'

I gestured. Why not? 'I don't want to,' I said.

The simulacrum said softly, 'I journeyed a great distance to be of assistance to you, Louis, I think in exchange you should do me a favor; I would enjoy hearing Mr Grant rendering the songs of the day. Would you be obliging enough to accompany me?'

'You're deliberately putting me on the spot.'

'I want you to visit the place where you will most likely see Mr Barrows and Miss Pris.'

Evidently I had no choice. 'All right, we'll go.' I began to look up and down the street for a taxi, feeling bitter.

An enormous crowd had turned out to hear the legendary Earl Grant; we were barely able to squeeze in. However, there was no sign of Pris and Sam Barrows. We seated ourselves at the bar, ordered drinks, and watched from there. They probably won't show up, I said to myself. I felt a little better. One chance in a thousand . . .

'He sings beautifully,' the simulacrum said, between numbers.

'Yeah.'

'The Negro has music in his bones.'

I glanced at it. Was it being sarcastic? That banal remark, that cliche – but it had a serious expression on its face. In its time, perhaps, the remark had not meant what it did now. So many years had gone by.

'I recall,' the simulacrum said, 'my trips to New Orleans when a boy. I first experienced the Negro and his pitiable condition, then. It was in, I believe, 1826. I was astonished at the Spanish nature of that city; it was totally different from the America I had grown up in.'

'That was when Denton Offcutt engaged you? That peddler?'

'You are well-apprised of my early life.' It seemed puzzled at my knowledge.

'Hell,' I said, 'I looked it up. In 1835 Ann Rutledge died. In 1841 – ' I broke off. Why had I mentioned that? I could have kicked myself around the block. The simulacrum's face, even in the gloom of the bar, showed pain and deep, pervasive shock. 'I'm sorry,' I said.

Meantime, thank god, Grant had begun another number. It was a mild, sorrowful blues, however. Feeling

197

increasingly nervous, I waved the bartender over and ordered myself a double Scotch.

Broodingly, the simulacrum sat hunched over, its legs drawn up so that it could place its feet on the rungs of the barstool. After Earl Grant had finished singing it remained silent, as if unaware of its surroundings. Its face was blank and downcast.

'I'm sorry to have depressed you,' I said to it; I was beginning to worry about it.

'It is not your fault; these moods come upon me. I am, do you know, grossly superstitious. Is that a fault? In any case I cannot prevent it; it is a part of me.' Its words emerged haltingly, as if with vast effort; as if, I thought, it could hardly find the energy in it to speak.

'Have another drink,' I said, and then I discovered that it had not touched its first and only drink.

The simulacrum mutely shook its head no.

'Listen,' I said, 'let's get out of here and on the rocket flight; let's get back to Boise.' I jumped from my stool. '*Come on.*'

The simulacrum remained where it was.

'Don't get so down in the dumps. I should have realized – blues singing affects everyone that way.'

'It is not the colored man's singing,' the simulacrum said. 'It is my own self. Don't blame him for it, Louis, nor yourself. On the flight here I saw down onto the wild forests and thought to myself of my early days and the travels of my family and especially of the death of my mother and our trip to Illinois by oxen.'

'For chrissakes, this place is too gloomy; let's take a cab to the Sea-Tac Airport and – ' I broke off.

Pris and Sam had entered the room; a waitress was showing them to a reserved table.

Seeing them the simulacrum smiled. 'Well, Louis, I should have heeded you. Now it is too late, I fear.'

I stood rigid by my barstool.

16

In a low voice in my ear the Lincoln simulacrum said, 'Louis, you must climb back up on your stool.'

Nodding, I clumsily got back up. Pris – she glowed. Stunning in one of the new Total Glimpse dresses . . . her hair had been cut much shorter and brushed back and she wore a peculiar eyeshadow which made her eyes seem huge and black. Barrows, with his pool-ball shaved head and jovial, jerky manner, appeared the same as always; business-like and brisk, grinning, he accepted the menu and began ordering.

'She is astonishingly lovely,' the simulacrum said to me.

'Yes,' I said. Around us the men seated at the bar – and the women too – had paused to give her the once-over. I couldn't blame them.

'You must take action,' the simulacrum said to me. 'You cannot leave now, I fear, and you cannot stay as you are. I will go over to their table and tell them that you have an appointment with Mrs Devorac later in the evening, and that is all I can do for you; the rest, Louis, is on your shoulders.' It stepped long-legged from the stool and made its way from the bar before I could stop it.

It reached Barrows' table and bent down, resting its hand on Barrows' shoulder, and spoke to him.

At once Barrows twisted to face me. Pris also turned; her dark cold eyes glittered.

The Lincoln returned to the bar. 'Go over to them, Louis.'

Automatically I got down and threaded my way among

the tables, over to Barrows and Pris. They stared. Probably they believed I had my .38 with me, but I did not; it was back at the motel. I said, 'Sam, you're finished. I've got all the dope ready for Silvia.' I examined my wristwatch. 'Too bad for you, but it's too late for you now; you had your chance and you muffed it.'

'Sit down, Rosen.'

I seated myself at their table.

The waitress brought martinis for Barrows and Pris.

'We've built our first simulacrum,' Barrows said.

'Oh? Who's it of?'

'George Washington, the Father of Our Country.'

I said, 'It's a shame to see your empire crumbling in ruins.'

'I don't get what you mean but I'm glad I ran into you,' Barrows said. 'It's an opportunity to thrash out a few misunderstandings.' To Pris he said, 'I'm sorry to discuss business, dear, but it's luck to run across Louis here; do you mind?'

'Yes I mind. If he doesn't leave, you and I are finished.'

Barrows said, 'You get so violent, dear. This is a minor point but an interesting one that I'd like to settle with Rosen, here. If you're so dissatisfied I can send you home in a cab.'

In her flat, remote tone Pris said, 'I'm not going to be sent off. If you try to get rid of me you'll find yourself in the bucket so fast it'll make your head spin.'

We both regarded her. Beyond the beautiful dress, hair-do and make-up it was the same old Pris.

'I think I will send you home,' Barrows said.

'No,' she said.

Barrows beckoned to the waitress. 'Will you have a cab – '

'You screwed me before witnesses,' Pris said.

Blanching, Barrows waved the waitress away. 'Now look.' His hands were trembling. 'Do you want to sit and have the vichyssoise and be quiet? Can you be quiet?'

'I'll say what I want, when I want.'

'What witnesses?' Barrows managed to smile. 'Dave Blunk? Colleen Nild?' His smile strengthened, 'Go on, dear.'

'You're a dirty aging middle-aged man who likes to peep up girls' skirts,' Pris said. 'You ought to be behind bars.' Her voice, although not loud, was so distinct that several people at nearby tables turned their heads. 'You put it in me once too often,' Pris said. 'And I can tell you this: it's a wonder you can get it up at all. It's so little and flaccid. You're just too old and flaccid, you old fairy.'

Barrows winced, grinned twistedly. 'Anything else?'

'No,' Pris said. 'You have all those people bought so they won't be witnesses against you.'

'Anything else?'

She shook her head, panting.

Turning to me Barrows said, 'Now. Go ahead.' He seemed still to have his poise. It was amazing; he could endure anything.

I said, 'Shall I contact Mrs Devorac or not? It's up to you.'

Glancing at his wristwatch Barrows said, 'I'd like to consult with my legal people. Would it offend you if I telephoned Dave Blunk to come over here?'

'All right,' I said, knowing that Blunk would advise him to give in.

Excusing himself, Barrows went off to phone. While he was gone Pris and I sat facing each other without speaking. At last he returned and Pris met him with a forlorn, suspicious expression. 'What vicious thing are you up to, Sam?' she said.

Sam Barrows did not answer. He leaned back comfortably.

'Louis, he's done something,' Pris said with a wild glance all around. 'Can't you tell? Don't you know him well enough to see? Oh, Louis!'

'Don't worry,' I said, but now I felt uneasy, and at the

bar I noticed that the Lincoln was stirring about restlessly and frowning. Had I made a mistake? Too late now; I had agreed.

'Will you step over here?' I called to the simulacrum. It rose at once and came over, stooping to hear. 'Mr Barrows is waiting to consult with his attorney.'

Seating itself the simulacrum pondered. 'I suppose there is no harm in that.'

We all waited. Half an hour later Dave Blunk appeared, threading his way to us. With him was Colleen Nild, dressed up, and after her a third person, a young man with crewcut and bow-tie, an alert, eager expression on his face.

Who is this man? I wondered. *What is going on*? And my uneasiness grew.

'Sorry we're late,' Blunk said as he seated Mrs Nild. Both he and the bow-tied young man seated themselves. No one introduced anyone.

This must be some employee of Barrows, I said to myself. Could this be the punk who would fulfill the formality of a legal marriage with Pris?

Seeing me staring at the man, Barrows spoke up. 'This is Johnny Booth. Johnny, I want you to meet Louis Rosen.'

The young man nodded hastily. 'Pleased to meet you, Mr Rosen.' He ducked his head to the others in turn. 'Hi. Hi there. How are you?'

'Wait a minute.' I felt cold all over. 'This is John Booth? John Wilkes Booth?'

'You hit the nail on the head,' Barrows said.

'But he doesn't look anything like John Wilkes Booth.' It was a simulacrum and a terrible one at that. I had just been browsing in the reference books; John Wilkes Booth had been a theatrical, dramatic-looking individual – this was just another ordinary flunky type, a *nebbish*, the kind you see in the downtown business sections of every major city in the United States. 'Don't put me on,' I said.

202

'This is your first effort? I've got news for you; better go back and try again.'

But all the time I was talking I was staring at the simulacrum in terror, for despite its foolish appearance it worked; it was a success in the technical sense, and what a dreadful omen that was for us, for every one of us; the John Wilkes Booth simulacrum! I couldn't help glancing sideways at the Lincoln to see its reaction. Did it know what this meant?

The Lincoln had said nothing. But the lines of its face had deepened, the twilight of melancholy which always to some degree hung over it. It seemed to know what was in store for it, what this new simulacrum portended.

I couldn't believe that Pris could design such a thing. And then I realized that of course she hadn't; that was why it had, really, no face. Only Bundy had been involved. Through him they had developed the inner workings and then they had crammed it into this mass-man container which sat here at the table smiling and nodding, a typical Ja-Sager, a yes man. They hadn't even *attempted* to recreate the authentic Booth appearance, perhaps hadn't even been interested, it was a rush job, done for a specific purpose.

'We'll continue our discussion,' Barrows said.

Dave Blunk nodded, the John Wilkes Booth nodded. Mrs Nild examined a menu. Pris was staring at the new simulacrum as if turned to stone. So I was right; it was a surprise to her. While she had been out being wined and dined, dressed up in new clothes, slept with and pretti-fied, Bob Bundy had been off in some workshop of the Barrows organization, hammering away on this contraption.

'All right,' I said. 'Let's continue.'

'Johnny,' Barrows said to his simulacrum, 'by the way, this tall man with the beard, this is Abe Lincoln. I was telling you about him, remember?'

'Oh yes, Mr Barrows,' the Booth thing said instantly, with a wide-awake nod. 'I remember distinctly.'

I said, 'Barrows, it's a phony business you have here; this is just an assassin with the name "Booth," he doesn't look or talk right and you know it. This is phony, lousy and phony from the bottom up, it makes me sick. I feel shame for you.'

Barrows shrugged.

To the Booth thing I said, 'Say something out of Shakespeare.'

It grinned back in its busy, silly way.

'Say something in Latin, then,' I said to it.

It went on grinning.

'How many hours did it take to whip this nothing up?' I said to Barrows. 'Half a morning? Where's any painstaking fidelity to detail? Where's craftsmanship gone? All that's left is schlock, the killer-instinct planted in this contraption – right?'

Barrows said, 'I think you will want to withdraw your threat to contact Mrs Devorac, in view of Johnny Booth, here.'

'How's he going to do it?' I said. 'With a poison ring? With bacteriological warfare?'

Dave Blunk laughed. Mrs Nild smiled. The Booth thing went right along with the others, grinning emptily, taking its cue from its boss. Mr Barrows had them all on strings and he was jerking away with all his might.

Staring at the Booth simulacrum Pris had become almost unrecognizable. She had become gaunt; her neck was stretched out like a fowl's and her eyes were glazed and full of splintered light.

'Listen,' she said. She pointed at the Lincoln. 'I built that.'

Barrows eyed her.

'It's mine,' Pris said. To the Lincoln she said. 'Did you know that? That my father and I built you?'

'Pris,' I said, 'for god's sake – '

'Be quiet,' she said to me.

'Stay out of this,' I said to her. 'This is between I and Mr Barrows.' I was shaking. 'Maybe you mean well and I realize you had nothing to do with building this Booth thing. And you – '

'For christ's sake,' Pris said to me, 'shut up.' She faced Barrows. 'You had Bob Bundy build that thing to destroy the Lincoln and you very carefully kept me from knowing. You crud. I'll never forgive you for this.'

Barrows said, 'What's eating you, Pris? Don't tell me you're having an affair with the Lincoln simulacrum.' He frowned at her.

'I won't see my work killed,' Pris said.

Barrows said, 'Maybe you will.'

In a heavy voice the Lincoln said, 'Miss Pris, I do think Mr Rosen is correct. You should allow him and Mr Barrows to discover the solution to their problem.'

'I can solve this,' Pris said. Bending down, she fumbled with something under the table. I could not imagine what she was up to, nor could Barrows; all of us, in fact, sat rigid. Pris emerged, holding one of her high heeled shoes, brandishing it with the metal heel out.

'Goddam you,' she said to Barrows.

Barrows started from his chair. 'No,' he said, holding up his hand.

The shoe smashed down on the head of the Booth simulacrum. Its heel burst into the thing's head, right behind the ear. 'There,' Pris said to Barrows, her eyes shining and wet, her mouth a thin contorted frantic line.

'Glap,' the Booth simulacrum said. Its hands beat jerkily in the air; its feet drummed on the floor. Then it ceased moving. An inner wind convulsed it; its limbs floundered and twitched. It became inert.

I said, 'Don't hit it again, Pris.' I did not feel able to stand any more. Barrows was saying almost the same thing, muttering at Pris in a dazed monotone.

'Why should I hit it again?' Pris said matter-of-factly;

she withdrew the heel of her shoe from its head, bent down, put her shoe back on again. People at the tables around us stared in amazement.

Barrows got out a white linen handkerchief and mopped his forehead. He started to speak, changed his mind, remained silent.

Gradually the Booth simulacrum began to slide from its chair. I stood up and tried to prop it so that it would remain where it was. Dave Blunk rose, too: together we managed to get it propped upright so that it would not fall. Pris sipped her drink expressionlessly.

To the people at the nearby tables Blunk said, 'It's a doll, a life-size doll, for display. Mechanical.' For their benefit he showed them the now-visible metal and plastic inner part of the simulacrum's skull. Within the puncture I could see something shining, the damaged ruling monad, I suppose. I wondered if Bob Bundy could repair it. I wondered if I cared whether it could be repaired or not.

Putting out his cigarette Barrows drank his drink, then in a hoarse voice said to Pris, 'You've put yourself on bad terms with me, by doing that.'

'Then goodbye,' Pris said. 'Goodbye, Sam K. Barrows, you dirty ugly fairy.' She rose to her feet, deliberately knocked over her chair; she walked away from the table, leaving us, going among and past the other tables of people, at last to the checkstand. She got her coat from the girl, there.

Neither Barrows nor I moved.

'She went out the door,' Dave Blunk said presently. 'I can see the door better than any of you; she's gone.'

'What am I going to do with this?' Barrows said to Blunk regarding the dead Booth simulacrum. 'We'll have to get it out of here.'

'We can get it out between the two of us,' Blunk said.

'I'll give you a hand,' I said.

Barrows said, 'We'll never see her again. Or she might

206

be standing outside on the sidewalk, waiting.' To me he said, 'Can you tell? I can't; I don't understand her.'

I hurried up the aisle along side the bar, past the checkstand; I pushed open the street door. There stood the uniformed doorman. He nodded courteously at me.

There was no sign of Pris.

'What happened to the girl who just came out?' I said.

The doorman gestured. 'I don't know, sir.' He indicated the many cabs, the traffic, the clusters of people like bees near the doorway of the club. 'Sorry, couldn't tell.'

I looked up and down the sidewalk; I even ran a little in each direction, straining to catch a glimpse of her.

Nothing.

At last I returned to the club and to the table where Barrows and the others sat with the dead, damaged Booth simulacrum. It had slid down in its seat, now, and was leaning to one side, its head lolling, its mouth open; I propped it up again, with Dave Blunk's help.

'You've lost everything,' I said to Barrows.

'I've lost nothing.'

'Sam's right,' Dave Blunk said. 'What has he lost? Bob Bundy can make another simulacrum if necessary.'

'You've lost Pris,' I said. 'That's everything.'

'Oh hell, who knows about Pris; I don't even think she knows.'

'Guess so,' I said. My tongue felt thick; it clung to the sides of my mouth. I waggled my jaw, feeling no pain, nothing at all. 'I've lost her, too.'

'Evidently,' Barrows said. 'But you're better off; could you bear to undergo something of this sort every day?'

'No.'

As we sat there the great Earl Grant appeared once more. The piano was playing and everyone had shut up, and we did so, too.

I've got grasshoppers in my
pillow, baby.

207

Was he singing to me? Had he seen me sitting there, seen the look on my face, known how I felt? It was an old song and sad. Maybe he saw me; maybe not. I couldn't tell, but it seemed so.

Pris is wild, I thought. Not a part of us. Outside somewhere. Pris *is* pristine and in an awful way: all that goes on among and between people, all that we have here, fails to touch her. When one looks at her one sees back into the farthest past; one sees us as we started out, a million, two million years ago . . .

The song which Earl Grant was singing; that was one of the ways of taming, of making us over, modifying us again and again in countless slow ways. The Creator was still at work, still molding what in most of us remained soft. Not so with Pris; there was no more molding and shaping with her, not even by Him.

I have seen into the *other*, I said to myself, when I saw Pris. And where am I left, now? Waiting only for death, as the Booth simulacrum when she took off her shoe. The Booth simulacrum had finally gotten it in exchange for its deed of over a century ago. Before his death, Lincoln had dreamed of assassination, seen in his sleep a black-draped coffin, and weeping processions. Had this simulacrum received any intimation, last night? Had it dreamed in its sleep in some mechanical, mystical way?

We would all get it. Chug-chug. The black crepe draped on the train passing in the midst of the grain fields. People out to witness, removing their caps. Chug-chug-chug.

The black train with the coffin guarded by soldiers in blue who carried guns and who never moved in all that time, from start to end of the long, long trip.

'Mr Rosen.' Someone beside me speaking. A woman. Startled, I glanced up. Mrs Nild was addressing me.

'Would you help us? Mr Barrows has gone to get the car; we want to put the Booth simulacrum into the car.'

'Oh,' I said, nodding. 'Sure.'

As I got to my feet, I looked to the Lincoln to see if it was going to pitch in. But strange to say the Lincoln sat with its head bowed in deepest melancholy, paying no attention to us or to what we were doing. Was it listening to Earl Grant? Was it overcome by his blues song? I did not think so. It was hunched over, actually bent out of shape, as if its bones were fusing into one single bone. And it was absolutely silent; it did not even seem to be breathing.

A kind of prayer, I thought as I watched it. And yet no prayer at all. The stoppage of prayer, perhaps; its interruption. Blunk and I turned to the Booth; we began lifting it to its feet. It was very heavy.

'The car's a Mercedes-Benz,' Blunk gasped as we started up the aisle. 'White with red leather interior.'

'I'll hold the door open,' Mrs Nild said, following after us.

We got the Booth up the narrow aisle to the entrance of the club. The doorman regarded us with curiosity but neither he nor anyone else made a move to interfere or help or inquire as to what was taking place. The doorman, however, did hold the door aside for us and we were grateful because that left Mrs Nild free to go out into the street to hail Sam Barrows' car.

'Here it comes,' Blunk said, jerking his head.

Mrs Nild opened the car door wide for us, and between Blunk and myself we managed to get the simulacrum into the back seat.

'You better come along with us,' Mrs Nild said to me as I started away from the car.

'Good idea,' Blunk said. 'We'll have a drink, okay, Rosen? We'll take the Booth to the shop and then go over to Collie's apartment; the liquor's there.'

'No,' I said.

'Come on,' Barrows said from behind the wheel. 'You fellows get in so we can go; that includes you, Rosen, and naturally your simulacrum. Go back and get it.'

'No, no thanks,' I said. 'You guys go on.'

Blunk and Mrs Nild closed the car door after them and the car drove off and disappeared into the heavy evening traffic.

Hands in my pockets I returned to the club, making my way down the aisle to the table where the Lincoln still sat, its head down, its arms wrapped about itself, in utter stillness.

What could I say to it? How could I cheer it up?

'You shouldn't let an incident like that get you down,' I said to it. 'You should try to rise above it.'

The Lincoln did not respond.

'Many a mickle makes a muckle,' I said.

The simulacrum raised its head. It stared at me hopelessly. 'What does that mean?'

'I don't know,' I said. 'I just don't know.'

We both sat in silence, then.

'Listen,' I said, 'I'm going to take you back to Boise and take you to see Doctor Horstowski. It won't do you any harm and he may be able to do something about these depressions. Is it okay, with you?'

Now the Lincoln seemed calmer; it had brought out a large red handkerchief and was blowing its nose. 'Thank you for your concern,' it said from behind the handkerchief.

'A drink,' I said. 'Or a cup of coffee or something to eat.'

The simulacrum shook its head no.

'When did you first notice the onset of these depressions?' I asked. 'I mean, in your youth. Would you like to talk about them? Tell me what comes to your mind, what free associations you have. Please. I have a feeling it'll make you feel better.'

The Lincoln cleared its throat and said, 'Will Mr Barrows and his party be returning?'

'I doubt it. They invited us to come along; they're going over to Mrs Nild's apartment.'

The Lincoln gave me a long, slow, queer look. 'Why are they going there and not to Mr Barrows' house?'

'The liquor's there. That's what Dave Blunk said, anyhow.'

The Lincoln cleared its throat again, drank a little water from the glass before it on the table. The strange look remained on its face, as if there was something it did not understand, as if it was puzzled but at the same time enlightened.

'What is it?' I said.

There was a pause and then the Lincoln said suddenly, 'Louis, *go over to Mrs Nild's apartment*. Waste no time.'

'Why?'

'She must be there.'

I felt my scalp tingle.

'I think,' the simulacrum said, 'she has been living there with Mrs Nild. I will go back to the motel, now. Don't worry about me – if necessary I am capable of returning to Boise on my own, tomorrow. Go at once, Louis, before their party arrives there.'

I scrambled to my feet. 'I don't – '

'You can obtain the address from the telephone book.'

'Yeah,' I said, 'that's so. Thanks for the advice, I really appreciate it. I have a feeling you've got a good idea, there. So I'll see you, then. So long. And if – '

'Go,' it said.

I went.

At an all-night drugstore I consulted the phonebook. I found Colleen Nild's address and then went outside onto the sidewalk and flagged down a cab. At last I was on my way.

Her building was a great dark brick apartment house.

Only a few windows were lit up, here and there. I found her number and pressed the button next to it. After a long time the small speaker made a static noise and a muffled female voice asked who I was.

'Louis Rosen.' Was it Pris? 'Can I come up?' I asked.

The heavy glass and black wrought-iron door buzzed; I leaped to catch it and pushed it open. In a moment I had crossed the deserted lobby and was climbing the stairs to the third floor. It was a long climb and when I reached her door I was panting and tired.

The door was open. I knocked, hesitated, and then went on inside the apartment.

In the living room on a couch sat Mrs Nild with a drink in her hand, and across from her sat Sam Barrows. Both of them glanced up at me.

'Hi, Rosen.' Barrows inclined his head towards a coffee table on which stood a bottle of vodka, lemons, mixer, lime juice and ice cubes and glasses. 'Go ahead, help yourself.'

Not knowing what else to do I went over and busied myself.

While I was doing that Barrows said, 'I have news for you. Someone very dear to you is in there.' He pointed with his glass. 'Go look in the bedroom.' Both he and Mrs Nild smiled.

I set down my drink and hurried in the direction of the door.

'How did you happen to change your mind and come here?' Barrows asked me, swirling his drink.

I said, 'The Lincoln thought Pris would be here.'

'Well, Rosen, I hate to say it, but in my opinion it did you a rotten favor. You're really bats to let yourself get hooked by that girl.'

'I don't agree.'

'Hell, that's because you're sick, all three of you, Pris and the Lincoln and you. I tell you, Rosen, Johnny Booth was worth a million of the Lincolns. I think what we'll do

212

is patch it up and use it for our Lunar development . . . after all, Booth is a good old familiar American name; no reason why the family next door can't be named Booth. You know, Rosen, you must come to Luna someday and see what we've done. You have no conception of it, none at all. No offense, but it's impossible to understand from here; you have to go there.'

'That's so, Mr Rosen,' Mrs Nild said.

I said, 'A successful man doesn't have to stoop to bamboozlement.'

'Bamboozlement!' Barrows exclaimed. 'Hell, it was an attempt to nudge people into doing what they're going to be doing someday anyhow. Oh hell, I don't want to argue. This has been quite a day; I'm tired. I feel no animosity toward anyone.' He grinned at me. 'If your little firm had linked up with us – you must have had an intuition of what it would have meant; you picked me out, I didn't pick you out. But it's water over the dam for you, now. Not for me; we'll go on and do it, possibly using the Booth – but anyhow in some manner, by some means.'

Mrs Nild said, 'Everyone knows that, Sam.' She patted him.

'Thanks, Collie,' Barrows said. 'I just hate to see the guy this way, no goals, no vision, no ambitions. It's heart-breaking. It is.'

I said nothing; I stood at the bedroom door, waiting for them to finish talking to me.

To me Mrs Nild said, 'Go ahead on in. You might as well.'

Taking hold of the knob I opened the bedroom door.

The bedroom lay in darkness. In the center I could make out the outlines of a bed. On the bed a figure lay. It had propped itself up with a pillow, and it was smoking a cigarette; or was it actually a cigarette? The bedroom smelled of cigar smoke. Hurrying to a light switch I turned on the light.

In the bed lay my father, smoking a cigar and regarding me with a frowning, thoughtful expression. He had on his bathrobe and pajamas, and beside the bed he had placed his fur-lined slippers. Next to the slippers were his suitcase and his clothes neatly piled.

'Close the door, mein Sohn', he said in a gentle voice.

Bewildered, I automatically complied; I shut the door behind me but not quickly enough to obliterate the howls of laughter from the living room, the roars from Sam Barrows and Mrs Nild. What a joke they had played on me, all this time; all their talk, solemn and pretentious – knowing that Pris was not in here, was not in the apartment at all, that the Lincoln had been mistaken.

'A shame, Louis,' my father said, evidently reading my expression. 'Perhaps I should have stepped out and put an end to the banter, and yet I was interested in what Mr Barrows said; it was not entirely beside the point, was it? He is a great man in some ways. Sit down.' He nodded toward the chair by the bed, and I sat.

'You don't know where she is?' I said. 'You can't help me either?'

'Afraid not, Louis.'

It was not even worth it to get up and leave. This was as far as I could go, here to this chair, beside my father's bed, as he sat smoking.

The door burst open and a man with his face on upside down appeared, my brother Chester, bustling and full of importance. 'I've got a good room for us, Dad,' he said, and then, seeing me, he smiled happily. 'So here you are, Louis; after all our trouble we at last manage to locate you.'

'Several times,' my father said, 'I was tempted to correct Mr Barrows; however, a man like him can't be re-educated, so why waste time?'

I could not bear the idea that my father was about to launch into one of his philosophical tirades; sinking down on the chair and pretending not to hear him I made

214

his words blur into fly-like buzzing. In my stupor of disappointment I imagined how it would have been if there had been no joke played on me, if I had found Pris here in this room, lying on the bed.

Think how it would have been. I would have found her asleep, perhaps drunk; I would have lifted her up and held her in my arms, brushed her hair back from her eyes, kissed her on the ear. I could imagine her stirring to life as I woke her up from her drunken nap.

'You're not paying attention,' my father said reprovingly. And I was not; I was completely away from the dismal disappointment, into my dream of Pris. 'You still pursue this will-of-the-wisp.' He frowned at me.

In my dream of a happier life I kissed Pris once more, and she opened her eyes. I laid her back down, lay against her and hugged her.

'How's the Lincoln?' Pris' voice, murmuring at my ear. She showed no surprise at seeing me, or at my having gathered her up and kissed her; in fact she did not show any reaction at all. But that was Pris.

'As good as could be expected.' I awkwardly caressed her hair as she lay on her back gazing up at me in the darkness. I could barely discern her outlined there. 'No,' I admitted, 'actually it's in terrible shape. It's having a psychotic depression. What do you care? You did it.'

'I saved it,' Pris said remotely, languidly. 'Bring me a cigarette, will you?'

I lit a cigarette for her and handed it to her. She lay smoking.

My father's voice came to me. 'Ignore this introverted ideal, mein Sohn – it takes you away from reality, like Mr Barrows told you, and this is serious! This is what Doctor Horstowski, if you'll excuse the expression, would have to call ill; do you see?'

Dimly I heard Chester's voice, 'It's schizophrenia, Dad, like all those adolescent kids; millions of Americans have it without knowing it, they never get into the clinics. I read an article, it told about that.'

Pris said, 'You're a good person, Louis. I feel sorry for you, being in love with me. You're wasting your time, but I suppose you don't care about that. Can you explain what love is? Love like that?'

'No,' I said.

'Won't you try?' she said. 'Is the door locked? If it isn't go lock it.'

'Hell,' I said miserably, 'I can't shut them out; they're right here on top of us. We'll never be away from them, we'll never be alone, just the two of us – I know it.' But I went anyhow, knowing what I knew, and shut and locked the door.

When I got back to the bed I found Pris standing up on it; she was unzipping her skirt. She drew her skirt up over her head and tossed it away from her, onto a chair; she was undressing. Now she kicked off her shoes.

'Who else can teach me, Louis, if not you?' she said. 'Pull the covers back.' She began taking off her underwear, but I stopped her. 'Why not?'

'I'm going mad,' I said. 'I can't stand this. I have to go back to Boise and see Doctor Horstowski; this can't go on, not here with my family in the same room.'

Pris said gently, 'Tomorrow we'll fly back to Boise. But not now.' She dragged the bedspread and blankets and top sheet back, got in, and, picking up her cigarette again, lay naked, not covering herself up but simply lying there. 'I'm so tired, Louis. Stay with me here tonight.'

'I just can't,' I said.

'Then take me back to where you're staying.'

'I can't do that either; the Lincoln is there.'

'Louis,' she said. 'I just want to go to sleep; lie down and cover us up. They won't bother us. Don't be afraid of them. I'm sorry the Lincoln had one of its fits. Don't blame me for that, Louis; it has them anyhow, and I did save its life. It's my child . . . isn't it?'

'I guess you could put it like that,' I said.

'I brought it to life, I mothered it. I'm very proud of that. When I saw that filthy Booth object . . . all I wanted to do was kill it on the spot. As soon as I saw it I knew what it was for. Could I be your mother, too? I wish I had brought you to life like I did it; I wish I had brought all kinds of people into life . . . everybody. I give life, and tonight I took it, and that's a good thing, if you can bear to do that. It takes a lot of strength to take someone's life, don't you think, Louis?'

'Yeah,' I said. I seated myself beside her on the bed once more.

In the darkness she reached up and stroked my hair from my eyes. 'I have that power over you, to give you life or take it away from you. Does that scare you? You know it's true.'

'It doesn't scare me now,' I said. 'It did once, when I first realized it.'

'It never scared me,' Pris said. 'If it did I'd lose the power; isn't that so, Louis? And I have to keep it; someone has to have it.'

I did not answer. Cigar smoke billowed around me, making me sick, making me aware of my father and my brother, both of them intently watching. 'Man must cherish some illusions,' my father said, puffing away rapidly, 'but this is ridiculous.' Chester nodded to that.

'Pris,' I said aloud.

'Listen to that, listen to that,' my father said excitedly, 'he's calling her; he's talking to her!'

'Get out of here,' I said to my father and Chester. I waved my arms at them, but it did no good; neither of them stirred.

'You must understand, Louis,' my father said, 'I have sympathy for you. I see what Mr Barrows doesn't see, the nobility of your search.'

Through the darkness and the babble of their voices I once more made out Pris; she had gathered her clothes in

217

a ball and sat on the edge of the bed, hugging them. 'Does it matter,' she said, 'what anyone says or thinks about us? I wouldn't worry about it; I wouldn't let words become so real as that. Everybody on the outside is angry with us. Sam and Maury and all the rest of them. The Lincoln wouldn't have sent you here if it wasn't the right thing . . . don't you know that?'

'Pris,' I said. 'I know it'll be all right. We're going to have a happy future.'

She smiled at that; in the darkness I saw the flash of her teeth. It was a smile of great suffering and sorrow, and it seemed to me – just for a moment – that what I had seen in the Lincoln simulacrum had come from her. It was here so clearly, now, the pain that Pris felt. She had put it into her creation perhaps without intending to; perhaps without even knowing that it was there.

'I love you,' I said to her.

Pris rose to her feet, naked and cool and thin. She put her hands to the sides of my head and drew me down.

'Mein Sohn,' my father was saying now to Chester, 'er schlaft in dem Freiheit der Liebesnacht. What I mean, he's asleep, my boy is, in the freedom of a night of love, if you follow me.'

'What'll they say back in Boise?' Chester said irritably. 'I mean, how can we go back home with him like this?'

'Aw,' my father said reprovingly, 'shut up, Chester; you don't understand the depth of his psyche, what he finds. There's a two-fold side to mental psychosis, it's also a return to the original source that we've all turned away from. You better remember that, Chester, before you shoot off your mouth.'

'Do you hear them?' I asked Pris.

Standing there against me, her body arched back for me, Pris laughed a soft, compassionate laugh. She gazed up at me fixedly, without expression. And yet she was fully alert. For her, change and reality, the events of her life, time itself, all had at this moment ceased.

Wonderingly, she lifted her hand and touched me on the cheek, brushed me with her fingertips.

Quite close to the door Mrs Nild said clearly, 'We'll get out of here, Mr Rosen, and let you have the apartment.'

From farther off I heard Sam Barrows mutter, 'That girl in there is underdeveloped. Everything slides back out. What's she doing there in the bedroom anyhow? Has she got that skinny body – ' His voice faded.

Neither Pris nor I said anything. Presently we heard the front door of the apartment shut.

'That's nice of them,' my father said. 'Louis, you should at least have thanked them; that Mr Barrows is a gentleman, in spite of what he says, you can tell more about a person by what he does anyhow.'

'You ought to be grateful to both of them,' Chester grumbled at me. Both he and my father glowered at me reprovingly, my father chewing on his cigar.

I held Pris against me. And for me, that was all.

17

When my father and Chester got me back to Boise, the next day, they discovered that Doctor Horstowski could not – or did not want to – treat me. He did however give me several psychological tests for the purpose of diagnosis. One I remember involved listening to a tape of voices which mumbled at a distance, only a few phrases now and then being at all distinguishable. The task was to write down what each of their successive conversations was about.

I think Horstowski made his diagnosis on my results in that test, because I heard each conversation as dealing with me. In detail I heard them outlining my faults, outlining my failings, analyzing me for what I was, diagnosing my behavior . . . I heard them insulting both me and Pris and our relationship.

All Horstowski said was merely, 'Louis, each time you heard the word "this" you thought they were saying "Pris".' That seemed to make him despondent. 'And what you thought was "Louis" was, generally speaking, the two words "do we".' He glanced at me bleakly, and thereupon washed his hands of me.

I was not out of the reach of the psychiatric profession, however, because Doctor Horstowski turned me over to the Federal Commissioner of the Bureau of Mental Health in Area Five, the Pacific Northwest. I had heard of him. His name was Doctor Ragland Nisea and it was his job to make final determination on all commitment proceedings originating in his area. Single-handed, since 1980, he had committed many thousands of disturbed people to the Bureau's clinics scattered around the country; he was considered a brilliant psychiatrist and diagnostician and it had been a joke for years among us that sooner or later we would fall into Nisea's hands; it was a joke everyone made and which a certain percentage of us lived to see come true.

'You'll find Doctor Nisea to be capable and sympathetic,' Horstowski told me as he drove me over to the Bureau's office in Boise.

'It's nice of you to take me over,' I said.

'I'm in and out of there every day. I'd have to make this trip anyhow. What I'm doing is sparing you the appearance in court and the jury costs . . . as you know, Nisea makes final determination anyhow, and you're better off in his hands than before a lay jury.'

I nodded; it was so.

'You're not feeling hostile about this, are you?' Horstowski asked. 'It's no stigma to be placed in a Bureau clinic . . . happens every minute of the day – one out of nine people have crippling mental illness which makes it impossible for them . . .' He droned on; I paid no attention. I had heard it all before on the countless TV ads, in the infinitely many magazine articles.

But as a matter of fact I did feel hostile toward him for washing his hands of me and turning me over to the mental health people, even though I knew that by law he was required to if he felt I was psychotic. And I felt hostile toward everyone else, including the two simulacra; as we drove through the sunny, familiar streets of Boise between his office and the Bureau, I felt that everyone was a betrayer and enemy of mine, that I was surrounded by an alien, hating world.

All this and much more had of course shown up in the tests which Horstowski had given me. In the Rorschach Test, for instance, I had interpreted each blot and picture as full of crashing, banging, jagged machinery designed from the start of time to swing into frantic, lethal motion with the intention of doing me bodily injury. In fact, on the drive over to the Bureau to see Doctor Nisea, I distinctly saw lines of cars following us, due no doubt to my being back in town; the people in the cars had been tipped off the moment I arrived at the Boise airport.

'Can Doctor Nisea help me?' I asked Horstowski as we slid to the curb by a large, modern office building of many floors and windows. Now I had begun to feel acute panic. 'I mean, the mental health people have all those new techniques which even you don't have, all the latest – '

'It depends on what you mean by help,' Horstowski said, opening the car door and beckoning me to accompany him into the building.

So here I stood at last where so many had come before me: the Federal Bureau of Mental Health, in its diagnostic division, the first step, perhaps, in a new era of my life.

How right Pris had been when she had told me that I had within me a deeply unstable streak which someday might bring me into trouble. Hallucinated, weary and hopeless, I had at last been taken into tow by the authorities, as she herself had been a few years ago. I had not seen Horstowski's diagnosis, but I knew without asking that he had found schizophrenic responses in me . . . I felt them inside me, too. Why deny what was obvious?

I was lucky that help, on a vast collective scale, was available for me; god knew I was wretched in such a state, close to suicide or to total collapse from which there might be no recovery. And they had caught it so early – there was a distinct hope for me. Specifically, I realized I was in the early catatonic excitement stage, before any permanent maladjustment pattern such as the dreaded hebephrenia or paranoia had set in. I had the illness in its simple, original form, where it was still accessible to therapy.

I could thank my father and brother for their timely action.

And yet, although I knew all this, I accompanied

Horstowski into the Bureau's office in a state of trembling dread, conscious still of my hostility and of the hostility all around me. I had insight and yet I did not; one part of me knew and understood, the rest seethed like a captured animal that yearns to get back to its own environment, its own familiar places.

At this moment I could speak for only a small portion of my mind, while the remainder went its own way.

This made clear to me the reasons why the McHeston Act was so necessary. A truly psychotic individual, such as myself, *could on his own never seek aid*; he had to be coerced by law. That was what it meant to be psychotic.

Pris, I thought. You were like this, once; they caught you there in school, picked you out and separated you from the others, hauled you off as I'm being hauled off. And they did manage to restore you to your society. Can they succeed with me?

And, I thought, will I be like you when the therapy is over? What former, more adjusted state in my history will they restore me to?

How will I feel about you then? Will I remember you?

And if I do, will I still care about you as I do now?

Doctor Horstowski deposited me in the public waiting room and I sat for an hour with all the other bewildered, sick people, until at last a nurse came and summoned me. In a small inner office I was introduced to Doctor Nisea. He turned out to be a good-looking man not much older than myself, with soft brown eyes, thick hair that was well-combed, and a cautious, apologetic manner which I had never encountered outside the field of veterinarian medicine. The man had a sympathetic interest which he displayed at once, making sure that I was comfortable and that I understood why I was there.

I said, 'I am here because I no longer have any basis by which I can communicate my wants and emotions to other humans.' While waiting I had been able to work it out exactly. 'So for me there's no longer any possibility

223

of satisfying my needs in the world of real people; I have to turn inward to a fantasy life instead.'

Leaning back in his chair Doctor Nisea studied me reflectively. 'And this you want to change.'

'I want to achieve satisfaction, the real kind.'

'Have you nothing at all in common with other people?'

'Nothing. My reality lies entirely outside the world that others experience. You, for instance, to you it would be a fantasy, if I told you about it. About her, I mean.'

'Who is she?'

'Pris,' I said.

He waited, but I did not go on.

'Doctor Horstowski talked to me briefly on the phone about you,' he said presently. 'You apparently have the dynamism of difficulty which we call the Magna Mater type of schizophrenia. However, by law, I must administer first the James Benjamin Proverb Test to you and then the Soviet Vigotsky-Luria Block Test.' He nodded and from behind me a nurse appeared with note pad and pencil. 'Now, I will give you several proverbs and you are to tell me what they mean. Are you ready?'

'Yes,' I said.

'"When the cat's away the mice will play."'

I pondered and then said, 'In the absence of authority there will be wrong-doing.'

In this manner we continued and I did all right until Doctor Nisea got to what turned out for me to be the fatal number six.

'"A rolling stone gathers no moss."'

Try as I might I could not remember the meaning. At last I hazarded, 'Well, it means a person who's always active and never pauses to reflect – ' No, that didn't sound right. I tried again. 'That means a man who is always active and keeps growing in mental and moral stature won't grow stale.' He was looking at me more intently, so I added by way of clarification, 'I mean, a man who's active and doesn't let grass grow under his feet, he'll get ahead in life.'

Doctor Nisea said, 'I see.' And I knew that I had revealed, for the purposes of legal diagnosis, a schizophrenic thinking disorder.

'What does it mean?' I asked. 'Did I get it backward?'

'Yes, I'm afraid so. The generally-accepted meaning of the proverb is the opposite of what you've given; it is generally taken to mean that a person who – '

'You don't have to tell me,' I broke in. 'I remember – I really knew it. A person who's unstable will never acquire anything of value.'

Doctor Nisea nodded and went on to the next proverb. But the stipulation of the statute had been met; I showed a formal thinking impairment.

After the proverbs I made a stab at classifying the blocks, but without success. Both Doctor Nisea and I were relieved when I gave up and pushed the blocks away.

'That's about it, then,' Nisea said. He nodded to the nurse to leave. 'We can go ahead and fill out the forms. Do you have a preference clinic-wise? In my opinion, the best of the lot is the Los Angeles one; although perhaps it's because I know that better than the others. The Kasanin Clinic at Kansas City – '

'Send me there,' I said eagerly.

'Any special reason?'

'I've had a number of close friends come out of there,' I said evasively.

He looked at me as if he suspected there was a deeper reason.

'And it has a good reputation. Almost everyone I know who's been genuinely helped in their mental illness has been at Kasanin. Not that the other clinics aren't good, but that's the best. My aunt Gretchen, who's at the Harry Stack Sullivan Clinic at San Diego; she was the first mentally ill person I knew, and there've been a lot since, naturally, because such a large part of the public has it, as we're told every day on TV. There was my cousin Leo Roggis. He's still in one of the clinics somewhere. My English teacher in high school, Mr Haskins; he died in a clinic. There was an old Italian down the street from me who was on a pension, George Oliveri; he had catatonic excitements and they carted him off. I remember a buddy of mine in the Service, Art Boles; he had 'phrenia and went to the Fromme-Reichmann Clinic at Rochester, New York. There was Alys Johnson, a girl I went with in college; she's at Samuel Anderson Clinic in Area Three; that's at Baton Rouge, La. And a man I worked for, Ed Yeats; he contracted 'phrenia and that turned into acute paranoia. Waldo Dangerfield, another buddy of mine. Gloria Milstein, a girl I knew; she's god knows where, but she was spotted by means of a psych test when she was applying for a typing job. The Federal people picked her up . . . she was short, dark-haired, very attractive, and no one ever guessed until that test showed up. And John Franklin Mann, a used car salesman I knew; he tested out as a dilapidated 'phrenic and was carted off, I think to Kasanin, because he's got relatives in Missouri. And Marge Morrison, another girl I knew. She's out again; I'm sure she was cured at Kasanin. All of them who went to Kasanin seemed as good as new, to me, if not better; Kasanin didn't merely meet the requirements of the McHeston Act; it genuinely healed. Or so it seemed to me.'

Doctor Nisea wrote down *Kasanin Clinic at K.C.* on the Government forms and I breathed a sigh of relief. 'Yes,' he murmured, 'Kansas City is said to be good. The President spent two months there, you know.'

'I did hear that,' I admitted. Everyone knew the heroic story of the President's bout with mental illness in his mid-teens, with his subsequent triumph during his twenties.

'And now, before we separate,' Doctor Nisea said, 'I'd

like to tell you a little about the Magna Mater type of schizophrenia.'

'Good,' I said. 'I'd be anxious to hear.'

'As a matter of fact it has been my special interest,' Doctor Nisea said. 'I did several monographs on it. You know the Anderson theory which identifies each subform of schizophrenia with a subform of religion.'

I nodded. The Anderson view of 'phrenia had been popularized in almost every slick magazine in America; it was the current fashion.

'The primary form which 'phrenia takes is the heliocentric form, the sun-worship form where the sun is deified, is seen in fact as the patient's father. You have not experienced that. The heliocentric form is the most primitive and fits with the earliest known religion, solar worship, including the great heliocentric cult of the Roman Period, Mithraism. Also the earlier Persian solar cult, the worship of Mazda.'

'Yes,' I said, nodding.

'Now, the Magna Mater, the form you have, was the great female deity cult of the Mediterranean at the time of the Mycenaean Civilization. Ishtar, Cybele, Attis, then later Athene herself . . . finally the Virgin Mary. What has happened to you is that your anima, that is, the embodiment of your unconsciousness, its archetype, has been projected outward, onto the cosmos, and there it is perceived and worshiped.'

'I see,' I said.

'There, it is experienced as a dangerous, hostile, and incredibly powerful yet attractive being. The embodiment of all the pairs of opposites: it possesses the totality of life, yet is dead; all love, yet is cold; all intelligence, yet is given to a destructive analytical trend which is not creative; yet it is seen as the source of creativity itself. These are the opposites which slumber in the unconscious, which are transcended by gestalts in consciousness. When the opposites are experienced directly, as you are experiencing them, they cannot be fathomed or dealt with; they will eventually disrupt your ego and annihilate it, for as you know, in their original form they are archetypes and cannot be assimilated by the ego.'

'I see,' I said.

'So this battle is the great struggle of the conscious mind to come to an understanding with its own collective aspects, its unconsciousness and is doomed to fail. The archetypes of the unconscious must be experienced indirectly, through the anima, and in a benign form free of their bipolar qualities. For this to come about, you must hold an utterly different relationship to your unconscious; as it stands, you are passive, and it possesses all the powers of decision.'

'Right,' I said.

'Your consciousness has been impoverished so that it no longer can act. It has no authority except that which it derives from unconsciousness, and right now it is split off from unconsciousness. So no rapport can be established by way of the anima.' Doctor Nisea concluded, 'You have a relatively mild form of 'phrenia. But it is still a psychosis and still requires treatment at a Federal clinic. I'd like to see you again, when you get back from Kansas City; I know the improvement in your condition will be phenomenal.' He smiled at me with genuine warmth, and I smiled back at him. Standing, he held out his hand and we shook.

I was on my way to the Kasanin Clinic at Kansas City.

In a formal hearing before witnesses Doctor Nisea presented me with a summons, asking if there was any reason why I should not be taken at once to Kansas City. These legal formalities had a chilly quality that made me more anxious to be on my way than ever. Nisea offered me a twenty-four hour period in which to conclude my business affairs, but I declined it; I wanted to leave at once. In the end, we settled on eight hours. Plane reservations were made for me by Nisea's staff and I left the Bureau in a taxi, to return to Ontario until it was time for me to take my big trip east.

I had the taxi take me to Maury's house, where I had left a good part of my possessions. Soon I was at the door knocking.

No one was home. I tried the knob; it was unlocked. So I let myself into the silent, deserted house.

There in the bathroom was the tile mural which Pris had been working on that first night. It was done, now. For a time I stood staring up at it, marveling at the colors and the design itself, the mermaid and fish, the octopus with shoe-button bright eyes: she had finished him at last.

One blue tile had become loose. I plucked it entirely off, rubbed the sticky stuff from its back, and put it in my coat pocket.

In case I should forget you, I thought to myself. You and your bathroom mural, your mermaid with pink-tiled tits, your many lovely and monstrous creations bobbing and alive beneath the surface of the water. The placid, eternal water . . . she had done the line above my head, almost eight feet high. Above that, sky. Very little of it; the sky played no role in the scheme of creation, here.

As I stood there I heard from the front of the house a thumping and banging. Someone was after me, but I remained where I was. What did it matter? I waited, and presently Maury Rock came rushing in, panting; seeing me he stopped short.

'Louis Rosen,' he said. 'And in the bathroom.'

'I'm just leaving.'

'A neighbor phoned me at the office; she saw you pull up in a cab and enter and she knew I wasn't home.'

'Spying on me.' I was not surprised. 'They all are, everywhere I go.' I continued to stand, hands in my pockets, gazing up at the wall of color.

'She just thought I ought to know. I figured it was you.' He saw, then, my suitcase and the articles I had collected. 'You're really nuts. You barely get back here from Seattle – when did you get in? Couldn't be before this morning. And now you're off again somewhere else.'

I said, 'I have to go, Maury. It's the law.'

He stared at me, his jaw dropping gradually; then he flushed. 'I'm sorry, Louis. I mean, saying you were a nut.'

'Yes, but I am. I took the Benjamin Proverb Test and the block thing today and couldn't pass either one. The commitment's already been served on me.'

Rubbing his jaw he murmured, 'Who turned you in?'

'My father and Chester.'

'Hell's bells, your own blood.'

'They saved me from paranoia. Listen, Maury.' I turned to face him. 'Do you know where she is?'

'If I did, honest to god, Louis, I'd tell you. Even if you have been certified.'

'You know where they're sending me for therapy?'

'Kansas City?'

I nodded.

'Maybe you'll find her there. Maybe the mental health people caught up with her and sent her back and forgot to let me know about it.'

'Yeah, maybe so,' I said.

Coming up to me he whacked me on the back. 'Good luck, you son of a bitch. I know you'll pull out of it. You got 'phrenia, I presume; that's all there is, anymore.'

'I've got Magna Mater 'phrenia.' Reaching into my coat I got out the tile and showed it to him, saying, 'To remember her. I hope you don't mind; it's your house and mural, after all.'

'Take it. Take a whole fish. Take a tit.' He started toward the mermaid. 'No kidding, Louis; we'll pry a pink tit loose and you can carry that around with you, okay?'

'This is fine.'

We both stood awkwardly facing each other for a time.

'How's it feel to be 'phrenic?' Maury said at last.

230

'Bad, Maury. Very, very bad.'

'That's what I thought; that's what Pris always said. She was glad to get over it.'

'That going to Seattle, that was it coming on. What they call catatonic excitement, a sense of urgency, that you have to do something. It always turns out to be the wrong thing; it accomplishes nothing. And you realize that and then you have panic and then you get it, the real psychosis. I heard voices and saw – ' I broke off.

'What did you see?'

'Pris.'

'Keerist,' Maury said.

'Will you drive me to the airport?'

'Oh sure, buddy. Sure.' He nodded vigorously.

'I don't have to go until late tonight. So maybe we could have dinner together. I don't feel like seeing my family again, after what happened. I'm sort of ashamed.'

Maury said, 'How come you speak so rationally if you're a 'phrenic?'

'I'm not under tension right now, so I've been able to focus my attention. That's what an attack of schizophrenia is, a weakening of attention so that unconscious processes gain mastery and take over the field. They capture awareness, very archaic processes, archetypal, such as non-schizophrenics haven't had since they were five.'

'You think crazy things, like everyone's against you and you're the center of the universe?'

'No,' I said. 'Doctor Nisea explained to me that it's the heliocentric schizophrenics who – '

'Nisea? Ragland Nisea? Of course; by law you'd have to see him. He's the one who sent Pris up back in the beginning; he gave her the Vigotsky-Luria Block Test in his own office, personally. I always wanted to meet him.'

'Brilliant man. And very humane.'

'Are you dangerous?'

'Only if I'm riled.'

'Should I leave you, then?'

'I guess so,' I said. 'But I'll see you tonight, here at the house, for dinner. About six; that'll give us time to make the flight.'

'Can I do anything for you? Get you anything?'

'Naw. Thanks anyhow.'

Maury hung around the house for a little while and then I heard the front door slam. The house became silent once more. I was alone, as before.

Presently I resumed my slow packing.

Maury and I had dinner together and then he drove me to the Boise airfield in his white Jaguar. I watched the streets go by, and every woman that I saw looked – for an instant, at least – like Pris; each time I thought it was but it wasn't. Maury noticed my absorption but said nothing.

The flight which the mental health people had obtained for me was first-class and on the new Australian rocket, the C-80. The Bureau, I reflected, certainly had plenty of the public's funds to disburse. It took only half an hour to reach the Kansas City airport, so before nine that night I was stepping from the rocket, looking around me for the mental health people who were supposed to receive me.

At the bottom of the ramp a young man and woman approached me, both of them wearing gay, bright Scotch plaid coats. These were my party; in Boise I had been instructed to watch for the coats.

'Mr Rosen,' the young man said expectantly.

'Right,' I said, starting across the field toward the building.

One of them fell in on either side of me. 'A bit chilly tonight,' the girl said. They were not over twenty, I thought; two clear-eyed youngsters who undoubtedly had joined the FBMH out of idealism and were doing their heroic task right this moment. They walked with brisk, eager steps, moving me toward the baggage window, making low-keyed conversation about nothing in particular . . . I would have felt relaxed by it except that in the glare of the beacons which guided the ships in I could already see that the girl looked astonishingly like Pris.

'What's your name?' I asked her.

'Julie,' she said. 'And this is Ralf.'

'Did you – do you remember a patient you had here a few months ago, a young woman from Boise named Pris Frauenzimmer?'

'I'm sorry,' Julie said, 'I just came to the Kasanin Clinic last week; we both did.' She indicated her companion. 'We joined the Mental Health Corps this spring.'

'Do you enjoy it?' I asked. 'Did it work out the way you had expected?'

'Oh, it's terribly rewarding,' the girl said breathlessly. 'Isn't it, Ralf?' He nodded. 'We wouldn't drop out for anything.'

'Do you know anything about me?' I asked, as we stood waiting for the baggage machine to serve up my suitcases.

'Only that Doctor Shedd will be working with you,' Ralf said.

'And he's superb,' Julie said. 'You'll love him. And he does so much for people; he has performed so many cures!'

My suitcases appeared; Ralf took one and I took the other and we started through the building toward the street entrance.

'This is a nice airport,' I said. 'I never saw it before.'

'They just completed it this year,' Ralf said. 'It's the first able to handle both domestic and extra-t flights; you'll be able to leave for the Moon right from here.'

'Not me,' I said, but Ralf did not hear me.

Soon we were in a 'copter, the property of the Kasanin Clinic, flying above the rooftops of Kansas City. The air was cool and crisp and below us a million lights glowed in

233

countless patterns and aimless constellations which were not patterns at all, only clusters.

'Do you think,' I said, 'that every time someone dies, a new light winks on in Kansas City?'

Both Ralf and Julie smiled at my witticism.

'Do you two know what would have happened to me,' I said, 'if there was no compulsory mental health program? I'd be dead by now. This all saved my life, literally.'

To that the two of them smiled once more.

'Thank god the McHeston Act passed Congress,' I said.

They both nodded solemnly.

'You don't know what it's like,' I said, 'to have the catatonic urgency, that craving. It drives you on and on and then all at once you collapse; you know you're not right in the head, you're living in a realm of shadows. In front of my father and brother I had intercourse with a girl who didn't exist except in my mind. I heard people commenting about us, while we were doing it, through the door.'

Ralf asked, 'You did it through the door?'

'He heard them commenting, he means,' Julie said. 'The voices that took note of what he was doing and expressed disapproval. Isn't that it, Mr Rosen?'

'Yes,' I said, 'and it's a measure of the collapse of my ability to communicate that you had to translate that. At one time I could easily have phrased that in a clear manner. It wasn't until Doctor Nisea got to the part about the rolling stone that I saw what a break had come about between my personal language and that of my society. And then I understood all the trouble I had been having up to then.'

'Ah yes,' Julie said, 'number six in the Benjamin Proverb Test.'

'I wonder which proverb Pris missed years ago,' I said, 'that caused Nisea to single her out.'

'Who is Pris?' Julie asked.

'I would think,' Ralf said, 'that she's the girl with whom he had intercourse.'

'You hit the nail on the head,' I told him. 'She was here, once, before either of you. Now she's well again; they discharged her on parole. She's my Great Mother, Doctor Nisea says. My life is devoted to worshiping Pris as if she were a goddess. I've projected her archetype onto the universe; I see nothing but her, everything else to me is unreal. This trip we're taking, you two, Doctor Nisea, the whole Kansas City Clinic – it's all just shadows.'

There seemed to be no way to continue the conversation after what I had said. So we rode the rest of the distance in silence.

18

The following day at ten o'clock in the morning I met Doctor Albert Shedd in the steam bath at Kasanin Clinic. The patients lolled in the billowing steam nude, while the members of the staff padded about wearing blue trunks – evidently a status symbol or badge of office; certainly an indication of their difference from us.

Doctor Shedd approached me, looming up from the white clouds of steam, smiling friendlily at me; he was elderly, at least seventy, with wisps of hair sticking up like bent wires from his round, wrinkled head. His skin, at least in the steam bath, was a glistening pink.

'Morning, Rosen,' he said, ducking his head and eyeing me slyly, like a little gnome. 'How was your trip?'

'Fine, Doctor.'

'No other planes followed you here, I take it,' he said, chuckling.

I had to admire his joke, because it implied that he recognized somewhere in me a basically sane element which he was reaching through the medium of humor. He was spoofing my paranoia, and, in doing so, he slightly but subtly defanged it.

'Do you feel free to talk in this rather informal atmosphere?' Doctor Shedd asked.

'Oh sure. I used to go to a Finnish steam bath all the time when I was in the Los Angeles area.'

'Let's see.' He consulted his clipboard. 'You're a piano salesman. Electronic organs, too.'

'Right, the Rosen Electronic Organ – the finest in the world.'

'You were in Seattle on business at the onset of your

schizophrenic interlude, seeing a Mr Barrows. According to this deposition by your family.'

'Exactly so.'

'We have your school psych-test records and you seem to have had no difficulty . . . they go up to nineteen years and then there's the military service records; no trouble there either. Nor in subsequent applications for employment. It would appear to be a situational schizophrenia, then, rather than a life-history process. You were under unique stress, there in Seattle, I take it?'

'Yes,' I said, nodding vigorously.

'It might never occur again in your lifetime; however, it constitutes a warning – it is a danger sign and must be dealt with.' He scrutinized me for a long time, through the billowing steam. 'Now, it might be that in your case we could equip you to cope successfully with your environment by what is called *controlled fugue* therapy. Have you heard of this?'

'No, Doctor.' But I liked the sound of it.

'You would be given hallucinogenic drugs – drugs which would induce your psychotic break, bring on your hallucinations. For a very limited period each day. This would give your libido fulfillment of its regressive cravings which at present are too strong to be borne. Then very gradually we would diminish the fugal period, hoping eventually to eliminate it. Some of this period would be spent here; we would hope that later on you could return to Boise, to your job, and obtain out-patient therapy there. We are far too overcrowded here at Kasanin, you know.'

'I know that.'

'Would you care to try that?'

'Yes!'

'It would mean further schizophrenic episodes, occurring of course under supervised, controlled conditions.'

'I don't care, I want to try it.'

'It wouldn't bother you that I and other staff members

were present to witness your behavior during these episodes? In other words, the invasion of your privacy – '

'No,' I broke in, 'it wouldn't bother me; I don't care who watches.'

'Your paranoiac tendency,' Doctor Shedd said thoughtfully, 'cannot be too severe, if watching eyes daunt you no more than this.'

'They don't daunt me a damn bit.'

'Fine.' He looked pleased. 'That's an a-okay prognostic sign.' And with that he strolled off into the white steam clouds, wearing his blue trunks and holding his clipboard under his arm. My first interview with my psychiatrist at Kasanin Clinic was over with.

At one that afternoon I was taken to a large clean room in which several nurses and two doctors waited for me. They strapped me down to a leather-covered table and I was given an intravenous injection of the hallucinogenic drug. The doctors and nurses, all overworked but friendly, stood back and waited. I waited, too, strapped to my table and wearing a hospital frock, my bare feet sticking up, arms at my sides.

Several minutes later the drug took effect. I found myself in downtown Oakland, California, sitting on a park bench in Jack London Square. Beside me, feeding bread crumbs to a flock of blue-gray pigeons, sat Pris. She wore capri pants and a green turtle-neck sweater; her hair was tied back with a red checkered bandana and she was totally absorbed in what she was doing, apparently oblivious to me.

'Hey!' I said.

Turning her head she said calmly, 'Damn you; I said be quiet. If you talk you'll scare them away and then that old man down there'll be feeding them instead of me.'

On a bench a short distance down the path sat Doctor Shedd smiling at us, holding his own packet of bread crumbs. In that manner my psyche had dealt with his

238

presence, had incorporated him into the scene in this fashion.

'Pris,' I said in a low voice, 'I've got to talk to you.'

'Why?' She faced me with her cold, remote expression. 'It's important to you, but is it to me? Or do you care?'

'I care,' I said, feeling hopeless.

'Show it instead of saying it – be quiet. I'm quite happy doing what I'm doing.' She returned to feeding the birds.

'Do you love me?' I asked.

'Christ no!'

And yet I felt that she did.

We sat together on the bench for some time and then the park, the bench and Pris herself faded out and I once more found myself on the flat table, strapped down and observed by Doctor Shedd and the overworked nurses of Kasanin Clinic.

'That went much better,' Doctor Shedd said, as they released me.

'Better than what?'

'Than the two previous times.'

I had no memory of previous times and I told him so.

'Of course you don't; they were not successful. No fantasy life was activated; you simply went to sleep. But now we can expect results each time.'

They returned me to my room. The next morning I once more appeared in the therapy chamber to receive my allotment of fugal fantasy life, my hour with Pris.

As I was being strapped down Doctor Shedd entered and greeted me. 'Rosen, I'm going to have you entered in group therapy; that will augment this that we're doing here. Do you understand what group therapy is? You'll bring your problems before a group of your fellow patients, for their comments . . . you'll sit with them while they discuss you and where you seem to have gone astray in your thinking. You'll find that it all takes place in an atmosphere of friendliness and informality. And generally it's quite helpful.'

'Fine.' I had become lonely, here at the clinic.

'You have no objection to the material from your fugues being made available to your group?'

'Gosh no. Why should I?'

'It will be oxide-tape printed and distributed to them in advance of each group therapy session . . . you're aware that we're recording each of these fugues of yours for analytical purposes, and, with your permission, use with the group.'

'You certainly have my permission,' I said. 'I don't object to a group of my fellow patients knowing the contents of my fantasies, especially if they can help explain to me where I've gone wrong.'

'You'll find there's no body of people in the world more anxious to help you than your fellow patients,' Doctor Shedd said.

The injection of hallucinogenic drugs was given me and once more I lapsed into my controlled fugue.

I was behind the wheel of my Magic Fire Chevrolet, in heavy freeway traffic, returning home at the end of the day. On the radio a commuter club announcer was telling me of a traffic jam somewhere ahead.

'Confusion, construction or chaos,' he was saying. 'I'll guide you through, dear friend.'

'Thanks,' I said aloud.

Beside me on the seat Pris stirred and said irritably, 'Have you always talked back to the radio? It's not a good sign; I always knew your mental health wasn't the best.'

'Pris,' I said, 'in spite of what you say I know you love me. Don't you remember us together at Collie Nild's apartment in Seattle?'

'No.'

'Don't you remember how we made love?'

'Awk,' she said, with revulsion.

'I know you love me, no matter what you say.'

'Let me off right here in this traffic, if you're going to talk like that; you make me sick to my stomach.'

'Pris,' I said, 'why are we driving along like this together? Are we going home? Are we married?'

'Oh god,' she moaned.

'Answer me,' I said, keeping my eyes fixed on the truck ahead.

She did not; she squirmed away and sat against the door, as far from me as possible.

'We are,' I said. 'I know we are.'

When I came out of my fugue, Doctor Shedd seemed pleased. 'You are showing a progressive tendency. I think it's safe to say you're getting an effective external catharsis for your regressive libido drives, and that's what we're counting on.' He slapped me on the back encouragingly, much as my partner Maury Rock had done, not so long ago.

On my next controlled fugue Pris looked older. The two of us walked slowly through the great train station at Cheyenne, Wyoming, late at night, through the subway under the tracks and up onto the far side, where we stood silently together. Her face, I thought, had a fuller quality, as if she were maturing. Definitely, she had changed. Her figure was fuller. And she seemed more calm.

'How long,' I asked her, 'have we been married?'

'Don't you know?'

'Then we are,' I said, my heart full of joy.

'Of course we are; do you think we're living in sin? What's the matter with you anyhow, do you have amnesia or something?'

'Let's go over to that bar we saw, opposite the train station; it looked lively.'

'Okay,' she said. As we started back down into the subway once more she said, 'I'm glad you got me away from those empty tracks . . . they depressed me. Do you know what I was starting to think about? I was wondering

241

how it would feel to watch the engine coming, and then to sort of fall forward ahead of it, fall onto the tracks, and have it pass over you, cut you in half . . . I wondered how it would feel to end it all like that, just by falling forward, as if you were going to sleep.'

'Don't talk like that,' I said, putting my arm around her and hugging her. She was stiff and unyielding, as always.

When Doctor Shedd brought me out of my fugue he looked grave. 'I am not too happy to see morbid elements arising in your anima-projection. However, it's to be expected; it shows what a long haul we still have ahead of us. In the next try, the fifteenth fugue – '

'Fifteenth!' I exclaimed. 'You mean that was number fourteen?'

'You've been here over a month, now. I am aware that your episodes are blending together; that is to be expected, since sometimes there is no progress at all and sometimes the same material is repeated. Don't worry about that, Rosen.'

'Okay, Doctor,' I said, feeling glum.

On the next try – or what appeared to my confused mind to be the next try – I once more sat with Pris on a bench in Jack London Park in downtown Oakland, California. This time she was quiet and sad; she did not feed any of the pigeons who wandered about but merely sat with her hands clasped together, staring down.

'What's the matter?' I asked her, trying to draw her close to me.

A tear ran down her cheek. 'Nothing, Louis.' From her purse she brought a handkerchief; she wiped her eyes and then blew her nose. 'I just feel sort of dead and empty, that's all. Maybe I'm pregnant. I'm a whole week late, now.'

I felt wild elation; I gripped her in my arms and kissed her on her cold, unresponsive mouth. 'That's the best news I've heard yet!'

She raised her gray, sadness-filled eyes. 'I'm glad it pleases you, Louis.' Smiling a little she patted my hand.

Definitely now I could see that she had changed. There were distinct lines about her eyes, giving her a somber, weary cast. How much time had passed? How many times had we been together, now? A dozen? A hundred? I couldn't tell; time was gone for me, a thing that did not flow but moved in fitful jolts and starts, bogging down completely and then hesitantly resuming. I, too, felt older and much more weary. And yet – what good news this was.

As soon as I was back in the therapy room I told Doctor Shedd about Pris' pregnancy. He, too, was pleased. 'You see, Rosen, how your fugues are showing more maturity, more elements of responsible reality-seeking on your part? Eventually their maturity will match your actual chronological age and at that point most of the fugal quality will have been discharged.'

I went downstairs in a joyful frame of mind to meet with my group of fellow patients to listen to their explanations and questions regarding this new and important development. I knew that when they had read the manuscript of today's session they would have a good deal to say.

In my fifty-second fugue I caught sight of Pris and my son, a healthy, handsome baby with eyes as gray as Pris' and hair much like mine. Pris sat in the living room in a deep easy chair, feeding him from a bottle, an absorbed expression on her face. Across from them I sat, in a state of almost total bliss, as if all my tensions, all my anxieties and woes, had at last deserted me.

'Goddam these plastic nipples,' Pris said, shaking the bottle angrily. 'They collapse when he sucks; it must be the way I'm sterilizing them.'

I trotted into the kitchen to get a fresh bottle from the sterilizer steaming on the range.

'What's his name, dear?' I asked when I returned.

'What's his name?' Pris gazed at me with resignation. 'Are you all there, Louis? Asking what your baby's name is, for chrissakes? His name's Rosen, the same as yours.'

Sheepishly, I had to smile and say, 'Forgive me.'

'I forgive you; I'm used to you.' She sighed. 'Sorry to say.'

But what is his name? I wondered. Perhaps I will know the next time or if not, then perhaps the one hundredth time. I must know or it will mean nothing to me, all this; it will be in vain.

'Charles,' Pris murmured to the baby, 'are you wetting?'

His name was Charles, and I felt glad; it was a good name. Maybe I had picked it out; it sounded like what I would have arrived at.

That day, after my fugue, as I was hurrying downstairs to the group therapy auditorium, I caught sight of a number of women entering a door on the women's side of the building. One woman had short-cut black hair and stood slender and lithe, much smaller than the other women around her; they looked like inflated balloons in comparison to her. *Is that Pris?* I asked myself, halting. *Please turn around*, I begged, fixing my eyes on her back.

Just as she entered the doorway she turned for an instant. I saw the pert, bobbed nose, the dispassionate, appraising gray eyes . . . it was Pris. 'Pris!' I yelled, waving my arms.

She saw me. She peered, frowning; her lips tightened. Then, very slightly, she smiled.

Was it a phantom? The girl – Pris Frauenzimmer – had now gone on into the room, had disappeared from sight. You are back here at Kasanin Clinic, I said to myself. I knew it would happen sooner or later. And this is not a fantasy, not a fugue, controlled or otherwise; I've found you in actuality, in the real world, the outside world that is not a product of regressive libido or drugs. I have not seen you since that night at the club in Seattle when you

244

hit the Johnny Booth simulacrum over the head with your shoe; how long ago that was! How much, how awfully much, I have seen and done since then – done in a vacuum, done without you, without the authentic, actual you. Satisfied with a mere phantom instead of the real thing . . . Pris, I said to myself. Thank god; I have found you; I knew I would, someday.

I did not go to my group therapy; instead I remained there in the hall, waiting and watching.

At last, hours later, she reemerged. She came across the open patio directly towards me, her face clear and calm, a slight glow kindled in her eyes, more of wry amusement than anything else.

'Hi,' I said.

'So they netted you, Louis Rosen,' she said. 'You finally went shizophrenic, too. I'm not surprised.'

I said, 'Pris, I've been here months.'

'Well, are you getting healed?'

'Yes,' I said, 'I think so. I'm having controlled fugue therapy every day; I always go to you, Pris, every time. We're married and we have a child named Charles. I think we're living in Oakland, California.'

'Oakland,' she said, wrinkling her nose. 'Parts of Oakland are nice; parts are dreadful.' She started away from me up the hall. 'It was nice seeing you, Louis. Maybe I'll run into you again, here.'

'Pris!' I called in grief. 'Come back!'

But she continued on and was lost beyond the closing doors at the end of the hall.

The next time in my controlled fugue when I saw her she had definitely aged; her figure was more matronly and she had deep, permanent shadows under her eyes. We stood together in the kitchen doing the dinner dishes; Pris washed while I dried. Under the glare of the overhead light her skin looked dry, with fine, tiny wrinkles radiating through it. She had on no make-up. Her hair, in particular, had changed; it was dry, too, like her skin, and no

245

longer black. It was a reddish brown, and very nice; I touched it and found it stiff yet clean and pleasant to the touch.

'Pris,' I said, 'I saw you yesterday in the hall. Here, where I am, at Kasanin.'

'Good for you,' she said briefly.

'Was it real? More real than this?' In the living room I saw Charles seated before the three-D color TV set, his eyes fixed raptly on the image. 'Do you remember that meeting after so long? Was it as real to you as it was to me? Is this now real to you? Please tell me; I don't understand anymore.'

'Louis,' she said, as she scrubbed a frying pan, 'can't you take life as it comes? Do you have to be a philosopher? You act like a college sophomore; you make me wonder if you're going to grow up.'

'I just don't know which way to go anymore,' I said, feeling desolate but automatically continuing in my task of dish-drying.

'Take me where you find me,' Pris said. 'As you find me. Be content with that, don't ask questions.'

'Yes,' I agreed, 'I'll do that; I'll try to do it, anyhow.'

When I came out of my fugue, Doctor Shedd once more was present. 'You're mistaken, Rosen; you couldn't have run into Miss Frauenzimmer here at Kasanin. I checked the records carefully and found no one by that name. I'm afraid that so-called meeting with her in the hall was an involuntary lapse into psychosis; we must not be getting as complete a catharsis of your libido cravings as we thought. Perhaps we should increase the number of minutes of controlled regression per day.'

I nodded mutely. But I did not believe him; I knew that it had been really Pris there in the hall; it was not a schizophrenic fantasy.

The following week I saw her again at Kasanin. This time I looked down and saw her through the window of the solarium; she was outdoors playing volley ball with a team of girls, all of them wearing light blue gym shorts and blouses.

She did not see me; she was intent on the game. For a long time I stood there, drinking in the sight of her, knowing it was real . . . and then the ball bounced from the court toward the building and Pris came scampering after it. As she bent to snatch it up I saw her name, stitched in colored block letters on her gym blouse.

ROCK, PRIS

That explained it. She was entered in Kasanin Clinic under her father's name, not her own. Therefore Doctor Shedd hadn't found her listed in the files; he had looked under Frauenzimmer, which was the way I always thought of her, no matter what she called herself.

I won't tell him, I said to myself. I'll keep myself from mentioning it during my controlled fugues. That way he'll never know, and maybe, sometime, I'll get to talk to her again.

And then I thought, *Maybe this is all deliberate on Shedd's part*; maybe it's a technique for drawing me out of my fugues and back into the actual world. Because these tiny glimpses of the real Pris have become more valuable to me than all the fugues put together. *This is their therapy, and it is working.*

I did not know whether to feel good or bad.

It was after my two hundred and twentieth controlled fugue therapy session that I got to talk to Pris once more. She was strolling out of the clinic's cafeteria; I was entering. I saw her before she saw me; she was absorbed in conversation with another young woman, a buddy.

'Pris,' I said, stopping her. 'For god's sake, let me see you for a few minutes. They don't care; I know this is part of their therapy. Please.'

The other girl moved off considerately and Pris and I were alone.

'You're looking older, Louis,' Pris said, after a pause.

247

'You look swell, as always.' I longed to put my arms around her; I yearned to hug her to me. But instead I stood a few inches from her doing nothing.

'You'll be glad to know they're going to let me sign out of here again, one of these days,' Pris said matter-of-factly. 'And get outpatient therapy like I did before. I'm making terrific progress according to Doctor Ditchley, who's the top psychiatrist here. I see him almost every day. I looked you up in the files; you're seeing Shedd. He's not much . . . he's an old fool, as far as I'm concerned.'

'Pris,' I said, 'maybe we could leave here together. What would you say to that? I'm making progress, too.'

'Why should we leave together?'

'I love you,' I said, 'and I know you love me.'

She did not retort; instead she merely nodded.

'Could it be done?' I asked. 'You know so much more about this place than I do; you've practically lived your life here.'

'Some life.'

'Could you work it out?'

'Work it out yourself; you're the man.'

'If I do,' I said, 'will you marry me?'

She groaned. 'Sure, Louis. Anything you want. Marriage, living in sin, incidental screwing . . . you name it.'

'Marriage,' I said.

'And kids? Like in your fantasy? A child named Charles?' Her lips twitched with amusement.

'Yes.'

'Work it out, then,' Pris said. 'Talk to Shovel-head Shedd, the clinic idiot. He can release you; he has the authority. I'll give you a hint. When you go up for your next fugue, hang back. Tell him you're not sure you're getting anything out of it anymore. And then when you're in it, tell your fantasy sex-partner there, the Pris Frauenzimmer that you've cooked up in that warped, hot little brain of yours, that you don't find her convincing

248

anymore.' She grinned in her old familiar way. 'See where that gets you. Maybe it'll get you out of here, maybe it won't – maybe it'll only get you in deeper.'

I said haltingly, 'You wouldn't – '

'Kid you? Mislead you? Try it, Louis, and find out.' Her face now, was deeply serious. 'The only way you'll know is to have the courage to go ahead.'

Turning, she walked rapidly away from me.

'I'll see you,' she said over her shoulder. 'Maybe.' A last cool, cheerful, self-possessed grin and she was gone; other people moved in between us, people going in to eat at the cafeteria.

I trust you, I said to myself.

After dinner that day I ran into Doctor Shedd in the hall. He did not object when I told him I'd like a moment of his time.

'What's on your mind, Rosen?'

'Doctor, when I get up to take my fugues I sort of feel like hanging back. I'm not sure I'm getting anything out of them anymore.'

'How's that again?' Doctor Shedd said, frowning.

I repeated what I had said. He listened with great attention. 'And I don't find my fantasy sex-partner convincing anymore,' I added this time. 'I know she's just a projection of my subconscious; she's not the real Pris Frauenzimmer.'

Doctor Shedd said, 'This is interesting.'

'What does it mean, what I've said just now . . . does it indicate I'm getting worse or better?'

'I honestly don't know. We'll see at the next fugue session; I'll know more when I can observe your behavior during it.' Nodding goodbye to me he continued on down the corridor.

At my next controlled fugue I found myself meandering through a supermarket with Pris; we were doing our weekly grocery shopping.

She was much older now, but still Pris, still the same

attractive, firm, clear-eyed woman I had always loved. Our boy ran ahead of us, finding items for his weekend camping trip which he was about to enjoy with his scout troop in Charles Tilden Park in the Oakland hills.

'You're certainly quiet for a change,' Pris said to me.

'Thinking.'

'Worrying, you mean. I know you; I can tell.'

'Pris, is this real?' I said. 'Is this enough, what we have here?'

'No more,' she said. 'I can't stand your eternal philosophizing; either accept your life or kill yourself but stop babbling about it.'

'Okay' I said. 'And in exchange I want you to stop giving me your constant derogatory opinions about me. I'm tired of it.'

'You're just afraid of hearing them – ' she began.

Before I knew what I was doing I had reached back and slapped her in the face; she tumbled and half-fell, leaped away and stood with her hand pressed to her cheek, staring at me in bewilderment and pain.

'Goddam you,' she said in a broken voice. 'I'll never forgive you.'

'I just can't stand your derogatory opinions anymore.'

She stared at me, and then spun and hurried off down the aisle of the supermarket without looking back; she grabbed up Charles and went on.

All at once I realized that Doctor Shedd stood beside me. 'I think we've had enough for today, Rosen.' The aisle, with its shelves of cartons and packages, wavered and faded away.

'Did I do wrong?' I had done it without thinking without any plan in mind. Had I upset everything? 'That's the first time in my life I ever hit a woman,' I said to Doctor Shedd.

'Don't worry about it,' he said, preoccupied with his notebook. He nodded to the nurses. 'Let him up. And we'll cancel the group therapy session for today, I think;

have him go back to his room where he can be by himself.' To me he said suddenly, 'Rosen, there's something peculiar about your behavior that I don't understand. It's not like you at all.'

I said nothing; I merely hung my head.

'I'd almost say,' Doctor Shedd said slowly, 'that you're malingering.'

'No, not at all,' I protested. 'I'm really sick; I would have died if I hadn't come here.'

'I think I'll have you come up to my office tomorrow; I'd like to give you the Benjamin Proverb Test and the Vigotsky-Luria Block Test myself. It's more who gives the test than the test itself.'

'I agree with that,' I said, feeling apprehensive and nervous.

The next day at one in the afternoon I successfully passed both the Benjamin Proverb Test and the Vigotsky-Luria Block Test. According to the McHeston Act I was legally free; I could go home.

'I wonder if you ever should have been here at Kasanin,' Dr Shedd said. 'With people waiting all over the country and the staff overworked – ' He signed my release and handed it to me. 'I don't know what you were trying to get out of by coming here, but you'll have to go back and face your life once more, and without pleading the pretext of a mental illness which I doubt you have or ever have had.'

On that brusque note I was formally expelled from the Federal Government's Kasanin Clinic at Kansas City, Missouri.

'There's a girl here I'd like to see before I leave.' I asked Doctor Shedd, 'Is that all right to talk to her for a moment? Her name is Miss Rock.' Cautiously I added, 'I don't know her first name.'

Doctor Shedd touched a button on his desk. 'Let Mr Rosen see a Miss Rock for a period of no more than ten minutes. And then take him to the main gate and put him outside; his time here is over with.'

The husky male attendant brought me to the room which Pris shared with six other girls in the women's dorm. I found her seated on her bed, using an orange stick on her nails. As I entered she barely glanced up.

'Hi, Louis,' she murmured.

'Pris, I had the courage; I went and told him what you said to me.' I bent to touch her. 'I'm free. They discharged me. I can go home.'

'Then go.'

At first I did not understand. 'What about you?'

Pris said calmly, 'I changed my mind. I didn't apply for a release from here; I feel like staying a few months longer. I like it right now – I'm learning how to weave. I'm weaving a rug out of black sheep wool, virgin wool.' And then all at once she whispered bleakly, 'I lied to you, Louis. I'm not up for release; I'm much too sick. I have to stay here a long time more, maybe forever. I'm sorry I told you I was getting out. Forgive me.' She took hold of my hand briefly, then let it go.

I could say nothing.

A moment later the attendant led me through the halls of the clinic to the gate and left me standing outside on the public sidewalk with fifty dollars in my pocket, courtesy of the Federal Government. Kasanin Clinic was behind me, no longer a part of my life; it had gone into the past and would, I hoped, never reappear again.

I'm well, I said to myself. Once more I test out perfectly, as I did when I was a child in school. I can go back to Boise, to my brother Chester and my father, Maury and my business; the Government healed me.

I have everything but Pris.

Somewhere inside the great building of Kasanin Clinic Pris Frauenzimmer sat carding and weaving virgin black sheep's wool, utterly involved, without a thought for me or for any other thing.

Random Acts of Senseless Violence
Jack Womack

'If you dropped the characters from *Neuromancer* into Womack's Manhatten, they'd fall down screaming and have nervous breakdowns' WILLIAM GIBSON

It's just a little later than now and Lola Hart is writing her life in a diary. She's a nice middle-class girl on the verge of her teens who schools at the calm end of town.

A normal, happy girl.

But in a disintegrating New York she is a dying breed. War is breaking out on Long Island, the army boys are flame-throwing the streets, five Presidents have been assassinated in a year. No one notices any more.

Soon Lola and her family must move over to the Lower East Side - Loisaida - to the Pit and the new language and violence of the streets.

The metamorphosis of the nice Lola Hart into the new model Lola has begun . . .

'Womack astounds and entertains'   *Publishers Weekly*

ISBN 0 586 21320 1

Only Forward
Michael Marshall Smith

A truly stunning debut from a young author. Extremely original, satyrical and poignant, a marriage of numerous genres brilliantly executed to produce something entirely new.

Stark is a troubleshooter. He lives in The City - a massive conglomeration of self-governing Neighbourhoods, each with their own peculiarity. Stark lives in Colour, where computers co-ordinate the tone of the street lights to match the clothes that people wear. Close by is Sound where noise is strictly forbidden, and Ffnaph where people spend their whole lives leaping on trampolines and trying to touch the sky. Then there is Red, where anything goes, and all too often does.

At the heart of them all is the Centre - a back-stabbing community of 'Actioneers' intent only on achieving - divided into areas like 'The Results are what Counts sub-section' which boasts 43 grades of monorail attendant. Fell Alkland, Actioneer extraordinaire has been kidapped. It is up to Stark to find him. But in doing so he is forced to confront the terrible secrets of his past. A life he has blocked out for too long.

'Michael Marshall Smith's *Only Forward* is a dark labyrinth of a book: shocking, moving and surreal. Violent, outrageous and witty - sometimes simultaneously - it offers us a journey from which we return both shaken and exhilarated. An extraordinary debut.'

Clive Barker

ISBN 0 586 21774 6

The World Jones Made
Philip K. Dick

'Dick was perhaps the first real genius to have worked in the science-fictional mode since the days of Stapeldon'

Brian Aldiss

After the war, amid the radiation and rubble, a world government is established based on Relativism. People can do whatever they like – take heroin, fornicate in the street – and believe whatever they like, so long as they don't tell anyone else what to do or what to believe in.

Underground police enforce the new Law. Dedicated people such as Cussick. Cussick hopes that God is a thing of the past, along with war – at last. What he doesn't expect is the rise of the devil.

Philip K. Dick remained a cult figure until Hollywood translated two of his stories into movies, *Blade Runner* and *Total Recall*, which defined for a generation a terrifying, and totally plausible, future. *The World Jones Made* is a hauntingly sinister place.

ISBN 0 586 21844 0